From the Point

BOOKS BY DON J. SNYDER

Veterans Park
A Soldier's Disgrace
From the Point

FROM THE POINT

*A Novel by
Don J. Snyder*

*Franklin Watts
New York/Toronto/1988*

Library of Congress Cataloging-in-Publication Data

Snyder, Don J.
From the point.
I. Title.
PS3569.N86F76   1988   813'.54   87-31623
ISBN 0-531-15081-X

Copyright © 1988 by Don J. Snyder
All rights reserved
Printed in the United States of America
6 5 4 3 2 1

For Colleen, My Wife

From the Point

Epitaph for Fire and Flower

You might as well haul up
This wave's green peak on wire
To prevent fall, or anchor the fluent air
In quartz, as crack your skull to keep
These two most perishable lovers from the touch
That will kindle angels' envy, scorch and drop
Their fond hearts charred as any match.

—Sylvia Plath

Prologue

Minute by minute our past gathers authority over us. Certain gestures, a glance across a room, phrases spoken under memorable shades of light, all possess the power to call us back.

"I can tell you everything about our past," she once said to Jack. "We were angry, running around in the streets, trying to change the world. We were young, very young it seems now—and don't you remember the old passion and ideals? Everything was alive then, Jack. It was like I'd carried around this ball of red yarn for years, and then suddenly it fell off my lap and dropped onto the floor, and pretty soon there was red yarn spilling everywhere, down the stairs, out the door. It went on and on, and nothing was ever the same again."

Casey Lawrence went crashing through those years of innocence and defiance with eyes so green you had to look again to be sure. She came of age in the late 1960s, and her youth was a time of urgency and discovery and extreme guilt and disillusion. Her youth became a part of the past she would forever try to recover or outrun.

"But we were a different kind of generation," she would declare when looking back. "We were young at precisely the time when the world was saying how fine it was to be young and reckless and pissed off. We didn't have to be careful about things. The time was perfect. I mean, there's no romance in *following* the American dream—the job, the pension plan, the house and backyard. The romance is in tearing it all down, and trying to make a new way."

She wanted to believe she had made a new way, and that she had lived out her youth with a particular grace. But when she looked back honestly over her past, she knew that her past had been defined not by ideals and a struggle for righteousness, but by men. Men who, for a little while, loved to hold her face in their hands when they kissed her, almost as if they were worshipping her. Then, soon enough, they didn't bother to hold her face anymore; they just wanted to get on top of her.

One of these men was really only a boy who said to her, "Every man wants to be a woman's first love, and every woman wants to be his last." For a while she believed this might be true. She was not much more than a girl when she used to sit with him in front of an old radio that looked to her then, with its scrolled doors and gabled roof, like a miniature church. She knew even then that he would change her life. Waiting for him to speak or to touch her, she would watch his hands fiddle with the lighted dials on the radio until suddenly there were men playing baseball or reading the news inside the little church.

This happened a long time ago, and when she thought back about the way they were in those days she could never be sure she hadn't made all of it up. That was the thing about the past: it was terribly difficult to get an

—2

accurate fix on it when you looked back at it to explain how your life had turned out.

If, in her past, passion and ideals were no more than a ball of red yarn, then happiness was even less substantial. She had learned that the world turning around her was dark and her happiness was just a piece of this yarn held between her fingers, and if she were to let go of this, she might spend the rest of her life down on her hands and knees searching for something that once promised a way out of the darkness.

BOOK ONE

Chapter One

She was nine years old when Jack moved to town. He came drifting into her backyard one summer evening when she was sitting in the branches of the weeping willow tree watching her father in his suspenders and gray-flannel trousers hosing down the vegetable garden. In the tiny square patch of earth there were only pale-green shoots where her father had planted pumpkins. She was watching the stream of water boring into the hard ground. She heard the faint whistling from the nozzle and then a boy's voice rising up into the branches of the tree. "I've lost my cat," she heard him say. "Have you seen a cat?"

She saw her father turn slowly toward him, turning only from his hips. The water splashed on the perforated toes of his shoes and caused him to glance down for a moment.

"What's your cat look like?" he asked.

"Battleship gray," the boy replied.

This made her father laugh lightly to himself. Casey saw his shoulders go back gently, the suspenders buckling a little where they crisscrossed his back.

The boy had a different way of saying things. Casey followed him that first summer evening, trailing at a distance as he went from house to house, backyard to backyard, in search of his gray cat. It was getting dark when he discovered she was behind him, following. He seemed eminently pleased to have her company. She stood at his heels while, with a little bow at the waist, he introduced himself to Mr. Shepard, Mrs. Turner, the old widow Martindale at the corner. It was the time of evening when people sat out on their porches, and Jack went up to each of them with his sad story about the battleship-gray cat he was missing.

It was a lie; he'd never owned a cat. In fact he was allergic to them. "They make my nose run," he confessed. And then in the same confessional tone he volunteered his life story. His father had been in the foreign service with the U.S. government. For years they had lived in strange places all over the world. It had never been easy to make friends or meet people under those circumstances, he explained. "I don't have brothers or sisters," he said, "so I have to get to know people." Living in some part of Paris, he had followed his fictional cat into courtyards in order to get to know the children playing there.

Casey liked him, and they began to roam the squared-off yards of their neighborhood of interchangeable ranch houses, houses put together in neat rows as if by someone with a farmer's understanding of space and order but without a farmer's heart. The world of grown-ups was a source of endless fascination to Jack. He studied them and developed theories about them. One night as they were passing down Clearspring Road on their way from a church fair, Jack pointed to all the grown-ups sitting out on their stoops. Though they were only a few yards from each other, separated by flimsy wire fences or stubby hedges, each adult seemed to be in his own world, smoking a cigarette or just staring up at the sky.

"They all think about the same thing," Jack said to her. "When they look up at the sky that way, they're thinking about how they got old so fast."

At school, in his pleated linen trousers and brightly polished shoes, he was something of an outcast. He was too smart for his age, too self-absorbed. He was terribly uncoordinated on the playground, and he possessed none of the toughness the other boys seemed to come by naturally. Casey tried to protect him in this world, and he led the way through the world of adults, where they encountered Casey's mother, an energetic woman whose great passion in life was shopping for bargains. Nothing pleased her more than taking Jack and Casey on countless shopping trips when she dickered with sales clerks in department stores like Woolworth's and J.C. Penney as if she were at some outdoor market in Istanbul. It almost always worked; she seldom failed to get them to lower their prices. They gave in once they figured out this was the only way to get rid of her.

At Sears she walked up to a record player which was out of its box and on display. Casey was looking right at it with Jack when her mother said to the salesman, "You can't be asking a hundred dollars for this. It's all scratched and dusty, look at it." Casey was shocked. She couldn't see a single scratch. "Come on, Mama," she said.

The clerk examined the record player incredulously. He held his ground for a while. Then Casey's mother went on again: "You know as well as I do that most of the life in this machine's already gone. Shelf life, sir. Look at the scratches in the dial here."

Eventually he went off to talk with the manager. Once she got them going to consult their managers and bosses she knew she had the inside track and it was only a matter of time.

She ended up paying sixty-eight dollars for the record player, then trying to console the clerk as he boxed it up for her. "You needn't feel bad, sir. Your manager knows these things aren't worth a penny over fifty dollars."

She talked a local Italian bakery into selling her their excess bread, the day-old rolls and the misshaped loaves. Wednesday afternoons she walked to Pearl Street with Jack at her side carrying an empty duffel bag, and then back home with more bread than she could eat in five months. She passed it out to neighbors and sent Casey to school with whatever was left to donate to the cafeteria. "We pay taxes so the school can buy its own bread," Casey's father argued. The logic of this made no difference to her mother. She had gotten an incredible deal on the bread, less than three cents a loaf. He shook his head at her and walked to his study.

Eventually Jack saw what was at stake here: Casey's mother derived great satisfaction from coming home with a bargain because it was her way of fitting into the world, which otherwise excluded her. She didn't care at all about material things; she ended up giving away much of what she bought. But she possessed this inscrutable talent for finding good deals, and so she exercised it whenever she had the opportunity.

Casey and Jack were sixteen years old when she began buying extras of everything, sometimes a dozen identical items—Christmas-tree stands, rolling pins with slightly cracked cylinders, beautiful shirts with buttons but no buttonholes. She began hoarding, piling this stuff in the basement. It was as if she knew her days of shopping were numbered with single digits and coming to an end.

One Saturday evening she came to the front door. A cab was parked at the curb. She needed Jack to help her unload its trunk. She had bought twenty pairs of spiked golf shoes, crazy-looking shoes with big, floppy frills sewed to their tongues.

"Just what we need," Casey said.

Her mother opened her purse, smiling slyly. She suddenly held up a small aluminum tool, like a bottle opener. "This removes the spikes!" she said triumphantly. "He wanted a dollar a pair, can you imagine? I got him down to twenty cents, plus he threw in this tool."

"Victory!" Jack said to her.

Later he said to Casey, "Victory over the way things are."

She saw what he meant. There was an enormous, complicated world beyond her mother's control, a world of high finance and staggering indifference, a world which decided how much everything was worth. And then along she would come, without any money to speak of, with no influence or power, and she would get her way.

That year Jack was in charge of the altar boys at Saint Vincent's Church, and he figured out a way to get into the priest's side of the confessional. He would coax Casey into the dark booth, then slide open the little door between them, and they would talk about how their lives were going to turn out. He spoke about discovering cures for the great diseases, and of becoming a painter. She never believed he would do these things, not because he wasn't capable but because she couldn't imagine knowing someone whose life was so celebrated. And when it was her turn to say what she was going to be, she made things up, things she knew would please him.

From time to time in the confessional booth he pretended to be a priest. "How have you sinned, my child?" he would ask.

By the time she had anything to confess, Jack had moved away to Boston to start college. That was the summer Casey turned eighteen, when she began wearing her hair up in braids and when she lived in dime-store sundresses. That was the summer her mother's illness began to take over everything. One afternoon in June, Casey fixed lunch on a tray and carried it upstairs to her mother's room. She looked up at Casey from the pillow, smiled, and said, "We should invite Jack over for lunch today." It was the first time in months she had mentioned Jack. She said his name again and smiled an aimless, evanescent smile. She had always smiled a great deal, showing a countenance full of patience and kindness, but this summer she was losing ground to hardened arteries and she smiled even more. Giddy smiles prompted by a gradual depletion of oxygen to her brain.

"Jack's not here anymore," Casey told her. "You remember, he moved to Boston."

She looked back vacantly, then reached under her pillow for something. "Well, it's cold in Boston, I'll need my hat today," she declared. She sat up suddenly in her bed and pulled an orange ski hat down over her head. It was a ludicrous hat, foisted onto her diminished capacity for discretion by a store clerk eager to make a sale. She had bought this hat on her last shopping trip to town to please her husband, for the first snowfall of winter had come and this meant he would soon go up into the mountains to ski. She wanted to go along with him. She had stood in the doorway calling out to him to take her along. "Captain, I can still ski, I can keep up with you!" She stood there in her nightgown, her hands knotting the flannel cloth at her sides, the ski hat propped crazily on her head of silver hair. He hummed some big-band swing tune as he packed the car, stopping once and coming up to her and trying to make her understand the hopelessness of her plea. "You're too sick now, Marianne. Don't please, don't make this any worse than it has to be."

Casey remembered how his voice that day was soft. She had watched her mother reach up and touch his tanned cheek. She touched it once before he turned and walked away. When he started the car, she leaned back against the door frame to steady herself.

Her father was a big man, a thinker, a reader, a philosopher, a Renaissance man with wide shoulders and a striking face. He moved with a kind of grace and seemed to go through his days with a dazed look in his eyes, as if to say this was not at all the way his life should have turned out.

Even as a young girl, Casey had been aware that she and her mother slowed him down, dragged him back, imprisoned him. He was so versatile and competent, it seemed a terrible waste for him to have to hold down a regular job selling insurance. He had the most restless blue eyes.

Her mother's eyes were the same color, but nothing like his. They burned with a slow blue anguish, all the anguish she had kept to herself, too proud or just too much in love with him to complain. The anguish had come as no surprise to her. From the beginning she had known how difficult life would be with him. She had tried to dissuade him from marriage. He had insisted. When they met she was working as a domestic for a wealthy family in New York City. The family was summering on Long Island when he arrived one weekend to be a guest in the house she was employed to clean. It was 1945, he was right back from the war and barely twenty-one years old. She was nineteen years older; her hair was already streaked with silver. He would return to that house many times and to her bed in the help's quarters. She had never been anywhere in the world, and she was puzzled by the attention he paid her, puzzled until he had told her a thousand times how beautiful she was and how he needed to make love to her. She finally admitted to herself that her only asset was her performance between bed sheets. She was in love with him; she could not control herself, she did everything he wanted her to do, things his girls would not consent to. He told her how he loved the fact that she was a woman. "Not a girl," he said inspiredly, "but a woman. There's a big difference." As often as she asked him, he never managed to explain what this difference was.

When she became pregnant with Casey she made plans to go off on her own and face whatever hardships were waiting. But instead, he insisted they marry. He said he wanted to do the honorable thing. He would have it no other way. She suspected from the start that he was one of those men who deliberately place themselves in impossible circumstances so that they can then stand back and marvel at their sad fate. He could have married any number of girls, girls she knew he was sleeping with when he wasn't sleeping with her. They were girls who spoke with a nasal arrogance when they ordered her around. They had met him at weekend parties in Cambridge and

New Haven and Princeton, where he and his Ivy League confederates migrated like exotic birds in pastel-colored jackets and bow ties. During the years after he had graduated from Harvard and gone off to war he kept in touch with his friends and planned reunions big and small. He seemed to live in perpetual anticipation of these gatherings, and she always encouraged them; though they usually excluded her, she knew how happy they made him and how he depended upon his friends to relieve the monotony of life. Once she showed Casey a poem he had written for a toast at a friend's wedding:

My dream is for a place by the sea,
where the men who were boys when I
was a boy can come and sit and talk with me.

He and his friends had all been singers and sailors in their youth. Whenever they gathered as Casey was growing up, they sang songs for her and her mother. She would always remember in particular a lovely Irish ballad which included one section where her father and his friend would turn and face each other, singing out a dialogue of some sort, gesturing expansively over the heartwarming lyrics as if in an opera. Once when they had finished this they were perfectly still for a moment and then they embraced.

It was the same friend who first called her father Captain. They had all gone to visit him on Cape Cod where he and her father sailed a sloop together in the August regatta. This nickname of Captain seemed perfect for him. Casey and her mother watched him standing in sunlight looking out over the harbor, his stiff baggy shorts held up by a length of rope, his feet brown from the sun, brown even between the toes. He looked invincible.

—15

As they watched him standing there, Casey's mother said with a smile, "I was lucky to find him. All the girls that wanted him, and he went off with me."

After the race there was a victory party that lasted late into the night, and Casey lay in her bed pretending to be asleep when her mother and father returned. She could see out into the room where her mother got undressed while her father went around the cottage putting things away. He did the dishes in the kitchen sink. He arranged things on top of the bureau. He was a compulsive man who liked to have things orderly. He always cleaned the house when he was nervous or upset. He stopped suddenly and said, "Look at me, I'm like some goddamned character in a cartoon, straightening up everything while I'm falling apart on the inside."

Casey's mother ran her hands along her thighs while he went on to say that of all his friends everyone had always believed he would do something fine with his life. "I haven't amounted to a row of beans," he said.

"You're too hard on yourself, Paul," she replied.

"I sell insurance," he said. Then he gazed into space for a minute.

In the silence he continued to line up magazines on the coffee table. "Ask any of them what I used to be like."

"I knew you before," she said, interrupting him. "You're the same man to me."

He turned and glared at her as she said she thought he expected too much of himself. "*You* could have been happy married to a damn mailman," he said.

Casey held her breath as her mother stood up and walked to his side of the bed. She placed a hand on each of his shoulders and slowly sat him down like a child, then she went down on her knees between his legs and began to kiss him. Casey heard him weeping, the only time she ever heard him cry until years later when he wept on the day President Kennedy was shot. That day he walked out of the house to cry alone over the loss of this friend who had sailed with him and given him the nickname Captain and sung the Irish ballad with him before his life became so busy there was no time left for her father.

He had gone to Washington for the funeral. On the television Casey and her mother spotted him at Arlington Cemetery standing off by himself with his arms folded in front of him, gazing straight ahead. This was the way he always stood when he burned leaves in the driveway and followed the smoke up toward heaven. On the TV screen he seemed suddenly within their reach. All his strength and his remoteness had been reduced on the screen to the image of a darkened figure, no more than half an inch tall, a man suddenly small and accessible to them. They watched him and examined him and were amazed by the sight of him there, as people are amazed by the sight of a ship inside a bottle until they figure out the trick behind the illusion.

"All I ever wanted was to make your father smile," her mother said.

"He'll come home soon," Casey told her.

Her mother simply nodded. "Why can't he smile a little for us?" she whispered.

Chapter Two

That was all before the summer Jack moved away and her mother's illness began to take over everything in Casey's life. It began with forgetfulness and spread to incompetence. There was a Sunday when she hit the clutch instead of the brake pedal, and the car went coasting right through the aluminum garage door. After that Casey's father wouldn't let her drive again. "I've driven all my life," she argued. He didn't answer this. His silence seemed intended to say her life, as far as he was concerned, was over.

Casey began dating that summer, and her father took great interest in this. He lectured her, he said for her own good. He began looking at her in a different way, in a way that made her take a little half-step back away from him whenever they were alone in a room.

"You need something more grown-up to wear," he said to her one day.

She shrugged her shoulders and he went on, "You know, if you could lose ten pounds on your bottom you'd be a real knockout, sweetie."

He walked up next to her and put his hand on her arm. "I remember when you used to be built like a little bird. You'd be curled up in my lap and I wouldn't even know you were there."

"I'll go on a diet," she said. "I'll do it for you, if that's what you want."

He picked up on this. "Do it for yourself, Love. Think about yourself."

"Yes," she said, nodding her head to show him she understood.

He stepped away from her, his hands clenched into fists. "Because I'll tell you something. Believe me, if you don't think about yourself in this world, nobody else will. The world is against you from the word go."

She watched as he opened his hands, and she interpreted this gesture to mean he was done talking. She started to turn away. Then he said, "The world is always trying to take away your choices, your . . . liberty. That *word*. I fought in a war to save that word. Can you believe it? I was a damn kid, and then it was over and we got drunk and celebrated. Only nobody was standing there telling me that liberty was something I'd have to keep fighting for."

When he stopped, she lied and told him she knew what he meant.

"Well, all I'm saying is do yourself a favor, hold on to liberty, don't ever foreclose on options. And you can make it a whole hell of a lot easier for yourself in this regard, Sweetie, by losing that weight on your butt."

This soon became his battle cry. He watched her chewing at the table and monitored her trips to the refrigerator. Casey felt his eyes following her around the house.

Then out of the blue he took her shopping one day for a dress. He took her to a boutique called La Bella Dame, where he picked out a dress for her date with a college boy who'd called to ask her out. It was a cotton dress, and when she came out from the dressing room with the belt fastened around her waist he look disheartened. "Can she wear that without the belt?" he asked the saleswoman.

"Oh sure," the woman replied.

"Why don't you take off the belt then, Sugar. Yes, there, that's a big improvement, don't you think?"

Casey watched him as he paid the full price for the dress then rolled up several bills in one hand and tipped the saleswoman on their way out.

Casey had three dates with the college boy, spending the last hours of each in his car, a beer-stained compartment with a smell that was pungent enough to overpower the cardboard spruce tree air-freshener that hung from the knob of the lighter on the dashboard. On the last night she let him touch her. He fumbled around with the buttons on her blouse, and while he was telling her about his football scholarship he laid her down on the seat and lifted up her legs and parted them with great tenderness. In the darkness of the car she tried to see his face or imagine his expression when he touched her bare skin. But he seemed very far off. Suddenly he asked if she was a virgin. She said yes she was. "Well, I have a rule," he said. "I don't do it with virgins. But you're real nice, Casey, and I'm going to have to do *something* or I won't be able to stand up straight for a week."

At her house he kept his malodorous car running. He told her he would write her from Texas. She watched him

—20

drive away, his taillights burning like hot coals in the darkness.

Her father was downstairs sitting in the living room with a book on his lap and a floor lamp pulled up next to his chair. "I was thinking about you," he said pleasantly when he saw her. He spoke very softly and said her mother was sleeping. "Do you remember me reading this to you, *Charlotte's Web*?"

"My favorite of all time," she said.

"Yes. Good old E.B. White up there on his saltwater farm in Maine put his finger on something. He struck the right notes and he's found permanence because of it."

He was silent then, and seemed lost. It was, Casey guessed, the prize of permanence that he had most ardently wanted in life. He must have believed at one time that there was something about him which would elevate him above the masses and bestow upon him a distinction which time and change would not impair. He expected a great deal of himself and his daughter. Sitting alone at night in his study as he had done for years, he must have thought back over his life and his own chances for permanence, back to a time when he was responsible only for himself, a time when life could still surprise him with possibilities.

He set down the book and looked up at her. Then a distracted expression swept over his face. His lips opened and froze. He beckoned her closer to the light. He squinted and stared hard at her. Then he rose from his chair and turned away. As he passed through the living room he called back to her. "You'd better soak your dress in something or it'll be ruined."

There was nothing she could say, nor any way for her

to explain how this had happened, and besides, he knew everything and she knew nothing. He knew what the college boy had done to her.

As he turned and walked away he hesitated only briefly, and he drummed the fingers of his left hand against the hardness of his thigh as if he considered saying something more. But then he left her.

The college boy had exposed her, she thought. He had uncovered her insufficiency. And from then on when her father's eyes followed her, when his admonition about her weight echoed through the house, she found a new implication in his disappointment: what he seemed to be telling her now was that if she had not been deficient in some way that college boy would have just screwed her and been done with it and no one would have known the difference.

When Casey cooked his favorite meal one night after this as part of her unremitting effort to regain his favor, he said nothing to her. She cooked him spare ribs, and set the table with their best dishes, the ones with bunches of blueberries hand-painted on a white background. He was tired from a hard day at work. He talked about the people in the insurance office, how they were all the same. "Pay people a few bucks a week and they'll cash in their youth and never know the difference." He spoke in a lifeless monotone as if there was no one else in the room. "I long for a certain time, certain things," he announced. "Everything's wasted."

Casey's mother interrupted. "Oh, Captain, we ought to go to the shore again!"

He shook his head at her and said the shore wouldn't make any difference. When he said this her face flushed. It was as if his words had physically struck her. He apologized and then he turned to Casey. "I'm going to take you skiing this winter and you're going to learn. Here . . ." He jumped up from the table to show her how it was done. "It's all in the hips and knees, like this. All the weight on the downhill ski, then lift the other one through the turn. And rotate the hips, rotate them."

"I bet I can still ski," Casey's mother cried out. "I remember how we skied together, Captain."

"No you don't," he said softly.

"Maybe she does," Casey said. She looked right into his eyes.

He looked back at her and for a moment the room was silent. Then he said, "No, she doesn't remember. And she doesn't know that I'm the one who's dying in this wasted house, dying on the inside where it counts. Neither of you seems to know that. Neither of you knows how to comfort a man when he's down."

Soon after he said this there was a clinking noise at the end of the table where Casey's mother was sitting. With a spoon in her hand she was trying to scrape the painted blueberries from her plate. "These berries look so good," she said happily. "I'm hungry for berries tonight."

He got up from the table. He seemed very calm. "Let me take you to bed, Marianne," he said. And he led her away.

Casey imagined that snow was falling in his mountains that night. In some ski lodge on the side of some mountain he had flown down on his waxed skis in his past, people were watching the snow blow past a giant window, the smoke from their fireplace curling up in the silent winter sky.

In the middle of the night her father came into her

—23

room. He came wearing no shirt. He sat down on the end of her bed and woke her with one hand on her shoulder. "Your mother's getting worse," he said. "There's nothing I can do."

He reached up and stroked her hair, stroked it again and again. "You're my angel," he said. He traced the palm of one hand across his jaw, his whiskers scratching the callouses on his fingers. "Ever since you were a baby I thought you were going to turn out to be like me, I mean being able to understand things." He shook his head. "I mean it's a great comfort to me, always has been. Whenever everything seems lost, I think about how you're going to go on. You know? Way farther than I've gone. It's a good thing." His hand pulled away suddenly, and she was filled with apprehension. He walked away from her bed, walked quickly, and she lay there thinking how he had always walked too quickly for her mother to keep up. Then reaching the door to her room, he pushed it shut and turned and came back to her. She couldn't open her eyes. "You're okay," he said. "Your mother's asleep. I'm just going to pull up your nightgown here. Lift up for me angel. You can pretend I'm that college boy."

She lay there thinking of the snow on his ski mountain, thinking of herself as an angel on her back in the snow, and for a few moments she seemed to have gained his love and his forgiveness. She seemed to have comforted him.

Chapter Three

That winter everything changed. One night Casey was awakened by her mother's screams. She ran down the dark hallway to her room and found her sitting up in bed, the sheets twisted around her shoulders. She pointed to the window. "I saw him there, that butcher. That fellow Oswald, I saw him."

Casey turned on all the lights and held her and told her everything was all right. "You had a dream, Mama, that's all it was." She walked to the window. "There's no one here, there's nothing at all."

Her mother shook her head. "He's gone," she whispered. "He's gone."

"Yes, gone. You were only dreaming."

"No, he's gone," she said sorrowfully. She turned her head to the closet and lifted one hand toward its opened doors. "He took his shirts, he isn't coming back. He took all his nice striped shirts. The beautiful shirts."

Casey walked to the closet and saw the empty space, a gap which even in its emptiness seemed to emanate her father's scent. "No," she said hopefully, "there are a few shirts here." And she pulled the sleeve of one and held it out for her mother to see. "Here, look."

"But it's a white shirt. He never cared for his white shirts." She motioned for Casey to come to the bed, her hand opening and closing quickly, then patting the mattress. "We have to figure out what to do now, and we'll be fine. We'll be fine. I'm going to get a job."

"Where's he gone, Mama?"

"I don't know where he goes when I wake up in the night and he's not here. But this time he took his shirts. This time is different."

There is a difference, Casey thought. A difference between his not being here in her bed and his being *gone*. It was more than the emptiness of his side of the closet, more than the bleak look in her mother's eyes. Casey looked far into her eyes, wondering if she knew what the difference was.

"Where does he go at night?" she asked again, brushing her mother's hair back from her face. "Do you know, Mama?"

"We don't know," she answered. "We'll never know. But you and I ought to go tomorrow and buy your father some nice new shirts."

It took Casey most of the morning to get her mother ready to go out. She laid out clothes but her mother wanted to dress herself and she kept coming down the stairs in crazy combinations, blouses over dresses, a slip for a skirt.

They rode the bus to town. In all the stores her mother was interested in only the men's clothing. "Your father would look handsome in this," she said in every aisle. Finally she picked out two striped shirts and paid the asking price. She just laid her money on the counter. The fight in her was gone. Casey thought she no longer believed in her ability to change anything in the big world.

He sent a small check each Friday, but weeks passed with no word from him. Whenever Casey and her mother went out of the house they returned and found more of his things gone. It was as if he had them under surveillance so he could get into his house and leave without being confronted.

"We ought to put all his stuff in a pile on the front lawn," Casey said as they stood facing the empty desk in his study. She heard her mother drop into the leather chair.

"Go and see, will you," she said. "See if he's taken his skis."

Casey found them in one corner of the basement, a block of wood wedged between them to preserve their camber. When she told her mother, her eyes brightened.

That night Casey heard her dragging the skis up the stairs to her room. She found her sliding them under the blanket on her bed. "When he comes back I'm going to be ready," she said cheerfully.

Casey stood in the doorway. "Aren't you happy with me?" she called out to her. "Can't we be fine, just the two of us? Can't we let him just go?"

Her mother turned and faced her. She was smiling grandly and she raised one hand with a finger pointed to the ceiling. "He's never forgotten his skis, he'll be back."

"He won't be back," Casey said.

"Oh, he will, he will. But I want you to promise me you won't tell him where his skis are." She raised her eyebrows, waiting. "Will you? Will you promise me?"

"You're going to make me promise?"

"Yes."

—27

"You don't trust me, Mama?"

"No," she said. She shook her head dramatically and said she couldn't afford to trust anyone. "Not anymore."

"But why not me?"

"You're so pretty," she answered. "All the pretty girls everywhere I go. I have to watch out for them."

Casey walked over to her and put a hand on her shoulder. "I want you to say you don't mean that," she said softly.

"Oh," she whispered, "but look how pretty you are." She reached up and her hand accidentally brushed over Casey's breasts. Then she closed her eyes. "It's so dark in here without your father," she said.

They spent many days cleaning the house and rearranging furniture together. Casey had the idea that she could somehow transform his house so that it would seem like he had never been there at all, that the new positioning of chairs and rugs would create an illusion of travel, that she and her mother had traveled to a place beyond his reach. But the more Casey tried to exorcize her father, the more her mother tried to re-create him. It wasn't long before she had replenished all his shirts. She pricked her fingers taking the straight pins out of the collars and cuffs. She washed and ironed them every Monday, then carried them back up to the closet one at a time and hung them in a row. She had moments of complete disorientation when she would have burned holes in the shirts and the house down around them if Casey hadn't intervened. Other times she was so lucid it seemed her disease had been reversed. In those moments she spoke generously of her husband, telling Casey again and again that he would be back. Once she said, "He's a romantic man. He'll surprise us, you wait and see. Romantic men surprise you when you least expect them to."

Casey could cope with her mother's dementia, but she dreaded those moments of lucidity when the unutterable secret between the two of them, the secret which had been caused by her illness and concealed by it, seemed suddenly to be near exposure. The secret seemed to have a physical presence in the house. And Casey was always waiting for her mother to say, "*You have the power to bring him back to me. It's not the shirts or the skis, it's you. You can keep him happy in this house.*"

The guilt Casey lived with had two sides: she had betrayed her mother, and she had failed to keep her father under their roof, the one thing which could have pardoned her betrayal.

When he finally came back it was Christmas Eve. He had a redhead named Shelly on his arm. They had been drinking. At the door they swayed together. He grinned and said, "I thought it was time to just live and let live. What do you say?"

This began the first of many visits. Casey's mother welcomed them into the house and baked pies for them and got down on her knees and rolled up the carpets in the living room for them so they could dance to his old records. She sat on the couch smiling up at them. He always took her in his arms once before the night was over and placed her feet on the perforated toes of his shoes and waltzed her around the room as if she was weightless. This seemed to be enough for her.

On one of these visits he came to Casey's bedroom. It was very late and she thought he had already left the house. He came into the room and closed the door behind him, just reaching behind his back and swinging it shut

—29

without even looking. He was a step away from her when she turned on her light. His hands flew up in the air and he shook his head. "No, no, I just want to make sure of one thing," he said. "I want to know if you ever said anything to your mother."

She wouldn't give him an answer. After a moment he said, "Okay then, don't talk to me, I don't blame you."

When he closed the door and had walked the length of the hallway, Casey got out of bed and followed him. From the top of the stairs she looked down at Shelly sitting on the carpet in her bra and panties. Her father got down on the floor and took her in his arms. He parted her thighs with one hand and then Casey saw him take hold of her panties and twist the material around two of his fingers. With a jerk of his wrist the material tore from her hip. Shelly's body seemed to go limp beneath him. Suddenly he raised himself up on his elbows and his voice drifted up the stairs. "I was sitting right here in this room one night when the president of the United States of America called me from the White House. He said, 'Paul, I'm in the Oval Office with two naked girls and I'm reading the fucking *Wall Street Journal.* Am I getting old?' That's exactly what he said. Two months later he was dead."

By the new year he was gone. He took his skis and said he was never coming back. "I've signed the house over to you," he told Casey before he left. "Be smart, get out of here. Life's short."

She watched him kiss her mother on the forehead, then go out to his car. He had already started the engine when Casey ran out into the driveway. "Don't ever tell anyone, yourself or anyone else, that I'm like you," she

—30

said to him. He stared at her, then rolled down the window. "You heard me," she said. "Don't pretend you didn't hear me."

"The office," he called to her. "If you ever want to get in touch with me."

As he was backing into the street she pictured Shelly waiting for him, or some other woman half-dressed and waiting, someone he would someday walk out on.

Casey turned nineteen the next week. One morning she and her mother were walking to mass, and when they passed Casey's old elementary school her mother stopped. She gazed at the low, rectangular windows where heads of George Washington had been cut from construction paper and pasted on the glass. "Easter's coming next," Casey said, to break the spell this scene had cast over her mother. She watched her standing there against the blue sky. She wondered what her mother believed about Easter, about the life and death of Jesus. When she was a girl her mother took her to Sunday school and Mass. It didn't seem so very long ago. And she seemed to know even then as a girl, even as she stood in her white confirmation dress to take her first Communion, that the day would come when she would believe none of it, when Jesus Christ would only be a character in some old, old story.

"What are you thinking, Mama?"

In the sunlight her mother's eyes glistened. The tiny broken capillaries were as red as rubies. "I came and stood here before," she said. "I watched you on the playground, over there. I saw a boy kiss you over there."

"Billy Andrews," Casey said. "My first kiss. I punched him for it."

Then her mother's expression became very sad. She

—31

lowered her eyes. "I came one day and you were all under your desks," she said with a heavy sigh. "I stood at the windows looking in. You were all curled up under your desks. The bombs."

"We had drills. There was a shelter in the basement."

"I thought, we've killed the fun for you."

That morning Casey's mother fell down the granite church steps and broke her hip. It was a beautiful young nun, Sister Tamara, who took Casey aside in the hospital and advised her to put her mother into a home run by the Catholic Diocese. "We'll look after her for you," she said. "God gave you a life, go and live it."

The house had to be signed over to the Church. But in exchange, Casey's mother was moved into a robin's-egg-blue room on the tenth floor of the Shelter of Mercy. "She'll be happy with us," Sister Tamara said, standing at the window.

"Mama, what do you think?" Casey asked.

She looked around the room and smiled. "Who wouldn't be happy in such a wonderful room?" She turned to Casey and asked how long she would be staying.

"As long as you wish," the Sister answered. "Your daughter's going off to college now. Don't you think that's just wonderful?"

"Oh yes. It is," she said.

Casey sat on the bed and told her all her plans. "I'll be back to see you. I'll come back whenever I can, whenever you want me to. You have to get well, get your leg strong again."

"I'm going to have her playing tennis with me by summer," Sister Tamara said.

They all laughed for a moment and then Casey's mother turned away. "How far am I from home?" she asked.

—32

"We're just a couple of miles, Mama. Right out there, that's Hammond Street. You remember I told you?"

"I thought I was up in the mountains," she said. "I'm so high up. I thought I was up in the mountains. Did you know, Sister, that I still ski?"

Chapter Four

Two days later Casey rode a bus to Boston and found her way to Jack's door.

"It isn't much to look at," he said as he swept her into his apartment. He looked at her with that great, open smile of his that she had always found reassuring. She thought he looked taller.

"Thinner," he said. "Eating my own cooking."

She told him the apartment was great. He said it wasn't much. "I started cleaning up the day I found out you were coming. It's been pretty much of a pig sty since my roommate bolted on me. But check this out, Casey." He took her hand and pulled her to a room of wide windows looking down on the city. "There it is," he said triumphantly, "over there. Where all of New England goes to worship."

She had to confess the view was very nice but she didn't know what he meant.

"Fenway Park! Here we are looking right down on the bosom of the old grande dame. And up there a ways, I pass it every day on my way to classes, the bargain basement at Filene's. I always think of your mom, how she'd be in heaven there."

Even before he said that, Casey had been looking down from his windows thinking of her mother, wondering if someone would take the time to set her chair next to a window and point out things for her.

"I'm going to pay for this, I think. Someday I'm going to pay for abandoning her."

He shook his head. She hoped he would tell her something that would absolve her guilt. He had always known what to say to her, she thought. The problems then had been so much smaller.

He draped one arm over her shoulder. She wondered if by his touching her he could tell that she was different, that things had happened to her since they were last together. "I should have written you more often," she said.

"That's what friends are for," he said. He reached out to the window and traced one finger across the glass. He asked her if she remembered the last thing he'd said to her before he left town a year ago. He had told her they were kindred spirits and they wouldn't be apart for long.

"When you wrote that you were coming," he went on, "I thought, God, isn't that great! We're going to be together before you meet some guy and get married and I never see you again."

"You make it sound pretty certain. Maybe I'll join the nunnery." She smiled at him.

"Pray for my soul if you do," he said. "But what I mean is it happens all the time, friends get split up, everything else gets in the way. There's no time once you get married and have kids. There's no such thing as just dropping in on each other. Everything's complicated. I was talking to my roommate about this before he jumped ship. You think about the way life is set up, almost nobody has time to keep old friends. And then you get old and you

—35

have more time than you know what to do with, and the old friends are gone. Right?"

"You make new friends, I suppose," she said tentatively.

He looked disappointed. "Maybe," he said. Later, over dinner, he started talking again about friendship. "People talk about making new friends, you know, as if it's that easy. They make it sound like friendship is as universal as love. But when I'm old and they've got me pissing into a plastic bag, I don't want some new friend there trying to console me. I want someone who remembers me from these days, someone who can say to me, Jesus, you look stupid! And we can laugh about it."

What he said made sense to her. But she told him her life was going to be different. "I may surprise you," she said. "I may move in here and never leave."

That night she stood naked in the shower thinking that she was too young for what Jack had said about friendship to have any urgency. She hadn't lived long enough to imagine life depriving them of each other.

They sat around on an old green couch eating fish sticks. They talked for a long time of her mother. "No one would be cheering harder for you to have your own life," he said.

"This last year . . . ," she said, but then she paused. She thought of some of the details she could recount for him, scenes she could describe for him which would, in their terrible grimness, show why she had to put her mother into the nursing home. She didn't have to explain anything to Jack. Even if the evidence had been against her, he would have held her blameless.

"What I kept hoping," she told him, "was that the sickness would erase her memory. I mean so she wouldn't be able to dwell on how he betrayed her." She stopped and looked at him and waited, wondering again if he would be able to tell by looking at her it was more than that.

She went on, "And now I hope for the same thing so she doesn't have any memory of me leaving her."

Jack wouldn't judge her, she knew this. She wondered if perhaps she wanted to be judged. If she could reveal her secret to someone and be pardoned, then it would be over. The guilt would be behind her.

They sat there on his couch. He had a pair of binoculars and they took turns watching the game. He said if she lived in Boston long enough she would become a Red Sox fan. "It's inevitable. There's a waiting list for this side of the apartment building. I had to bribe the real estate agent and the landlords. It ended up costing me more than a season ticket in a box seat. But that's the price of getting what you really want in this town."

She figured it must have been his parents' money financing the bribe. In his retirement Jack's father had played the stock market, and she'd always known them to have plenty of money.

"Your father—" she started to say.

"My father cut me off. Didn't I write and tell you the gory details?"

"No."

"I got in some academic trouble. Probation. Dad got pissed, he called me a libertine. I tried to explain to him that there's a kind of gallantry in this town associated with academic probation. Half of Harvard is on academic pro. The idea is that since there's a war on and since we should be over there fighting in it instead of over here living it up, you've got to walk a fine line."

"I don't understand."

"Well, it has to do with manhood. With the war and the draft to Vietnam you don't want to look like you're intentionally avoiding getting your ass shot off. You know, hiding behind good grades. So you just fuck off, and if the professors want to save your neck then it's on their conscience. All the really brave boys are about one-tenth of a grade point from getting snapped up by the Army and shipped to the rice paddies."

Jack had changed, she thought. He had become glib about things. "You were always a great student," she said.

He pretended to tip a hat, mocking himself. "My only claim to fame, I know. I had to overcome my natural brilliance. It took a concentrated effort. Dad called it sloth. He's disappointed." Jack cast his eyes down at the floor. "Shit, I didn't want to disappoint him, but I'm tired of trying to please everybody. Maybe I want to just hack around for a while."

Casey barely heard him. She was thinking about her own father, about how she was really freer than Jack. Now that her father had left she wouldn't have to worry about disappointing him. This thought filled her with an incredible lightness. The feeling quickly passed.

"Anyway," Jack went on, "that explains these rubber fish sticks for dinner. Now that I'm paying my own way the gruel's been pretty thin."

"I'm going to help out."

He waved her off and told her there was nothing to worry about. He was working at a record shop in Cambridge and selling his plasma once a month. "The proverbial pound of flesh," he called it.

"And the draft, Jack?"

He shook his head derisively. "Don't worry, the Army wouldn't want me."

—38

Jack was suddenly quiet. He pushed open the window and told her he could sometimes hear applause from the ball park if the wind was right. They listened together. There was nothing. He said this meant the Red Sox were losing. "Sometimes I swing a bat in front of the windows and imagine they're cheering for me."

She thought about how unknown he had been at school, how he had never drawn applause from anyone. But quietly, almost secretly he had been working away on his own, getting himself into Harvard. She remembered how her father had made a big deal of this when Jack received his acceptance letter. "Best days of your life will be right there, right there in Cambridge," he had said to him. "It'll be worth millions to you. Millions."

Looking carefully at Jack now, she saw he was trying too hard to convey self-confidence. While she answered his questions he drifted off, and a worried look, tense and apprehensive, came over him. Then he caught himself and recovered for the next question.

She said, "Do you remember we used to sit on that big couch in your parents' basement and pretend we were on a raft in the Mississippi? Make for the big water, Jim!"

Jack pulled his feet up onto the couch and played along. "Right, Huck, I done seen what they did to that abolitionist. We gots a heap of runnin' away to do."

The curtains blew in at the windows. It's true, Casey thought. I am running away.

"You need a plan," Jack said cheerfully.

"A plan to justify everything," she said. "I have no plan."

"A strategy then," he said. "A plan of attack. But first some fun. We're entitled to some fun."

It was almost morning when she fell asleep in the bed

—39

vacated by Jack's roommate. She thought back to each of the nights she had spent away from home. There weren't that many for a girl nineteen years old. She tried then to think about what was ahead, what tomorrow would be like waking up here. Thinking about tomorrow, and the day after that, would make it seem like she was running toward something new.

When she fell asleep she dreamed about her father.

She dreamed about the time he took her to the Montgomery County Air Show. It was spring. She was in sixth grade, and he just came walking down the corridor at school and into her homeroom and the two of them walked out of the building together. All the other kids watched them pass.

At an abandoned airport twelve miles away, amateur pilots were gathered to fly remote-control planes made of incredible, weightless wood. She spent the day looking up into the sky with her father; their hands shaded their eyes from the sun. The small planes circled overhead like birds. The rasping of the tiny gasoline engines filled the air. The first scent of spring blew in across the runways, blowing through the grass that had grown up through the cracks in the macadam and granite.

This was their first outing together. And the wonderful thing about it, the thing she would never forget, was that all the other fathers had sons at their sides.

Her father held her hand and marched her back and forth along the edge of the runway where the pilots had little booths and workbenches set up like street vendors. They all spoke to her father. They didn't seem to know him, but still they shared a common knowledge or passion. There was excitement in their eyes.

At the end of the day they walked to the car together.

Instead of opening the doors and getting in, her father unlocked the trunk. He had a tent and sleeping bags, and he said they would be camping out. They cooked beans and stew over a kindling fire. He showed her how to brew coffee by cracking open an egg and dropping it, shells and all, right into the boiling water with the coffee grounds. And then he let her drink some to show her how all the grounds adhered to the egg at the bottom of the pot.

They pitched the pup tent under one wing of a rusting Army transport that was moored to the ground with giant concrete blocks and heavy chains.

Before they fell asleep he told her about the war. This was the first time he'd ever spoken to her of this. He told her about going to the draft board the day after Pearl Harbor and lying about his age. He named all the places the Army had shipped him to, pausing between each with a little sigh of resignation and pride. The way he described the war made it seem like nothing more than a great Boy Scout adventure, the kind of adventure he hungered for.

Casey wondered if that's why they were camping out at the airport in sleeping bags when their house was only a few miles away. Perhaps he had gone to the trouble of bringing her along so that she would remember something nice about him, a nice scene—at night, sleeping in the grass under the wing of an airplane. Was he covering his bets, giving her a pleasant scene to countervale the dark ones ahead of her? Or perhaps he had no idea then what was ahead.

But while she slept away the morning under Jack's roof she dreamed her father was watching her that night at the airport. In the grass, the shadow of the plane's wing spread over her, she slept while he was propped up on one elbow watching her, and waiting.

Chapter Five

She found work, part-time at a delicatessen three blocks from Jack's apartment. When she wasn't there behind the counter, or sitting in on Jack's classes at Harvard, or riding the bus back and forth to visit her mother, she and Jack were walking the streets of Boston and Cambridge. They were vaguely aware of some energy gathering in the city, something restive and magnetic. Inside Jack's apartment they seemed always to be near the windows, monitoring the activity in the streets. One day they watched a procession of blacks carrying banners, their chanting voices as weightless as cinders rising up to the windows. "They have a plan," Jack said. "A plan to change things. I've been blind to all the things we need to change, all the things that matter."

"Tell me," she said. "Tell me, what does matter?"

He didn't answer her directly. "Something's heating up down there. People are pissed off. They're pissed off at people like me. Do you realize how blind I've been all my life?" Jack shook his head disconsolately and pressed his forehead against the window frame. "I was a kid and we were living all over the world with the Foreign Service, and I had that fantastic chance to learn about life, about people, and instead all I did was read comic books."

She told him he was just being hard on himself.

He shook his head. "I was a numb kid, a real peckerhead. I hardly have any memory of that time in my life, there's nothing that registered up here in my brains. All I remember is the maid standing in front of me every morning, holding out my underpants for me to step into. Every day the same self-indulgence, the same privilege."

He went on to condemn his privileged past. He told her he wanted to atone for it. "The time is coming in this country when no one will get away with being numb anymore. People will have to face things. The bums, the people I meet at the plasma center, I feel guilty as hell about the way things are for them. I wish I could give them a way out."

"Are they looking for that?" Casey asked. "A way out?"

"We all are, aren't we? Them from their poverty, me from privilege."

"And me?"

He turned, took a step closer to her and placed his hands on her shoulders. He held her at arm's length and looked at her. She began to remember her father standing in front of her like this when she was very small, examining her before she went off to school. Jack went on talking then. "These people living off the street, you want to give them something though, some word or something they can believe in and follow out of the gutter."

He looked into her eyes, then released her and walked into the kitchen. The room was silent but for the noise from the streets. When he came back to her he was eating

—43

cold baked beans from a can. She asked him if they would end up that way. "In the gutter, I mean."

He smiled at her curiously. He said it was too soon to know how they would end up. "But we won't be in the gutter because I'd save you from that and you'd save me."

"Then, they don't have anyone? That's it?"

"People give up on you after a while. They help you out of gutters only so many times. The longer you go on making mistakes in this world the fewer the places where you're welcome to come."

He shrugged his shoulders. She said, "I think it's up to you. No one can save you from that."

"Maybe," he said. He held the can of beans up and joked that he was preparing himself for a long life of deprivation.

She turned and looked down into the street. One black boy left the procession and went running ahead, wildly swerving through the traffic, and smashing the windshields of parked cars with a big stick. He stopped at each car for just an instant and brought his stick down with such force that his feet lifted off the pavement. Then he ran on. The entire procession stopped to watch him, all the marchers suddenly paralyzed by the boy's defiance. Casey saw two policemen running far behind, chasing him. She watched the boy disappear, then she saw the policemen return, walking with their hands on their hips. That night she lay awake in bed thinking that the black boy would never be caught, that his defiance was *his* way out.

It was already August when Casey found work at Children's Hospital and began making plans for fall. She quit the delicatessen job and signed up for courses at Northeastern University.

"You don't have to organize your whole life overnight," Jack said. "There's no rush. Take some time to relax. We were going to have some fun, remember?"

"I want to get moving," she told him. She wanted to tell him how she planned to get her own room somewhere, to be on her own, to test herself. But she could see that Jack was already afraid of losing her.

In the hospital many of the children she worked with were dying. She would see them one night, helping the nurses get them ready for surgery at sunrise. By the time she returned to her shift the next afternoon they were dead.

She worked all the overtime hours the hospital would give her. She spent free time drawing up what she told Jack was her secret agenda. She kept a journal and filled it with columns of numbers that represented a strict budget which would allow her to be independent by Christmas. She needed clothes, tuition money, and things for her mother. And she wanted to pay Jack back. He kidded her about this and told her that if she wasn't careful she was going to turn into a banker. "Like half of this city," he said.

She pointed out the one great difference between the two of them, that he always had money and she never had. Just like her mother, she had always been without money.

"I remember she kept quarters in the iced tea pitcher in the second cupboard to the right of the sink," Jack recalled.

"She used to stand me up on the counter. We'd count her money, then she'd go on a shopping spree."

"Twenty pairs of spiked golf shoes," Jack remembered, smiling.

—45

"She fought to get a good deal. *He* never gave her enough money." It was the first time Casey had spoken of her father. She turned from Jack when she mentioned him. She leaned away from him and drummed her knuckles on the arms of the chair. Something was becoming clear to her. "He had all the money, and the keys. Do you remember his key ring full of keys? It was clipped on his belt. They jingled when he walked." She thought that was the great difference between her father and mother; he had doors he could open and lock behind him. He could leave her on the outside.

One night after that they talked for a long time about what she could and could not change in her mother's life. She ended up telling Jack what she wanted most of all. "In the hospital I think all the time how I'd like to have a lot of children. I have this picture in mind of lots of kids running around. If I could have one for her before she's gone."

"I don't know anything about kids," Jack said.

"Well neither do I, but what do you have to know?"

"How to make money, lots of it. And you have to get married first."

"I'll always be poor," she said calmly. "And if I didn't get married I'd still find some way to get pregnant."

Jack looked at her a moment. "I believe you," he said. "I think you would."

She was lost in her own thoughts about her mother, what it would be like to walk into her room carrying a baby, to lay the baby down in the bed next to her. The thing about a baby, she thought, the best thing was that once you became a mother you were a mother for life, no one could ever take that away from you.

She turned to the windows. The lights were on in Fenway Park. The sky above the field was incandescent.

—46

For a minute she felt confident and renewed. Then suddenly everything seemed wrong to her. It was like her idea was turning to an illusion right in front of her eyes, like she already knew too much about herself and about her past to believe certain things.

Jack spoke softly. "You'll do it, you'll have kids."

She had started to answer him before he said that. "The past," she said, "you can't let the past get in the way. You can't pass it on to your kids." She turned back to the windows and gestured down to the streets.

"Yes," Jack said hopefully. "We're the generation that's going to bury the old, corrupted past."

"And we'll be free then?"

"Yes, all of us," he told her. "We'll all be free. We'll have things our own way. We'll go running around changing everything, making it all better."

Two weeks before her classes began at Northeastern she went back home for her mother's birthday. The nuns at the Shelter of Mercy baked a chocolate cake and set up a movie projector in her room. They ran a Laurel and Hardy film to the disjointed applause and the vacant laughter of other residents who gathered to celebrate the occasion. Casey sat among them. There was the hairless man with one bandaged ear, and the lady with red cat's-eye glasses and plastic rings on her fingers. They wore cone-shaped party hats held on their heads by elastic bands that cut into the pads of flesh under their chins. Casey wanted to believe her own mother was nothing like these other people. She watched them, thinking that children were supposed to spare their parents this kind of ending.

Casey gave a small box to her mother and watched as she turned the box in her hands. She seemed reluctant to open it. Casey noticed that her mother's fingernails were very long. They were beautiful really, like those of a young fashion model. In her neglect of them they had flourished.

She had trouble with the ribbon on the box. Casey finally helped her. "It's a necklace," she told her. "You see here . . ." she placed a small silver sand dollar on a silver chain in her mother's opened hand. "Let's put it on and have a look." Casey draped it around her mother's neck. When she tried to fasten it, it slipped from her fingers and dropped inside her mother's dress. Giggling like a schoolgirl, she looked up at Casey and started unbuttoning her dress. "It's okay," Casey said to her. "We'll get it later, Mama. They're going to start the movie now."

In the darkened room many of the old folks nodded their heads and fell asleep. Casey's mother stared at the screen with a bemused look on her face. Suddenly she whispered to Casey, "Paul, come and sit close to me. Come and touch me again."

Casey moved her chair closer to her mother. "Is that what you want? You want to be touched?"

"Oh I know you're angry at me," she said sadly. "I was spoiled for you." She pulled Casey's hand and placed it against one of her breasts. "You boys, you all want virgins. I don't know what to say."

"Don't apologize," Casey said.

"You know how I was spoiled," she went on. "I told you how that boy ripped my stockings. I couldn't help it." She frowned and lowered her head.

Casey looked at her for the longest time and finally she touched her mother's hair and told her, "It never mattered to me. It never mattered at all."

It was late September. They were sitting on a park bench in the Commons watching some Irish-looking men pass around a bottle of beer when Casey told Jack about her mother. "What kind of life lets you end up apologizing for not being a virgin? He walked all over her and she's apologizing to him."

This was only the second time since coming to Boston that she had mentioned her father to Jack. She went on and on. She could tell that Jack was just letting her get something off her chest.

After a while Jack said, "Your father did one thing you'll have to give him credit for. He finally overruled your mother about the accordion lessons."

"Only because I was getting stoop-shouldered from lugging the thing around and my tits were hanging down. He wanted me to pull my shoulders back so they'd stick out. That's what mattered most to him."

"Maybe you're being too hard on him, Casey."

"That's impossible," she said. "Don't ever accuse me of being too hard on him." She stared back at him for a minute, then stood up and walked away. When he rose to follow her she began running. She yelled back at him to let her alone.

She was in front of his window wrapped in a blanket when he got home. She heard the door opening and turned to find him standing there with his head down, a bottle of whiskey in one hand. He looked up at her then. As he started towards her she apologized for running away from him. He shrugged his shoulders and held the bottle out to her.

"What is it?" she asked.

"Nerve," he said. "I'm getting up my nerve to tell you something."

He told her the whole thing. It was more than offering her an explanation; he was making a confession. He spoke

—49

with a certain determination, however, as if he were sure she would be lenient. And she thought, all our lives we will tell each other things we tell no one else.

"Do you remember back in seventh grade, I was thirteen and I came to you and told you the hoods were going to get me? Percy Sergeant and his gang."

She remembered. She remembered his fear at the time, how he'd taken a different route to and from school to avoid the boys he said were after him.

"Days went by," he continued. "A couple weeks. Then they came for me. They came to my house one night after supper. My parents had just left. They came into the house and grabbed me. They flushed my head in the toilet. They took me up behind the water tower and ripped off all my clothes. Then they held me down in the grass and painted me. They painted me green, every inch of me."

Jack paused for another swallow of the whiskey. He looked down at the lighted streets of Boston. Off in the distance there was the muted sound of a police siren, the night soaking it up like a stain.

"They took my clothes. I waited until all the lights were out in the neighborhood, then I walked to your house. I was coming to you for help, I didn't want anybody else to see me. But I was going through the garage and your father was sitting there, sitting out on the hood of the car, just sitting in his underwear smoking a cigarette.

"The reason I stood up for him tonight about the accordion, is because of the way he treated me. He never questioned me that night. He pulled the garage doors shut and helped me. He got some kerosene and rags. He did my back, the places I couldn't reach."

A moment later he started in again. "I never had to

tell anyone what happened. Your father got me off the hook."

"Why did they do it to you?"

He shook his head. "We took those tests in gym class. Push-ups, pull-ups, you know, and they give you a score. They posted the scores in the locker room and sent them home to your parents. I got something, I don't know, I was ranked as the world's weakest kid, something like that. They told my parents they had to be careful with me."

He stood then without saying anything else. She wanted to touch him, to reassure him, but he stepped away. "I owe him for that anyway," he said.

"My father, you mean?"

"Yes."

"No you don't, Jack." She thought back to her mother, the way she had regretted not being a virgin for him. "It's the same thing she was saying. The same trap. She's going to go to her grave thinking she owes him something because she opened herself up for somebody before he came along. Why should anybody owe anybody for that? And this whole virginity thing is another trap. I'd give mine away to the first person who asked for it." She paused then said, "I'd give it to you Jack."

He barely turned to acknowledge her. She led him over to the couch. She sat with his head in her lap, the blanket drawn around them.

Finally he said to her, "It'll be like the blind leading the blind."

She knew what he meant. She didn't answer. Instead, she leaned down and kissed his forehead. She took his hand in hers and clenched it. She was thinking to herself that this would be the perfect time to put the whole stupid question of virginity behind her. It would answer certain questions about herself, and Jack.

He looked up at her. "I guess in the old days it was a virtue maybe to people like your mother. When you lost your virginity you lost a certain virtue too, something you could never get back."

"Well then," she said, "I've got nothing to lose because I've already lost my virtue."

"Me too," he said with resignation. "We're in the same boat."

"And where are we headed?" she asked.

"I was going to ask you that."

Casey thought when they were kids and they pretended to be on Huck Finn's raft they just had to pick some place downriver and off they went. But they never got anywhere really. They just made themselves believe. They couldn't do that anymore. Even as she thought this she wondered if they had already exceeded the time in their lives when they could believe in certain self-deceptions. Or, were there lies about yourself you always had to believe? Maybe that's what losing your virginity was all about. Maybe it exposed certain lies about yourself, things you would never again be able to believe about yourself no matter how desperately you wanted to believe them. She wondered what her mother had once believed about herself, what she had lost even before she married her father. She wondered what he took from her.

"She always waited on him," Jack said. "That's what I remember. Every time I was at your house she was working like a slave, scrubbing something, cleaning up."

Jack recalled when they were in ninth grade, how Casey's mother had organized the schoolchildren in a parade for John Kennedy's campaign for president. "You remember the big signs and banners she made? She marched us all the way to school shouting, 'Nixon's a bum! Kennedy's the one!' "

Casey hadn't thought of that in years. But now she remembered the scene vividly, as if it had happened only a few days earlier. It was a cold day, they were all bundled up and marching behind her mother like little ducks. Her mother had worn those thick stockings with dark seams, seams that ran down the center of both legs dividing them each in half.

"I wonder if she was doing it for my father because he was an old friend," Casey said.

This was just another question. When Casey looked down at Jack thinking he might have answers, he was just staring across the room. The only light in the room had risen up from the city streets and fallen in through the big windows. She squeezed Jack's hand. She felt a great warmth for him.

"I know where to begin," she said softly. She opened her blouse for him. She rolled over and kissed him. She pulled down her jeans, and then unbuttoned his. When she looked at him she saw his eyes were closed. She felt his body relax against hers. She waited, listening to his measured breathing. She thought back to the times they had pretended to be floating on Huck Finn's raft. She tried to recapture that wonderful feeling of floating, gliding along without a care in the world. Instead she felt as if they were being pushed down by some great weight, down below the surface of the river. She just lay there with her arms around him until he fell asleep.

—53

Chapter Six

Casey was aware that anyone who took one long look at Jack and her would know they were both drifting. They passed through the rest of summer, Jack standing at the windows looking down into Fenway Park where the Red Sox were losing their final games. "Gallantry in the face of perpetual loss," he declared once. "This team is a metaphor for my life."

"That's dumb," she told him. His brooding had begun to annoy her, maybe because she was brooding too, but she was determined to jolt him out of it. "You say things like that all the time. It's ridiculous the way you talk about your life as if it's out of your hands."

"Maybe it is, maybe it's all predetermined. We're like pieces on some game board. God just moves us around to amuse himself."

"Goddamn him then," she said. "If that's what kind of god he is."

By September she had made plans to move into a tiny efficiency apartment above The Crosstown Bar & Grill on

Beacon Street. When she told Jack about this, he nodded his head listlessly and shrugged his shoulders in a gesture he must have meant to convey how he had always known this was going to happen, how he was predestined to be abandoned. Casey felt too sorry for him to do anything but put her arms around him and tell him everything would be the same between them.

"You think I could live without your fish sticks?" she said.

"No, you'd perish without my cooking."

"Well, you can maybe bring over a box lunch every once in a while."

"Yeah."

"I'll be right around the corner, Jack."

"Yeah."

"It's not really a big deal."

He looked at her. He told her her eyes were getting greener. "Boston brings out the Irish in you," he said. They laughed at this. "You're going to be one of those girls whose life gets better and better," he said.

Just before she moved into her apartment, she rode the bus back home once more to get a few things she would be able to use to furnish the new place.

She found her mother sitting up in bed. All of the letters Casey had written her in the last six months were scattered over the sheets and she was voraciously reading one after the other while Casey stood in the corridor looking in at her. She was frowning down at the pages, searching them, her eyes narrowed and intensely blue.

Casey entered the room. Her mother looked up at her and quickly beckoned her to her side. "Oh Casey, I can't find it anywhere. I've been reading for hours, ever since I woke up. I've looked through all these."

—55

She reached for another envelope and said, "I'm trying to find out about you."

"What about me?"

"You said you were going to start college. You wrote to me about your plans. I know that was weeks ago but I've been looking through these to find out exactly what you wrote." She looked up suddenly and said with surprise, "But you're here now. I can ask you."

Casey looked at her for some clue. "You remember I wrote you?"

"Yes of course I remember, and I've thought of you at college, how wonderful, like your father. Did you know he took me once to see Harvard. I always wanted to see the Harvard Yard. The ivy, Casey, the ivy was so wonderful and green, growing up the brick walls, reaching right across the windows. He showed me his old room, all the old places."

"You had a good time?" Casey asked her tentatively.

"We always had a good time. Or I only remember the good times. When you're alone as much of the time as I am you have to rely on good memories. He stood out on the steps singing to me."

"Only good memories then? Only good memories of me?"

"Yes. You only did what had to be done."

"Putting you in this place you mean?"

"And before that," she said plainly.

Casey shuddered. She turned slowly to her mother. And what she meant to do next, as soon as she caught her balance, was look into her mother's eyes and say, "Now you *tell* me exactly everything you know about what went on between Dad and me." But that next moment eluded her when her mother began speaking.

—56

"We'll have a long talk," she said. "But first, I'd love a cup of tea. Wouldn't you like a nice cup of tea. Why don't you go down to the Captain's room and get us some tea?"

"Captain's room?"

"Oh, I meant to say the nurses' room. Go—will you go and get the tea, Casey?"

She walked down the carpeted corridor thinking about her father's room, his study on the first floor, the room they had called the Captain's room. The dark-red leather chair pushed into one corner. His albums of classical music. A pipe rack on one corner of his desk. His books from floor to ceiling. The gold, wire-rimmed glasses he wore only when he was in that room.

She carried the tea on a tray. The sisters had said nothing about her mother getting better. Perhaps these periods of lucidity came and then vanished without anyone's knowledge. Perhaps she purposely kept them to herself, told no one about them. Her access to the real world had been reopened, like a path dug through the snow.

When Casey returned to the room, the snow had drifted again and the path was blown shut. She lay on her bed, a vacant, listless expression on her face. When Casey offered her the tea, she turned and examined her as if she were a stranger, and there was nothing more to say.

Back in Boston she moved into her flat and registered for three courses at Northeastern University. For several weeks she didn't see Jack. He stopped by her apartment once when she was on duty at the hospital. When she came home there was an old plaid couch pushed up against the window in her living room. He'd left a note: "Compliments, the Red Army."

She had already discovered the Salvation Army and had replenished her wardrobe there.

A few weeks into the semester, Jack seemed to vanish from her life. For the longest time she didn't see him. Then one afternoon he was waiting outside the door to her composition class. There was a terrified look on his face. "I've got to talk to you," he said. "Something terrible has happened; I did something awful."

He took her outside to a parking lot and led her over to a red pickup truck with a shattered windshield, a crushed top and mashed fenders. "It was a close call," he said just above a whisper.

He told her he had borrowed the truck from his friend and had fallen asleep when he was driving alone on the way up to the North Shore. "I rolled it over in a ditch," he said. "This guy's going to have my ass in a sling."

Then he told her about the owner of the truck, a friend he called Shep. "Short for Shepherd. Only he sort of leads us around, his flock of sheep."

He was a man in his early thirties, a onetime Harvard student who now had elaborate plans to tear the college apart. Jack was attending meetings he conducted in a laundromat in Cambridge, two blocks from Harvard Square. Shep presided over these meetings with a hooded falcon clamped on his left arm. He passed around a hash pipe and talked about his revolution.

Casey went to him before the next meeting to try to intercede on Jack's behalf. She found Shep on the roof of the laundromat. He had built a trap there to catch pigeons. He baited the trap while Casey watched, then took her behind a chimney where they waited.

"I don't want you to take this out on Jack," she told

him. "I've got a job. I can pay you for the damage to the truck."

"It's gone," Shep said glibly. "Totaled." He peered around one corner of the chimney and looked disappointedly up at the sky.

"Well then, a new truck."

"Where do you come up with that kind of cash, sister?"

"It'll take me a while, but—"

He raised his hand in front of her face and snapped his fingers for silence. Two pigeons coasted in over the roof. A moment later there was a loud clapping sound as the trap sprang shut. Shep began to smile.

He left her and when he returned he was holding one of the pigeons in his cupped hands, pinning its wings back with his fingers.

"Jack's ass is grass," he muttered.

"That's why I'm here talking to you," Casey said. "I want to help him out of this."

Shep looked at her and sneered. He looked at the pigeon and made a little cooing noise at it, and it blinked its eyes doubtfully at him. Then he held it down on the tarred roof with one hand. He brought his right foot up in the air slowly and then slammed it down violently, crushing the bird's head.

"I've got to feed my falcon," he said complacently. "You can come with me if you want."

She followed him down a dark flight of stairs into a back room off the laundromat, where there was a cot with a stained army blanket draped across it, some rudimentary cooking appliances, and the falcon on its stand. She turned away when the bird began tearing off the pigeon's wings.

Shep watched. "So you're Jack's public then," he said laconically. "Everybody's got a fucking following these days."

"He's a friend."

Shep laughed. "Well if you're here to ransom Jack's soul I'll put you to use, I'll get some use out of you, sister. But tell me, are you spoiled, bored, and privileged like the rest of my legion?"

Casey tried to persuade Jack that he was being manipulated by Shep. She scorned their revolution. "They're like children, they're all just trying to find limits. Just like my father was."

When Jack tried to defend Shep and his causes, she raised her voice.

"That's a mystery to me, Jack. How can you believe in that loser? You stand here—"

"But if you can break apart the apathy at a place like Harvard, you can get somewhere. We're trying to pry open peoples' eyes to see the truth."

This sounded to her like Shep's lines. "He's trying to swallow you up, Jack. He's got the right words, but they don't add up to any truth."

"Okay," he said, "but they symbolize something important."

"Well go ahead then, go ahead and fall for his symbols. I want to see things that are real, not just symbols. There's nothing real inside the symbols, except confusion maybe. There aren't any answers for the world inside his symbols. Shep doesn't have answers for anyone. He's another empty symbol."

It was raining. They were sitting in a coffee house on Marlboro Street. Fog was drifting up from the river. Even before Jack said it, Casey knew what he was going to tell her. It was not only Shep; there were other equally exotic and crazy boys he had told her about, people to whom he had some strange allegiance. Whenever she had questioned him about these friends of his, he evaded her questions in a way that seemed to be saying to her, "Please, I can't tell you about this."

He put both his hands down on the table and pushed back in his chair. Then he told her that he had been searching for something. "An answer," he said. "An answer about myself." He lowered his eyes and then looked up at her. "I'd like to just put it behind me and walk away."

She didn't say anything. But later when he said he had to go and he got up to leave the coffee house, she told him to wait. She walked with him, listening to his side of things. She was thinking Jack was testing himself, he was trying to be tougher. Boys never forgive each other for not being tough. Right now he must have thought that proving his manhood would be a way out of his past, a simple way out. She thought that nothing so far in her life had been simple and probably nothing ever would be.

Jack was expelled from school that winter when he and two of his cohorts from Shep's gang sabatoged the Winter Carnival ice-sculpting contest at Radcliffe. In the dead of night they constructed an enormous penis in the Quad, aiming it at the office of the woman dean of students. They hollowed out the inside of the sculpture and rigged up a fire extinguisher which shot a stream of foam at the dean when she made her way to the office. Jack was huddled inside when the campus police arrived.

"So what now?" Casey asked him. "There's the draft."

"I told you before, the Army wouldn't know what to do with me. There's a lot to do right here in this town. There's a war to fight right here."

She asked him if he really believed this was the war. "Isn't it inside you? Isn't that the war you have to fight?"

"One war at a time," he said, smiling at her.

"And Shep, he's just giving you something to lash out at. He's using you."

"No one uses anybody against his will."

"You have the will to fight, but I'm not convinced Shep's war is the right war and I don't think you're convinced either."

"You said it once," Jack went on. "You said defiance was a way out."

They walked along the Charles. Jack sailed his student ID card out into the river. "I'm a free man now, Huck," he said.

She walked ahead. They passed the boathouse, its shingles silver in the dappled sunlight, its windows boarded up until spring. She was aware of his great confusion. When he told her that he wanted to learn how to sail, she resisted the urge to tell him that he was holding up some phony romantic image of himself, like the image her father had. "Just be yourself," she said. "Be happy with yourself." Empty words. There should be something better to tell someone you love, she thought.

"Maybe I said that for myself," she explained. "I'm sorry."

He told her she didn't have to be sorry for anything. He looked off at the river. "Tell me though, did he teach you to sail?"

"Bits and pieces," she said.

—62

"Enough to pass on to me?"

"He taught me just enough to probably get us both killed."

"Well," he said, "next summer we have to both sail right out there on the river."

She thought about summer, how far off it was. "I'd like to get Mama near the ocean again," she said. "One more time near the ocean. They ought to have some kind of federal program in this country where every old person gets to spend one last summer by the sea."

"We can start it ourselves," Jack said. "We'll buy a big mansion on the shore and fill it with old people. Someday we'll check in ourselves."

The thought of this, the thought of getting old, filled her with fear, and then defiance. "I don't want to get old, Jack."

"You won't."

"No, but if I do . . . " She stopped short of asking him, begging him not to let her end up alone like her mother. Then she said, "I have to get her out by summer. I can't leave her in there another summer."

They turned twenty-one years old that winter of 1967. They celebrated her birthday in a small Italian restaurant, where they drank a bottle of wine and toasted the idea of summer. Casey drank too much for the first time in her life, and if Jack had asked her to tell him honestly why she was feeling melancholy she would have had to admit that it was because she felt completely and hopelessly at sea with her life. She was skeptical of everything. All around her in that city there were multitudes of young college students banding together under the power of defiance. They had many causes which united them and she wanted to be a part of them, to be carried away by their causes. She was held back by her own skepticism. They seemed to her to have velocity, a great and urgent velocity, but no direction. She wanted to find a direction most of all, a new direction which led straight away from the past into her future.

Chapter Seven

One April afternoon Ross Peterson came bounding onto her ward at the hospital with his shirttails out and a puppy zipped inside his leather aviator's jacket. He looked down over rimless sunglasses. "I've been watching you," he told her. "We've got to get some life in this place."

The expression on the faces of the children when he set the puppy loose was something she would never forget. It was like they were witnessing a miracle. After he left they watched the door for days hoping he would return. A week passed. Then he sent Casey a note:

I knew the little tykes would go for the dog. I'm trying to catch a bird. I'll be back.
Ross.

When she read the note to Jack he told her he'd already met him. "I was caught in traffic last week and this guy came up to my window and asked me if I was in a hurry. He said, 'Just tell me one thing and I'll get you out of here fast.' Then he asked me if I was married to you, or in love with you or both. I told him, and he ran up ahead and started waving his arms, directing traffic like a cop."

"So what did you tell him?"

"I told him I was your culinary advisor. I was fattening you up on fish sticks to get you ready to face the world."

"So, what did you think?"

"What do you mean, what did I think?" Jack looked at her carefully, then clapped his hands. "Hey, you're interested in this fellow, aren't you? I can tell."

"I don't think interested is the right word. I mean . . . " She looked over at him and his lips were moving comically. He was pantomiming her.

"What's so funny?"

"You're interested," he said. "Admit it!"

"Well, okay then, interested."

For the next month when Casey was on duty at the hospital on Saturday mornings he flew over. She brought all the children to the windows and he flew over and tipped his wings for them. They waved back and he dipped low in the sky and their faces lit up. He had a magic and power with children; like them, he seemed to have no sense of time or convention, no artifice or vanity. He showed up looking like Ichabod Crane, his shirt hanging out below his jacket. He was roguish and boyish. She saw a kind of heat in his eyes. His blond hair was wild, in shafts and clumps. He told her he cut it himself. He apologized for the way he looked. He was an orphan, he explained, so he had never learned about clothes. He had a light about him and the kind of looks that could overpower a scene so that when he had left all she could remember was the sight of him.

The spring turned into a succession of cool, sunlit mornings. She awakened early, her eyes wide open when the world was still silent and calm. Its calmness began to inspire a calmness of her own. Spring spread through her. She stood before the window and let the sunlight enter her. They were mornings like she had never seen. Under their influence she began to wonder if she was learning something new about life. She had allowed herself to think about this boy, to hope certain things. Perhaps *hope*, not defiance, was the way out.

The first place they went alone together was South Station. They walked the rain-drenched streets down to the docks, where they stood watching trains pull in and out.

"I used to play a game with the lady who raised me," he said. "She'd never traveled anywhere in her life but she had this terrific romance with trains. She would start the game by saying there was this man riding on this train, and then I'd have to finish the story for her. I think it was her way of imagining how the rest of the world lived."

They picked out a character together, a bald man in a shiny brown suit, carrying a leather briefcase. They walked along the platform following him the length of five cars until he chose a seat and they found his face in a window.

"Okay, here we go," Ross said. "There's this man riding on this train."

"Now what am I supposed to say?" she asked.

"Whatever comes to mind."

"I suppose he's heading west then."

"Ah, the American dream. Go west, young man, go west."

"He's dreaming of a new life, a ranch maybe, where he discovers oil in the backyard."

"One morning while he's shaving?"

"Yes, why not? But the trouble with oil wells is that

they run dry. And one day soon after he buys his fancy car and his mansion in Beverly Hills, his well runs out."

"And his fiancée, whose heart was set upon a life of idle pleasure, leaves him high and dry?"

"So to speak," Casey said.

"And so, is his dream over?"

She thought for a minute. "No. He says farewell and takes the next train back east to the ocean, where he recuperates fully."

"And so, the American dream is restored?"

"Yes, why not?" she said. "But what is the American dream? That was your idea."

He told her the dream was *composed* mostly of greed, that in America greed was the only passion that counted anymore. "Greed and hunger for the great life everyone agrees is worth any price to get. It's the dream that's made this country so great, the dream of slaughtering the Indians and taking their land, working kids to death in the factories—you know, all the good stuff." He told her no one achieved this dream without stepping on someone, and that it was the old story of good people doing terrible things to other people and then spending their lives seeking forgiveness, but being filthy rich. "And in this dream the hero is our man with his oil well."

A speech, she thought. He was silent. She recalled her father talking about the American dream, telling her about his classmates from Harvard who had died in the war, dying to preserve a way of life in America.

She told Ross about this. "Whenever my father spoke of the dream, he was bitter. He had expected life to measure up, to justify the sacrifices."

He watched her and didn't speak. She asked him, "So then, you don't subscribe to the dream either?"

—68

Ross turned back to the man on the train. "Christ, let's make him a plumber or a ditchdigger, anything to get me off my high horse."

"What do you mean?"

"I mean if we keep talking about the American dream, my social commentary is going to get pretty thick. I get up on a high horse and you'll get sick of it."

"How do you know I'll get sick of it? And besides, plumbers and ditchdiggers, aren't they entitled to some version of the American dream?"

He shrugged his shoulders, then looked at her with delight. His eyes widened. "I better go ask him," he said. He ran off yelling, "Stop the train! Stop the train!" He ran past five cars until he found the man at the window. The train was rolling but he skipped alongside it banging on the window and hollering at the man. Finally the train pulled away.

When he came back to Casey he was out of breath. "Well," he said, "your question goes unanswered."

He put his arm around her. They walked for hours, talking. He described in great detail the places where he had traveled. He was familiar with train stations in Paris, cathedrals in Rome. He was only two years older than she but he seemed to have lived on a different planet.

She discovered what he'd told her was true; he was quick to get up on his high horse. He began to explain to her how he was different from most people; he told her he didn't explore his interior, but was wholly devoted to searching the world outside himself. To be great, he said, you have to act. "What I mean is, life scares us all to death, and it's this fear that keeps us from acting. But if you can get angry enough you can act, and the fear is resolved."

"It's a theory," she said. "But what do you have to be angry about?"

"The American dream," he replied. "It's like a piece of fruit that's rotted in the sun."

She smiled at him, acknowledging the beginning of another speech.

"Alright," he said, smiling. "Another sermon. I give up. I should have been a Southern Baptist."

She stood there smiling back at him and feeling incredibly thankful that he had a sense of humor and he could laugh at himself, because this was the thing that enabled her to decide at this moment that he was not like the Captain. And what a relief it was for her to decide this.

Ross couldn't really resist the speeches though, and they were music to Jack's ears. Everything Ross said inspired Jack, and he tried from the start to be like him. He gave up shaving and began dressing like a hobo. But as hard as he tried to mimic Ross's irreverence, it seemed unnatural; he was too neat and concerned, and next to Ross he looked too young and inexperienced. Casey knew he was anxious about everything to be reckless, and it was recklessness that gave Ross his energy. Unlike his peers, Ross didn't seem to be testing his own limits, but the limits of the world and those around him. He knew of the people Jack was hanging around with and called them the street generation. "First there was the jazz generation, then the beat generation, now your street generation," he said. He went on to explain how he was trying to resist belonging to anything. Instead, he wanted to stay on the outside where he could be at the center of everything. "This new generation in the streets," he said, "is a lot of people trying to fight out their ambivalence. It's not for me. I'm just living, I can't get caught up in their fight, Jack."

He lived by his wits, by the seat of his pants, as he put it. He found a calmness beyond the anger, and this calmness, more than anything else, is what drew Casey to him.

He sometimes spent days in his apartment reading, coming out only for their company. Once he appeared at Casey's door looking exhausted but incredibly pleased. "I've discovered that no single factor has had a greater influence upon the development of civilization than this." He held out a potato in one hand, and said, "It's true, it's absolutely true."

She discovered that he could entertain her. She began to look forward to this, and gradually she fell into his orbit. On the days she spent with him that spring, she didn't look back. At the end of those days she felt satisfied, exhausted. They had discovered a used-book shop in Harvard Square called The Eaves, where they sat on the floor reading for hours. Entire days passed here. He often read to her from Thomas Wolfe's novels, telling her that nobody in America was writing anymore like Wolfe.

"Just listen to this," he said, holding open a book and reading aloud to her.

> He knew his life was little and would be extinguished. And that only darkness was immense and everlasting. And he knew that he would die with defiance on his lips, and that the shout of his denial would ring with the last pulsing of his heart into the maw of all-engulfing night.

He asked her, "Who has the courage to write like that anymore?"

"But do you believe it?" Casey asked. "The darkness, the hopelessness?"

"You just have to fight against it, that's all he's saying. It's just like the fear I've been talking about."

"But it doesn't always work. You can't believe it always works?"

"I don't know what you mean?"

"This darkness, it got the better of Wolfe didn't it?"

Ross thought for a minute and then said, "Maybe he didn't fight hard enough."

He looked at her. When he said this it sounded to her like a confirmation of all she had begun to believe to be true about defiance. She kept to herself the thought that maybe poor Thomas Wolfe *hadn't* fought hard enough to overcome the darkness, but he had fought as hard as he could.

They often played checkers in the front window of the book shop. One afternoon he leaned down over the table and kissed her. When she looked up she saw a mob of students forming out on the sidewalk. At first she thought they were watching her, but then they began unfolding a large American flag. They opened the flag and held it at the corners, then started walking in a circle with it and chanting like children playing a schoolyard game.

"That's for all the times you could have jumped me but didn't," Ross said. "I know you've been letting me win."

She looked at his mischievous grin. "There is this boy riding this train," she said.

"And he's lousy at checkers?"

"Yes, hopeless."

"Because he can't concentrate on the game."

"Whatever. But his opponent is charitable." As she

said this she watched him turn his attention from her to the street, where the students had set fire to the flag. They were kicking it into a ball so it would burn better. Then they stood back and stared down at the flames, their faces luminous and stern. Casey had never seen such stern faces, such serious expressions.

She spent a lot of time talking with him about her mother. But it was a long while before he said anything about his past. The three of them were in Jack's apartment the night Ross spoke of his parents. His father had died when he was a year old; he had no memory of him. His mother met a man who hated children and so they'd placed him in an orphanage in Philadelphia.

"It was run by the Lutheran Church," he said. "They whipped my behind in the belief that it would turn me into a Christian man. The people who ran the place tried to persuade me that my mother was a sinner and I would inherit her sin if I wasn't careful."

"What did you believe?" Casey asked him.

"I guess I believed some of that. The bit about the sins of the parents being visited upon their children—I believe there's something there."

"Is that what the Lutherans believe?" Jack asked.

"The Catholics too," he replied. "You're both good Catholics."

"Not when it comes to that," Casey said. "You're saying we're held accountable for a life we had no power over. We're always paying off some debt to the past, like one of those Greek tragedies?"

He said he didn't really know. "But so what if we inherit a little sinfulness, is that such a big deal? It's the people without sins, those are the ones you have to watch out for. In France during the reign of terror, one man sent

—73

twenty-five thousand people to the guillotine. He lived alone in one room, a completely sinless man reading his Bible and praying day and night while he composed the death lists."

"It depends upon the sin," Casey said.

"But there has to be some . . . some supreme effort at moral virtue," Jack said. "That's heroic in itself, and without that effort there's nothing."

"But the three of us are sinless," Ross told them. "We have the immunity of our youth. We're too young to have done anything really wrong."

That night after Jack went off with his friends, Ross and Casey sat looking down at the lights of Fenway Park. She told him she was worried about Jack. She told him about his trouble with Shep. Ross just took it all in. He didn't say anything. When she had finished he reached out and touched her.

"I don't know about you yet," she said.

"I'm the man riding on the train," he said.

"You deal in riddles."

"Yes, like the sphinx. No straight answers. I come to you with all the disclaimers of a laundromat—Not responsible for articles lost or stolen. But I wouldn't steal anything from you."

"Are we talking about my innocence?" She waited, and when he didn't answer she stopped his hand and said, "Just wait."

He apologized. "I've been pressing you. I'm the kind of guy who just charges at something."

"I guess that's not such a big sin," she said.

"The sin would be not to live a life, don't you think?" he said. "I mean if you're going to really live, you're going to sin a little here and there."

This time she didn't stop him. What he had said to her and now what he was doing to her were enough to overcome her questions. On Jack's couch they made love awkwardly. He was tender and soft with her, but it was over very quickly, she thought. She began to cry and couldn't tell him or herself why. While he tried to console her, she thought about her mother lying on her back in the blue room. She wondered whether her mother ever believed as a young girl that she would end up alone. She held on to Ross. Maybe this hadn't been all that she had imagined it would be, but still, holding him was wonderful and reassuring, and feeling him inside her made her feel complete in a way.

She asked him if he knew it would come to this.

He said, "I had high hopes."

"Isn't that terribly presumptuous of you?"

"Yeah, probably," he said. "But you have to hope for certain things, don't you?"

"Well you're the first," she told him.

He said it was only a matter of time before the first person came along. She asked what he meant. And then before he could answer, she said, "Never mind, don't say anything, but now that the damage is done, let's just do it again."

She was thinking to herself that he had found a way into her which would be exclusively his. He had made a discovery. Despite her fears, so had she. They had found a way of getting beyond everything, a way of claiming space that no one else walked in. She felt him embrace her knees. He didn't speak. Her cheeks were stinging from his whiskers. There was no longer any noise in the streets. She gave in totally, she felt transported. It ended in one great burst of energy. She wanted it to go on and on. Then they lay in silence. He seemed to be gathering his strength. She wondered if now she would be pregnant. It would be wonderful, she thought, a whole life like this.

He spoke softly while he stroked her back. "Kansas," he whispered. "I was living in Kansas when it happened. I was in high school. We were at basketball practice. Punk Ryder was the coach. He was tough, a hard man with the face and body of a street fighter. He had no mercy on weaklings.

"Practice was finished and we were in the shower room and he came around the corner and said, 'The president's been shot, you boys better head on home now.' So we got dressed. When we walked out past his office, I looked in and he had his head in his hands, his shoulders were shaking. I knew then that—well, I don't know what I knew. It was just a feeling that nothing would be the same after that. And I had a date that night with a girl I'd been chasing around for months. I wasn't getting anywhere with her, but that night at the drive-in she just gave in completely. It was the night I lost my virginity."

"Why are you telling me about this?"

"Because I always wondered after that if the only reason she gave in was because the president had been assassinated."

He went on to say how incredible it was that the great big events of the world found their way into the most private scenes.

"I suppose we'll all remember," he said. "I mean, years from now we'll all remember exactly where we were, what was said."

"When we lost our virginity?" she asked. "Or when he was shot?"

He looked at her thoughtfully. He held her face in his hands. His palms were calloused and when she opened his hands and held them to the light she asked what he did to get so many callouses.

"I'm a stevedore," he said.

"No. Seriously, what do you do?"

"Seriously, I play a lot of golf."

She laughed and told him golf seemed like an old man's game.

He shrugged his shoulders. She thought, years from now they would remember where they were and what they said to each other tonight.

Chapter Eight

Despite what he had said about their generation, it was only a short time before Ross insinuated himself into the chaotic flow of Jack's life in the street. He spoke to Casey of going after Jack to rescue him. It was a mission, he said. He read to her from Conrad of Marlow's trip up the River to find Kurtz.

She suspected it was more than that. That time they were sitting in the bookshop when the mob of students had set fire to the American flag, she had seen something in Ross's eyes. It was as if he were beginning to acknowledge that his generation had finally grown serious, and that the fight in the streets couldn't be ignored any longer.

When Shep ran into trouble with the police and was forced into hiding, Ross took over the meetings in the laundromat. He drew in the others, Jack's old comrades. They sat on the floor listening to him as he walked back and forth with his brown-leather aviator's jacket draped over his shoulders. He talked mostly about the war in Vietnam. He said he had no answers, only questions for them to ask. He was going to reshape their fight, clarify

—78

the causes. He told them they had the power to change things if they were willing to make a sacrifice.

They all ran around in bell-bottom pants that spring, and boots, high leather boots with thick wooden heels. It was a kind of uniform they wore. They raised hell in the streets. Casey took a pair of crutches from the hospital, and they put on a charade to raise money for their causes. Ross would dress in a black overcoat and black hat. He would stand out in the middle of Commonwealth Avenue reading a Bible at the top of his lungs, shouting scriptures at the passing pedestrians. Then Jack would come along on the crutches, and Ross would throw the Bible at his feet and shout that the good Lord could heal him. He would run in circles around Jack while people gathered to watch. Then he would take the crutches out from under Jack's arms and throw them to the ground. "Walk! Walk, oh man of faith!" And Jack would walk, and the two of them would jump up and down shouting that it was a miracle. And the onlookers would throw money which they needed for two-way radios, and drugs and beer and Ross's relief fund for the children of North Vietnam.

"These people who give money," Casey said. "They know it's just a show; they don't believe you're a healer."

"They don't believe," Ross said. "But they *want* to believe."

"Or they need to believe," Jack said.

When they were alone, Casey pressed Ross to tell her what he believed. He kept telling her he had no answers, and that he only believed in the questions.

"Well I have a question for you then," she said to him one night. "What's going to happen to us?"

He had no idea, he said. "I only know that if we're

not together in the future it won't matter. Whatever we discover together now, whatever truth we figure out will go on. And I'll show up at your door one day and no matter what kind of life you're living, I'll find my way back to you. Just like this, I'll take you just like this."

He knew it wasn't an answer. And she knew it. But because he had no answers, because neither of them had answers, they ended up in bed, making love, resolving everything or nothing.

Ross soon had a following, students, even some professors who wanted someone to inspire them. In bars around Cambridge he performed. He would drink half a bottle of beer and then, to underscore some point he was trying to make, he would slam his palm down so hard on the mouth of the bottle that the bottom would fall out. He made speeches and kept them spellbound while he talked.

Casey watched one night as he stood on top of a table and spoke about Ho Chi Minh. He seemed to believe so completely in what he was telling them. "All the man wants," he shouted, "is for the fucking U.S. of A. to get its bloody nose out of his country. We're killing his people, destroying their culture. It's our old trick, we kill the people in order to set them free from communism."

When they applauded him it made Casey feel uncomfortable. She watched their faces, the way they reflected his gestures. They were devoted to him. When Ross was performing this way, she wasn't sure she knew who he was. All over Boston she had seen young men making angry speeches, and often they were surrounded by girls, beautiful, emaciated girls who seemed to hang on every word. Casey had watched these girls and she had felt sorry for them because they looked so helpless and lost. Now,

—80

with Ross standing on the table, his fist raised in the air, she felt sorry for herself. She listened to him tonight and for many other nights as he called for a complete dismantling of the American establishment, and the American dream.

As the days went on he organized demonstrations in the Commons and out on the streets. Casey dressed in black and stood at his side. They ran from police; they lived like anarchists. She gave away her days to the wild currents in the streets, and at times Ross's defiance had the same marvelous power to overcome her doubts as their lovemaking had.

But there were times when she questioned his motives and when she pushed him for more answers.

"You're changing," she told him.

"It sounds like an accusation."

"You have an audience now."

"No," he said. "It's more than that. I have you and Jack."

"We're part of your audience."

"I care about you."

"And them, you don't care about them?"

"Don't be crazy. I care about them, but it's different."

"Well, with all your power, can you do anything for them, or us? Can you give us any answers, or do you just tear everything down to the ground?"

He reached out and touched her. "We tear it all down until we find the truth."

"The truth about what?"

"Christ, Casey. Can't we just be skeptical about everything for a while, and wait and see what turns out to be true and what doesn't?"

She looked at him carefully. She had already asked

—81

him once before what was going to happen to the two of them. It was one thing for him to be skeptical about the world around them, but it bothered her that he was skeptical about them. Still, she wouldn't ask him again what was going to happen, at least not now. She would try to be stronger, more self-sufficient, more reckless. More like him.

Casey worked alone for weeks using her status as a part-time student to help plan an assault on the ROTC department at Northeastern University. By Easter they were ready. They assembled in the laundromat at midnight. "Carry no identification, no rings or jewelry," Ross commanded. "Tonight we belong only to the gods. We're ambassadors from the heavens."

Jack and Casey were at his side. They were all dressed in black. They blackened their faces with shoe polish. It was just after 1 A.M. when they broke into Wheaton Hall through a basement window. Casey held the flashlight. When her hand began shaking, someone came up from behind and steadied her. "Someday we can tell our kids about this night," Ross whispered.

They stood over a file cabinet. "This is it," Casey said. "These are the ones who'll go to 'Nam right after graduation."

"Shut off the supply of killers and the whole fucking war will close down," Jack said.

She watched Jack's hands prying open the cabinet. She thought how completely devoted to Ross he had become.

"We're going for more than one file cabinet," Ross said. It was a departure from the plan they had agreed upon. "We're going to shut down this operation completely."

Ross threw a bunch of papers into a wastebasket, then lit a match. "I want to put them out of business," he said.

"Jesus," Jack gasped. "Burn the place down?"

Someone behind them began to object. But it was too late. Ross told them all to go out. "I'm going to stay here until I'm sure it catches. I'll find you."

Casey wouldn't leave. She saw Jack move to the door, then stop and turn back. "We're in this together," he said. This seemed to Casey to be a rite of passage for Jack.

They ran down the corridor with an alarm shreiking in the darkness. In the Commons outside, two security cops were running straight toward them. Casey heard Jack yell for Ross. Then she was tackled to the ground by one of the guards. His hand grabbed at her throat and then between her legs. She bit into his wrist, her teeth sank into his flesh. He cried out. The next second Ross's boot caught him in the temple and his eyes closed.

Later that night in a bar in Porter Square they waited for word about the fire. Ross had a contact inside the police department who eventually called. Ross left the table and took the call at the pay phone. When he returned he relayed the message. The fire had not spread beyond the wastebasket.

"Shit," Jack exclaimed. He looked up at Ross. "We'll get another shot at the bastards."

Ross nodded. "You might have gotten me a prison sentence tonight," he said softly to Jack. "You yelled out my name back there. They've got my name at headquarters."

Jack lowered his head. "It's just that when those pigs came up on us, Christ, I . . ." His voice trailed off.

Ross tried to console him. "It's alright, but I'm going to have to get out of here for a while. I'll have to leave town."

Casey watched Jack put his head in his hands. Then he got up and left the table. Ross called to him, and got up to start after him, but Casey told him to let Jack go. "He wants to be alone," she said.

"I shouldn't have made a big thing of it," Ross said. "Jesus, poor Jack takes it all so hard."

Casey thought about how Jack had seemed to be getting stronger, gaining confidence in himself. He had told her just a few days earlier that he was making progress. When she'd asked him what he meant by this, he had told her that he was putting one foot in front of the other, moving forward. Now she thought that if Jack was making progress it was because he was giving himself away to the cause, he had lost himself in the defiance of the street, he had lost his uncertainty.

She told this to Ross. He was silent for a long time.

"I want to take care of him," he said.

"Can you take care of him? The deeper we get in this . . . it's only a matter of time, it's going to drive us all apart."

He waited, then said he was going to go after Jack. "I have an idea where he went. I'll find you later."

"There's no way I'm just going to sit here," she said.

Eventually they found him in a fraternity house at Boston University. When they arrived he was in the basement sitting at a table across from Shep. They were both bare-chested. The room was crammed with people. Someone turned the lights down before Casey and Ross could get through. Jack laid his right arm down on the table. Shep put his arm down next to it. Someone lit a candle and asked for silence. He lit a cigarette from the candle, held it in the air for a second. Casey's eyes were drawn to its red coal. The coal moved slowly down until it lay against their bare arms.

A little puff of smoke went up when their hair was singed. A murmur spread through the crowd. Casey stared at Shep. There was a wide scar on his forehead she had never seen before. The cigarette burned slowly. Soon she could smell their flesh. The cigarette burned down until it went out. Neither Jack nor Shep had moved. A second cigarette was lighted and Casey turned and pushed her way out through the silent crowd. She walked along the Charles River. A police siren split the sky above her. Ross had told her just the day before that America was coming apart at its seams. Another year or two and the streets will be on fire, he had said. She had not believed him. She had wanted all along to believe that Ross would elevate himself above everything happening in the streets, that he would take Jack and her along with him into some sanctuary of calmness, and they would be bigger than the conflicts surrounding them. They would have more than the raw strength of their youth, they would have restraint as well, and discretion, and the chance for a future.

She stopped to gaze at the dark river. She saw herself in a new way. She saw that she had been looking to Ross to save her, to make life simpler for her and Jack. There is this man riding on this train, she said to herself. And the train is moving too fast and no one can stop it.

Just before dawn she found them both in Jack's apartment. On Jack's arm there was a hole as big around as a quarter. She touched his shoulder. She looked down and saw the blackened gristle.

"Two cigarettes," Jack said. "He wasn't going to flinch—you know Shep. So how could I give in?" He smiled faintly, but with satisfaction.

"What does it prove?" Casey asked. She looked over at the windows where Ross stood looking out, raking his hair with his fingers.

—85

"Actually," Jack said, "once you kill the nerves you don't feel anything."

"What good does it do?" she asked. She raised her voice and turned to Ross. "What's the purpose for any of this?"

"You want some explanation for everything," he said.

"You don't explain anything."

"Well, I could give you my life-is-short theory. That justifies just about everything."

She dropped down into a chair. "Please, spare me any more theories." She looked at Jack. "Spare us both any more of your theories."

"I can't give you an answer," Ross called out to her.

"Everything has to be so vague with you," she said. "As vague as your man riding on his train."

"Not vague," he said. "You're wrong, Casey."

Then she saw that he was right. Nothing with him was vague; it was just that nothing was explained.

"I don't have any answers," Ross went on. "Tell me one person who knows anything about anything anymore." He said the answers didn't matter anyway—it was the questions that counted. "You have to feel the pain and anger behind the questions and that's all. And if you can't, then don't blame me. Blame the way you grew up, blame the fucking 1950s. Why don't we all blame the 1950s when everyone had all the answers. There was the president of the United States out on some damn fucking golf course. Good old, bald Ike over and over again. Ike with the answers. You think there's nothing wrong with your world when the president is smiling up at everyone from a sand trap. His answers—they were the dream, the dream that's dead now."

He became silent. He went to the refrigerator and took out a beer.

"Christ, Ross," Jack said. "We—"

Ross turned on him and cut him off. "You're pissed off too? Of course you're pissed, you had it made before I came into the picture. The two of you giving each other sweet, perfect answers, handing them out like sugar pills."

"Go to hell," Casey said to him.

"You're being an asshole," Jack said. He walked to the door.

"Oh come on, Jack, what's your problem? What the hell are you hanging around for anyway? She's mine—I win, you lose. You had the answers but I got the girl."

Jack walked out. He pulled the door behind him trying to slam it, but it hit his shoulder and swung open.

"Shit, I didn't mean that," Ross said. He called out to him.

Casey heard Jack going down the stairs. "You got the girl because she doesn't have the guts to throw you out," she said.

Ross walked over to her. "I didn't mean that. Damn it all, I'm a fucking fool." He touched her arm, he told her he had to go after Jack. "I can't let him just take off."

"He'll come back. That's the thing about us—we want answers so we keep coming back for more."

He kept telling her he was sorry, that he would make it right for them all. Finally she told him to go. "Just leave," she said.

She sat alone for hours. She thought about how she had never had any answers to the crazy things that had happened to her. She thought about something her mother said to her years ago. When life is bad for you, you have to forget all the crazy things you can't bear to remember, and remember everything you can't bear to forget or else you'll never make things right. And this, Casey thought, this becomes the truth, the truth you rely on. The truth, the answers, are what you make from what you choose to forget and to remember. The truth becomes the dream. A dream, a lie.

Ross and Jack came back together. They stood in front of her. Ross had his arm draped over Jack's shoulder. "We've decided I'm an asshole," Ross said. He turned to Jack.

Jack smiled and nodded. "He's lost too. We're all lost together."

They joked around for her. While they tried to make up for what had happened she thought to herself that the answers meant more to her than they should. When you don't have the answers, you want them. She looked at Ross and searched his face and she thought maybe he understood this. She thought that maybe they would find some kind of truth. She thought how their love had become a kind of blaze and they were drawn into it again and again, they were being charred by it. They didn't give themselves to each other's ideas, they allowed themselves to be taken. They seemed to see in each other the things they really wanted to see in themselves. He was centerless, always tearing around with his reckless self-confidence, and she was still pragmatic, careful in a way. She asked her questions never out of a superficial curiosity but to pin him down and to get at the exact truth about things. She knew she had become the sort of girl who holds herself back so that somehow you had to reach towards her to get a clear picture of how she really felt.

"Anyway," Jack said to her, "we've been discussing things."

"Yeah," Ross said eagerly. He stepped toward her and took hold of her arm.

"We're going to split this crazy scene, Casey," Jack said. He gestured at the room. "Give all this shit back to the Salvation Army and blow this town. It'll be like we were never even here."

He sounded so hopeful. She stopped him and asked where they would go. Then she watched Jack turn to Ross, both of them grinning. Ross put his hands on her shoulders and pulled her to him. Just then, down in the street a police car tore around the corner with its blue lights flashing. When the car screeched to a stop, Casey felt the breath rush out of her.

Ross walked to the window. He waited until the car drove off. "We're out of here," he said softly. His eyes turned from the street to her face, then back to the street. He was smiling. "This old city will never be the same."

"Because of us?" she asked.

He thought for a while. Then he said maybe it *was* because of them, maybe they had helped change some things about the city, the world. He turned to Jack. "And maybe now you'll be out from under something. You had to put yourself up against Shep."

"He used to talk like this was a war," Jack said.

"If it was a war we wouldn't be able to leave until it was finished," Ross said.

"And we can?" Casey asked. "We can just leave?"

Ross turned to her, smiling again. "Yes," he said.

"But if we don't stay and fight, what will it mean about us?"

"There'll be other wars," he said to her. "And besides, I have to get out for a while. The pigs will zero in on me before long if I stay around."

Casey watched Ross and wondered if this was the real reason they would leave the city behind. Or if it was just that they were still young and could change their minds overnight about things.

"There's this man riding on this train," Ross said. "He's riding all the way to Maine, right to the end of the line, where the tracks just stop." He held her at arm's length and said, "You'll like me better up in Maine—all demagogues just shrivel up and blow away in Maine."

He knew a place they could go, an isolated seaside town on the northern coast. He had worked there in an old hotel the summer he turned sixteen. "I may be an asshole," he said, "but I've got some money stashed away. I can rent us a cottage for the whole damn summer. We'll live like real people."

While the sun reddened the sky over Boston he described the cottage in great detail, the kind of place where they would kick open the door and find rooms filled with old books whose covers had faded in the sunlight. "It'll have to have a porch," he said. "We'll sit out on the porch and listen to ball games on the radio at night. We'll smoke cigars for God's sake. Imagine us just smoking cigars."

"I've got a job, remember?" Casey said. She was conscious of trying to come up with some opposition, something to test his new idea. But really she was assenting to it, her skepticism had vanished.

"Quit the job," he said. He smiled at her. She felt his hands on her skin. "Come to Maine and smoke cigars with us."

"Just quit?" she said. Then she thought, Yes, with enough defiance you can quit anything, leave anything behind. She looked at him while he made his pitch. She remembered her mother telling her how certain people could turn everything upside down in your life without a minute's warning. Now she acknowledged that this was true, but only if you were susceptible, only if you were looking for answers and a way out.

Ross made all the arrangements. In a week they were ready.

The morning they were leaving Boston, Casey watched Ross packing his things and she had a vision of her father. She hadn't thought of him in some time. But now she had a vivid picture of him. It was autumn and her father was outside the garage, preparing the car for winter, running the garden hose into its radiator, flushing green liquid out into the driveway. "Get back now, sweetie. Here, stand over here." How old was she then, six or seven? He seemed to like having her around him. He never made her feel physically uncomfortable in those days. But there had always been some vague discomfort; she could recall it now. There was something about the very way he moved when he split wood for the fireplace and stacked it neatly in rows along the back porch by the sliding glass doors. He was meticulous. He kept stopping to wipe his hands clean with the white handkerchief he carried in a back pocket. When he raked leaves he did the same thing. It was her job to get down on her knees and push the leaves into piles for him. He would wait for her and while they were talking back and forth about what a nice job she was doing, he would be wiping his hands clean. In some way this habit of his had disconcerted her even as a little girl. There was something troubling about it. Maybe she had suspected that the chores around the house really annoyed him. Cleaning his hands was like taking one step in the opposite direction, one step away from the house, the chores, one step away from her. All those autumn afternoons, had she really suspected something even then? Now it seemed she had. She had never been confident of his loyalty to her. But perhaps this was true of all daughters. Wasn't there something uncertain about fathers, and wasn't that part of their allure to daughters? Didn't all daughters wonder from time to time if their fathers were coming back home at the end of the day from wherever they had gone? A father stops what he is doing, takes out his handkerchief, and wipes his hands clean. It is like saying good-bye, isn't it? And now she looked to Ross as he packed his suitcase, and she wondered how much of what was true about daughters worrying that their father's might just leave them was also true about women and men.

Ross looked over at her. "People leaving," he said. "Packing up and leaving. That's one thing about this country, you can just go wherever you want to go." He began packing again, and then stopped and seemed to drift away from her. He glanced around the room. He started talking about his childhood. He talked about the man his mother had married, how they had decided to give him up to the orphanage. "Charlie didn't want kids around," Ross said. "But he was alright though, he could really make me laugh. He was a juggler. He used to juggle three of anything. And he could walk all over the place on his hands. He kept trying to teach my mother how to do it. She tried and tried. Then one morning I woke up—it was a spring day, the windows were open. I woke up hearing Charlie clapping. I looked out the window and there she was up on her hands, her dress hanging down inside out over her head. She was laughing underneath it. I think I knew then they were leaving."

Chapter Nine

There are summers that ask questions and summers that ignore them. That summer of 1967 they planned to turn their backs on the mounting questions and escape to a cottage on Frenchman's Bay at a place called Hancock Point.

It was a place with ancient stone walls wandering through the woods, and dunes feathered with lime-green grass, and English bicycles ticking like geiger counters beyond the hedges. It was one of those fine summer places where you expect to find gold mornings, blue afternoons, silver nights, and a hint of permanence, for things seldom change here from one summer to the next. You expect to find seclusion, stillness, and repose. Having found all of that you expect perhaps to find yourself.

Ross walked around like a duke showing them his estate. They followed him through the grassy meadows of sweetfern and juniper. He led them to the boats up on their wooden cradles at the end of Ferry Lane, their big white bellies sagging between wooden planks. He took them to the lighthouse, which swept its red beam across the bay at night.

This place, the Point as it was called, had been settled and claimed at the turn of the century by a few dozen wealthy families who would always be called summer people. They were more than wealthy, their wealth was immense and indestructible. They were the people who owned those things everyone wonders who owns—diamond mines and railroads and the Empire State Building. And they had laid their claim to Hancock Point, turning it into a summer colony with a tiny post office of its own, a library, a wooden chapel standing among white birch trees, a yacht club, and the handsome houses they called cottages that stepped right down to the edge of the ocean and were visible only from out on the water. They were houses with many chimneys and vine-covered turrets and balconies hung in the sky. Privacy meant everything to the summer people. Once they arrived for the season, they seldom went off the Point. In the early 1950s the federal government threatened to shut down their little post office for lack of business. The families got together and made an arrangement among themselves; at the end of each summer they would buy in lump sum all the postage stamps they would need for the following year. The plan worked and the post office was spared. The summer people almost always had things their way.
    Ross rented a cottage for them on a tree-lined lane that led to the dock. A tall, wide-shouldered place with many windows, it had once belonged to a sea captain and was named Four Winds. It was distinguished by a blue porch that wrapped around the house following exactly the contour of each wall. The sun and shadows played on the cottage's silver cedar shingles. The trees seemed to lean into the living rooms. You could see right through the rooms out to the green tailored hedges in front and

the blue sea rolling in back. It was like looking at the world through a crystal glass.

There were two dozen rooms inside, rooms of all sizes and shapes, each with a stamped-tin ceiling and oak floorboards and dark wainscotting that ran up the plastered walls. There was a glass knob on every door, and on the first floor the dining room, living rooms, and terrace were separated by fantastic French doors that threw prisms of light in all directions at once. There was stained glass in the dining room where a chandelier hung like a crown above the dining room table. Staircases were wide with scrolled banisters. Couches in the living rooms had been covered with soft shades of blue and cranberry material that was bleached by years of sunlight. On the walls there were Wyeth watercolors and Edward Hopper oils. A broad stone fireplace dominated the living rooms downstairs, and six brick fireplaces upstairs burned off the night chill in the bedrooms. Sunlight flooded the kitchen, its warmth ramifying the scent of spices that had seeped into the grain of the walnut cabinets. Off the pantry a narrow door opened to an elevator. There were servants' quarters on the fourth floor and a panel of bells and lights whose circuitry had once been connected to buttons placed strategically throughout the rooms below. The cottage told of a way of life, a history.

They stood below it, barefoot in the grass, looking up. Ross said, "Try forgetting a place like this."

"They're going to have to pry us out of here," Jack said. Then he walked away from Ross and Casey. "At last I'm living in a style my father would approve of. But that's okay, I have a job to do here."

"Wait a minute," Ross said. "We agreed, no jobs, nothing serious this summer. This is on me."

—95

Jack went on. It was one of the few times Casey saw him oppose an idea of Ross's. Jack walked up the front steps to the blue porch, then turned and faced them. "You're probably wondering why I called you all here this morning," he joked. Then he became serious. "I'm the chronicler," he said. "I'm here to keep a record of our vanished past. When you forget, I'll be able to tell you what it was like."

Jack bowed at the waist when he was finished saying that. And then the summer began.

They were Ross's days. He weighed them and planned them and handed them out like coins. He knew the history of the place, he knew the geography. The tides and stars. He taught them to dig clams and make strawberry jam. He put an old record player in an upstairs bedroom window and started each morning by blasting the theme from *The Man of La Mancha*, "The Impossible Dream." It ran through their heads the rest of the day. They sang the song together under the influence of marijuana. They took walks around the big hotel where Ross had worked. At night they sat in the dunes looking back at its lighted rooms while Ross told them stories about the people he had met there.

"I was promoted to busboy by August," he recalled. "That got me out of the stinking kitchen, into the dining room, the civilized world. There were all these old ladies who came back summer after summer. Each of them had her own private table around the edge of the dining room, against the windows. They all had illustrious backgrounds. One had been the private secretary to J.P. Morgan. One lady from Virginia had a hundred house servants on her payroll. They were so old but they still dressed to the hilt, still made an effort. And each night they'd come down to

—96

dinner at six-thirty exactly, and they'd hobble over to their tables and wait for the arrival of Alfred King Chapman, their god. Now *there* was a man, a legend. He was in his eighties but he was still incredibly handsome. He'd sit out in the sun all day and then dress in his brick-red trousers and double-breasted navy blue blazer, and he'd walk into the dining room with his great head of thick white hair. You could hear the ladies gasp."

Casey listened to all his stories, trying to piece together a picture of his life before she met him. They had been together three months, but here at the Point she knew she was just discovering him, and day by day herself as well. She discovered she could make him laugh. When he played his Mozart records she staged a performance for him and Jack, using a warped tennis racket and a stick of driftwood for a violin and bow. She stood on a chair and didn't stop until they were doubled over on the floor.

Ross was financing all of this by playing golf. Every day the sun was shining, Jack and Casey walked him to the dock just before noon, helping him into a blue wooden dinghy. He would ask them how much they wanted him to come back with, then he would row across the harbor to the private club in Sorrento with his bag of clubs in the stern of the boat, their aluminum shafts sticking out over the gunwale and shining brightly in the sun. He came back every day toward dusk, his pockets stuffed with cash.

One afternoon he didn't come back. Jack and Casey were waiting for him on the porch when they heard a plane going back and forth, flying low in the sky. Out on the lawn they looked up, shading their eyes. The plane dipped its wings. "It's him," Casey said, thinking back to that day at the air show with her father and to those first days with Ross when he flew low over the hospital for the

—97

children. She was trying not to acknowledge to herself this love of airplanes that Ross and her father shared.

"Look out," Jack said. "He's probably going to drop his golf clubs down on the porch."

They watched the plane sweep low and make one last pass above them before it banked in the west and then wheeled out of sight.

On the porch they waited for him to return. It was nearly dark. Casey said, "There's this man riding on this train, or this plane. He's convinced the couple sitting across from him that he can do everything. He does his magic tricks for them, and he entertains them and then he leaves them at the next stop while they're sleeping. He leaves them with a romantic image, a vision of himself."

"You're talking about your father," Jack said. "Not Ross. He'll be back."

"You could be wrong, Jack," she said. She told him she already had a history of people leaving her. She looked at Jack and wondered how much she could tell him before he would stop believing in her chance for happiness. If she were to tell him what had happened last night he might give up all hope.

Last night she and Ross were walking the beach, laughing together. They stopped at the lighthouse. He leaned her back against the concrete foundation. He brushed her hair away from her face and asked her to stand still as if he were going to take her photograph. She heard the sea churning behind her, then his voice telling her to unbutton her blouse. "Slowly," he said. "I want to show you something." He seemed so confident. He reached across the space between them and unzipped her jeans. She felt his fingers on her skin. He spoke softly to her. She could

—98

barely hear him above the sea. She strained to hear every word he was saying. "Pretend I'm going inside you," he said. "You love when I go inside you. You think about it all the time, don't you? Don't you?"

"Yes." In this instant she recalled days when she had thought of nothing else.

"I want to tell you something. You might not always love me as completely as this, but you'll never be able to forget what it was like."

The perfect cadence of his voice and his fingers was suddenly shattered. She opened her eyes and looked at him. His expression was so earnest. "What kind of thing is that to tell me?" she said. He seemed surprised. She pushed his hand away and fastened her jeans while he told her something about how unrealistic she was.

"I'm just saying we should take the moment for what it is," he said.

"That's what it is to you—it's just a moment."

"Come on, Casey, ease off. What do you want it to be?"

"*You* ease off." She was thinking how unsatisfactory the moment was. She didn't want a moment, she wanted to be guaranteed a future. She thought to herself, I have the right to want this.

"These things we do," she told him, "I don't take them as lightly as you. I'm not just passing through town, another girl you can tell somebody about, like the girl you got to screw because John Kennedy was killed."

She tried to walk away but he grabbed her shoulder and threw her down in the wet sand. He ripped open her blouse. He took her breasts in his hands. He began kissing her nipples. At the end he was on top of her and slowly going inside her, more slowly and purposefully than he ever had before. She felt herself passing through stages, opposition giving way to ambivalence, then resignation. A passage. A transformation.

She looked up at Jack suddenly and she could tell he was waiting for her to explain. She thought to herself, you *do* have a right to know.

"All right then," she began. "He gives me this summer here at this beautiful place where everything is supposed to be so perfect. And it is perfect but I can't stop wondering what happens next, when the summer is finished. Is this a one-way ticket on his train, or does it go round-trip? I keep pushing him and he has nothing to say. His answer is to take off my clothes. Last night he told me he was as scared as I am about what will happen." She grimaced as she told this to Jack.

"Maybe he is," Jack said.

"I don't want him to be scared," she said. She could feel the resentment in her voice. "When you're scared, no one else can be sure about you, about what you'll do next. My father was scared. I remember how scared he was that no one would think highly of him. What a joke."

It was already late when they lit a fire in the living room hearth. Casey went on to acknowledge certain things about Ross and herself. Making love for them had always been best when they were surrounded by adversity, by the unanswered questions, the cold uncertainty. They could conquer these things in bed. And even though they had known each other only a few months, they loved so fully, so fitfully, because they recognized now in each other their own failings and deficiencies. She told Jack that when they fought they were really lashing out at what they hated about themselves.

"His recklessness, Jack, I give him hell for it. But isn't that what *I* want? He's up there flying through the stars and we sit here like two old hens. We hardly know him at all, but can you imagine if he didn't come back?"

Jack said something she didn't hear. She put another log in the fire and then walked to the screen door.

She told Jack that while they were fighting she had her mind on the reconciliation. Her heart was never in the fighting.

Jack asked her if she would regret coming here.

She turned back and looked at his face. His question had startled her because she was thinking exactly the same thing. "Maybe I'll regret that I couldn't just let go of the questions and take what's here in front of us without worrying about a future."

Jack said he had once asked his mother about her regrets. "She told me she had dreamed of being a veterinarian. She loved animals and wanted to go to college and then veterinary school. But her father only had enough money to send one kid, so naturally he sent her brother. Next thing that happens is she gets married to a good enough guy, but a tyrant really, has a kid, and spends most of her youth changing diapers and cleaning slop off the kitchen floor. She never complained much. I mean, I hardly remember her complaining at all. She got to do some traveling, but you talk about consolation—I can't believe that was any real consolation for the loss of her dream."

"What did she say to you though, about regrets?"

"Well, she wanted *me* to be the veterinarian. She tried to turn her kid into the thing she'd wanted to become. I told her I didn't have it in me. She told me she didn't want me to think she held any grudges against my father

—101

or anyone else. She said she had a good life. I told her it wasn't too late, she could go to school. She's fifty-three, she could still have her dream, be practicing by the time she was sixty-three and have twenty years to live out her dream."

"And you believe that, that it isn't too late for her?"

"Well, she said she has other things anyway. I don't know what—a garden and a college drop-out for a son."

"That's what happens, Jack. We find other things to fill the emptiness."

"Maybe."

"But what I want to know is why some people can accept the loss and just go on and live, but others are swallowed up in regret."

He didn't have an answer. They sat for hours. Jack said he was worried something might have happened to Ross. But Casey had figured out where he had gone. "I'm pretty sure he's gone to get Mama. He's been telling me he wanted to bring her here. You remember your idea about old people getting one last summer next to the sea?"

"*Your* idea," he reminded her.

"Well, it doesn't matter. But Ross has been building it up in his imagination, this great scene where he takes the castle by storm and liberates her from that nursing home." She pictured him sneaking her past the nurses, the lies and deceptions he would come up with in order to get her out of there.

"It's what he did to me," she said.

"And to me."

She stopped and thought to herself for the longest time until Jack asked her what it was.

"I want to know about regret. I want to know why some people lose things and get over it."

—102

"Well, my mother grew up without much of anything. Maybe that conditioned her in a way. Maybe it conditioned her not to expect too much, and plus that, she'd seen a lot of people get over things, worse things. She must have learned that it's just something you have to do if you're going to have any kind of life at all. You and I—"

She interrupted him. "He's increased our expectations. My father had the same effect on me when I was a girl. Hell, Jack, sometimes I feel like I'll always be seven years old, waiting for someone to pat me on the top of my head. But maybe you should, Jack . . . maybe you should become a veterinarian."

He laughed. "The first Doberman pinscher that came through the door would know I was an imposter. You know Ross was right about something. He said we were standing on the dividing line, and we are. I can feel it. It's not just us, the three of us, I mean. It's the time we're living in right now. The things that happen now, we won't be able to forget."

"Well don't tell me," she said to that. "Not tonight." She didn't want to regret anything; she wanted to be able to let go of all these things she wanted but couldn't have.

Ross telephoned the cottage in the morning. He asked them to go down to the dock and wait. They spotted him way out by the bell buoy, and when he saw them he stood up in the dinghy and waved.

"Holy God," Jack said as Ross neared the dock.

He called out to them, "The Queen has been restored, long live the Queen!"

Casey's mother was behind him in the boat. Next to her were his golf clubs and a white wicker wheelchair he

—103

had appropriated by some trick. Ross's expression changed when he jumped onto the dock and came up to Casey. He stood there a moment with his aviator's jacket draped over his shoulders. "She's not talking," he said.

Casey looked past him to her mother. As she waited, Jack went up to her. He only stood there at first, but then he reached out and took her hand and her eyes lit up right away, and when she smiled at Jack, Casey knew at once that she had drifted back in time and was seeing him as she had known him long ago. Then Jack turned and walked away. Casey could tell his feelings were hurt. *He* was the one who should have had the chance to rescue her mother. *He* was the one she and her mother had relied on before Ross came along. Ross had taken over. She watched Jack standing by himself. She thought, I'll find a way to make it up to you.

She went up to her mother. As they were lifting her from the boat she told her she was going to be happy here with them. "We'll make you happy again," she said. "Everyone here is happy now."

—104

Chapter Ten

There were days when Casey felt steady and strong, when she believed they were all prospering. Other days nothing could persuade her their lives would turn out well. Ross had fixed the outdoor shower behind the kitchen, where they washed after coming up from the beach. She memorized the outline of their bodies standing there naked in the low, late afternoon sun, the water splashing off their shoulders beading on the petals of the geraniums. In June the beads of water made her think of crystals of dew. By the end of July she thought of them as tears. Her own tears. This one detail, for the joy and sadness it conveyed to her, would remain one of the most enduring details of her summer.

They pushed her mother all around the Point. They faced her towards sunsets, a plaid blanket draped over her knees. They brought her to the tennis courts so she could watch them play. Ross put a Panama hat on her head and wheeled her to the pitcher's mound at the abandoned baseball field, where they hit tennis balls over a red-slatted snow fence in the outfield. She never really responded to them, but her skin turned brown in the sun.

They found her a pair of wild sunglasses, and Jack, who was collecting drugs in a box he called his medicine chest, mixed a concoction of crushed opium and hash and this made her sleep peacefully through the nights. Ross bought Moxie by the case and gave it to her straight from the bottle with a straw.

One afternoon Casey was alone in the cottage when someone drove up in an old, black Cadillac convertible. He introduced himself as a General Blake. He held up a finger and thumb and said, "Two wars." Then he dropped the keys to the car into her hand. He explained that Ross had won the car from him in a golf match. "He made the damndest fuckin' shot I ever saw. Excuse me, but I still can't believe the shot he made. One minute he's marching into the woods to get his ball, the next thing I know the ball's rollin across the green right smack into the fuckin' hole."

She told him she was sure Ross hadn't been serious about taking his car.

"Oh, he was serious all right. I bet the damn car on the match and he won it from me. I got three more of them back home anyway. You enjoy it."

In a few minutes a woman drove up in an identical Cadillac convertible and beeped her horn for him. "I gotta go now," he said. "That boy of yours though, he's a damn legend around the club."

That afternoon Casey drove her mother around the Point. They drove very slowly up and down the lanes. Her mother put her head back against the seat and held her face up to the sun. Casey watched her as they rolled along past the old weathered cottages. She thought about Ross saying that life was a riddle. Her mother's skin was cracked and drawn. Growing old is a riddle, Casey thought. Do you grow old gracefully like these old cottages? Do you grow old looking out at the sea? She recalled how her mother once took care of her skin with cream, some kind of cream in a milky-white bottle. A precaution, Casey thought. A precaution against being left alone. If you stay pretty, they don't leave you alone. You can have anything you want.

They drove down along the shore, past the beach. Casey wondered how she would look years from now. Would she become one of those women who no longer dared to wear a bathing suit in public, one of those women no one wanted. Forgotten, betrayed. For a moment she felt angry, unaccountably angry, and then strong, and she told herself if she became fat she would not give in. She pushed down on the gas pedal and this brought a faint smile to her mother's lips. She would go to the beach anyway like those marvelous fat ladies, happy as larks, kicking up sand as they flounced along, their baskets full of candy, not a care in the world, everyone looking at them and wondering how they made love with all that fat. Oh, to be like them, Casey thought. Defiant enough not to care.

She turned and looked again at her mother. The same man had touched them both. This thought came into her head. The same man had left them both. When the thought finally passed she realized that she had pulled her foot off the gas pedal and they were sitting still in the road. It surprised her the car had stopped, that they were going nowhere. Later she would tell Jack about this, describing the moment as if it had been an epiphany, and telling him that after you've been betrayed you're always caught between two extremes, between recklessness and inertia, between rebellion and wanting to be safe.

With Ross behind the wheel they drove the topless Cadillac straight through the end of July and into August. The four of them drove in the open pasture behind the dunes at Homer's Meadow, bumping along with the radio at the top of its lungs. They drove in circles, ever-widening circles. Every generation has its own word for going fast; theirs was *booking*. "We're really *booking* now," Jack would yell.

One of those times in the meadow when they were bombing along under a high sun, Casey reached her hands up and pulled back her hair, and her breasts lifted in the front of her shirt and she looked over and saw Ross looking at her with a satisfied expression.

"What is it?" she asked.

"Just then," he said. "I was just watching you and thinking."

"I can guess what you're thinking," she said.

He told her she was wrong. He told her he was thinking how things happen in life: they happen and then they never happen again in the same way.

She told Ross to stop the car. "I want us to have a picture," she said. Even before Ross had spoken about things happening and then never happening again she had decided that she wanted a permanent record of this afternoon.

They shot a whole roll of film under a cloudless sky. They took turns posing and horsing around in front of the lens. Then Casey said she wanted one serious picture. She gave Jack the camera and stood in front of the car with

Ross. She told him to look at her face. "Just look at me like you adore me," she said teasing him.

Then, just as Jack was about to take the picture she turned her head slightly and looked off across the meadow. She was trying to look independent and contented and defiant and reckless, because she had decided that she would send this one photograph to her father's insurance office on State Street. This one picture would be evidence that she had gone beyond his life and influence to a life of her own.

She turned to Ross and put her arms around him and laid him back on the sun-baked hood of the car. She felt completely free. Ross rolled on top of her and yelled to Jack to get behind the wheel.

"Take us for a spin," she called to Jack. Then she took Ross into her arms and laid her head back. Jack punched the gas peddle and they were off again, Casey and Ross lying over the hood, the engine pulsing beneath them.

Ross was reading her the poetry of Sylvia Plath and trying to write some of his own. He pressed Casey for her opinions. One night he read a long poem and then stood with an arm draped along the fireplace mantle while he affected the accent of a British literary critic. He fluttered his eyelashes and raised his eyebrows archly. "How does he do it? How *does* this kid do it?"

"Do *what*?" Casey asked.

"How does a boy so young, so frightfully new in this world of letters, compose such exquisite verse? Again and again in this, his first stab at it, he has demonstrated astonishing breadth, consummate technique, an unrivaled intensity. He is superb. He is utterly without peers!"

"He is modest too."

"Ah yes, *that* too."

"Then why, dare I ask *why*?"

"Dare, please."

"Then why does he leave things so up in the air?" she asked.

Suddenly Ross was all business. "Answers," he said. "You still want more answers."

"I'm only saying your stuff would be much stronger if it wasn't so vague. That's all I'm saying."

Ross walked out of the room. The screen door wheezed shut behind him. After she put her mother to bed Casey went out and found him sitting on the rocks at the end of the Point. When she came up to him he apologized.

"You look cold," she said.

He nodded. "Lonely, windswept, epic in a way." He laughed. "We still leave too much to chance for you?"

"I'm learning to live with it. Slowly."

He put his arms around her. They talked about life. He told her he thought much of life had to be *lived* without trying to figure out what it meant. They heard the sound of the ferry blowing her great horn as she passed behind the Porcupine Islands. The *Evangeline*, the ferry from Bar Harbor to Nova Scotia, was moving ponderously across the black sea, surf splitting at its bow. Casey and Ross could make out people standing on her upper deck, people probably looking toward the mainland, looking to Hancock Point, probably wondering if someone was looking back at them. Maybe the passengers out on the water tonight wondered what sort of charmed lives the people lived in the great cottages on this point of land, houses that seemed to have sprung up from the sea. Maybe the passengers on the ferry imagined that the lives on this point of land were ones less troubled, less tedious than their own. Or, Casey thought, maybe they knew better, knew there were arguments around the fine dining room tables, that someone old was alone and frightened of dying or living, that someone was fumbling behind a hedge where he'd hidden a bottle, that someone was promising someone something he could never give just to get what he wanted, that there was a father worrying that he might lose his son, or a father wondering if he would ever find the son he'd already lost, and a woman was dressing to make a man want her, a man who hadn't wanted her for a long time but who once could not get enough of her. The *Evangeline* would take almost an hour to pass the Point on her way to Canada; her iron hull full of automobiles, her cabins incandescent with honeycombs of white light, light as bright as the stars and as faint as memory, light that strayed from the ship and was lost at sea.

"You drive a hard bargain," Ross said. "You want life to add up in some way."

"Who doesn't? Everyone does."

"I don't want us to be like everyone. We should do everything most people never do."

"Still," she said, "there's the part when you have to be like everyone else, when you have to come down from the mountain, down to earth."

He thought a moment. "Well then, I'll worry about us getting up, and you worry about us getting down."

That night Jack opened his medicine chest and showed them the mescaline he had bought from one of the bellhops at the hotel. They all swallowed some. They played baseball in the grass.

"I think this team's going all the way," Jack said.

"The Red Sox?" Ross said. "Never. They'll choke in the end."

"Not this year. They've got it this year."

"Come on Jack, you're talking like a man on drugs."

Casey pitched them old tennis balls. They were hitting them up into the trees, across the lane. "Hit one into the Atlantic and you win!" Ross cried out.

"Win what?" Jack asked.

"The girl!"

"I can't be won," Casey said. It struck her that being won was the worst thing because if she could be won then she could be abandoned, betrayed. She was thinking about this while Jack and Ross went running around the lawns chasing fireflies. Ross pretended to be a plane and he swept by them with his arms out like wings. Casey asked him to stop and when he kept going she began screaming. She collapsed in the grass, sobbing. Ross went over to her and held her and laid down next to her in the grass. But she kicked him and rolled away. She pulled her hair down over her eyes. "I'll never see you again," she said. "My two lost boys, I'll never see you again."

Chapter Eleven

In those days of early August Jack resurrected an old radio from the servants' quarters. It was an enormous contraption, and Ross fooled around with the tubes in back and eventually got it working and carried it out to the porch, where they sat in the evenings listening to Red Sox games, their faces illuminated by the light from its dial. Soon the Red Sox began losing every game, and the radio told them the war was getting worse. It was all bad news. Ross said, "We ought to drop this sucker in the harbor and watch it sink to the bottom with all its doom and gloom."

Ross began writing down the numbers of dead soldiers. He kept a chart inside the cover of Sylvia Plath's book. "Both sides," he said, "I'm keeping both sides."

It was turning cool at night. The wind was often from the north. They walked the beach in sweaters.

"I'm not playing golf today," Ross announced to Casey one morning as they walked past the empty tennis courts. "Wind like this could cost me a lot of money, the way I slice the ball."

He told her he had been up early with her mother. "I had to clean her up a little," he said somberly. "She soaked her clothes."

Casey looked at him. "I should take her back, Ross," she said.

"A few more weeks," he said.

She knew this was all the time any of them had left. At the dock a family from New Jersey was already taking their boat out of the water. Its wooden cradle was in the sand waiting for the tide to rise.

"That first time you came into the hospital," Casey said to him, "I should have known." She thought how they had had their ups and downs, how Ross had made her feel like her life was beginning, and how, during her last two years at home, she had been waiting for this feeling.

"Known what?" he asked.

She smiled at him, then turned her face into the wind, and he stood still next to her.

"I wonder, when my father first walked up to her if she felt like her life was beginning. They were a bad match. I always knew that, but even if you can tell this at the beginning it's not always something you can stop."

He told her, "Whatever it was, you can't compare us to them. We have our own choices."

"I know," she said. "I know." She chose not to tell him how she felt connected to them in a way. It was like Jack had said; there were these things you couldn't do anything about which still had a power over you.

"There's nothing right now, right here, to keep us from doing whatever we want to do," Ross said.

She looked at him and then back at the bay. Out on

—114

the water the sunlight was broken into bits of glass. "We'll go back to Boston at the end of the month," Casey said. She told him she was going to try to work out something with the Catholic Church so she could move her mother closer. When she looked up at Ross again there was an emptiness in his eyes she had never seen before.

He began telling her something. "That summer I worked at the hotel there was a man named Eagleton, a guest who'd spent thirty summers here. He was in his eighties when I met him. I guess he was quite a dashing figure in his younger days, there were rumors about him and certain chambermaids young enough to be his granddaughters. But he'd had a stroke over the winter and it left him crippled. He could barely walk, and one corner of his mouth drooped. One hand was twisted like a claw. He checked into the hotel a week before the season started. He took a room up on the fourth floor where the staff lived, one room at the end of the hallway. His door was always closed and locked. We all thought it was just another storage room. But he was in there. And he'd come out late at night and walk all over the Point, back to all the places he'd been a thousand times in better days. No one knew he was back for the summer. When I became a busboy in the dining room I'd hear the old guests speaking of him, how sad it was that he had died. He kept up his nocturnal life, his fiction, the whole summer. I met him after Labor Day, after all the other guests had checked out. I'd seen him at night from a distance, out on the beaches and at the end of the dock. After I met him I kept thinking about how he must have sat at his window all those summer days, looking out at the real world, his old friends, the women he had made love to here, too

—115

proud or vain or something to come down from the fourth floor and show his face. He wanted them to remember him as he was when he was at his best. But he loved this place too much to stay away, and he had to have it on his own terms. Can you see how much it must have meant to him to have a place like this to come to?"

"He was lucky to have things on his own terms," Casey said.

Ross said it was more than luck. "He just did what had to be done, and he didn't give up. I mean, that's the whole huge difference between people—some people give up, and others take the worst kick in the teeth and still get back up. They live, no matter what."

"They don't need anyone," she said.

"What?"

"Those people who never give in, they don't need anyone." She wouldn't go on any further. He asked her to explain what she meant, but she wouldn't. She couldn't really explain it to herself, and if she had been able to, she might not have told him anyway because it would have made her even more vulnerable to him. She looked at his profile as he stood a few feet from her along the side of the lane where they had stopped. She smelled the sea breeze salting the pine trees above her head and for an instant she tried to recall the smells of this summer and to fix them in her memory so that if she were ever telling her story to someone she wouldn't leave out the smells. She knew a great deal about herself, much of it she had discovered here this summer. She knew that her father had driven a hole through her, and only Ross had filled it. From time to time he had filled it. For a moment or an hour now and then. The more often he failed to fill it, the more she wanted to be defiant of him, the more desperately she felt she needed him.

One of those last nights of the summer Jack cooked them a special dinner, a last supper, he called it. They drank wine and did a war dance in front of the old radio when the Red Sox won in the tenth inning on a home run by Carl Yastrezmski. "One day we'll be sitting in Fenway Park," Jack said, "and this guy Yastrezmski will be playing his last game and they'll be calling him the greatest player on that team since Ted Williams. And we'll be middle-aged, fat, and happy."

"Our kids will think we're square," Ross added. "We'll have compromised like everyone else. We'll wear argyle sweaters and worry about the tires on the station wagon. We'll ride off into the sunset, sucked up by the life we'll all say is so great and marvelous."

"We'll own lawn mowers," Jack added.

"What other kind of compromises?" Casey asked.

Ross slumped down in his chair and swung his feet up onto the table. "No, I was only joking. We'll hang on to our ideals right till the bitter end. They'll have to pry our hands off, finger by finger."

Jack lighted a joint and listened for a while. Then he began talking about his father. Casey realized it seldom took more than a few minutes on one kind of drug or another before Jack started talking about his parents. He said he could remember when one of his father's old girlfriends came to visit him at their house. "She called the house and said she was passing through town, that sort of deal. But when she got to our place she was all dressed up, completely decked out and smelling of perfume. She told my father she'd been divorced. She sat in our backyard on a lawn chair talking with Dad. Mom stayed inside, she looked out the window from time to time. I remember wondering what this lady wanted from my father."

"She probably wanted to talk," Casey said. "See how he was, after so many years."

"More than that," Ross said. "She wanted to hear him tell her she was exactly how he remembered her. She wanted him to look across at her and say, 'You haven't changed at all, Sheila,' or whatever her name was. She wanted to see if any of the old promise was still there."

Ross let his feet fall from the table to the floor. He looked to Jack and then Casey and then her mother.

"It's all promise," Ross went on. "That's what you miss when you're not young anymore. I saw it in the old people at the hotel. The promise is what you leave behind. You spend a lot of time on all the elaborate self-deceptions and illusions that seem to restore any little bit of that promise."

"Promise of what?" she asked.

He said he didn't know. "I guess just the chance for anything to happen. I think that's the reason people make love until they die, to try and capture the feeling of being young and strong again. If she could have made love to Jack's father the way they used to when they were sixteen—"

"Maybe they never even made love," Casey said. "Aren't you jazzing up this story?"

"Okay then, that's even more reason. Don't you get it? If he could lay her down and make love to her, she could feel, for a few minutes anyway, like she'd beaten the odds, and isn't that what we want? We all want to go back and beat the odds that beat us."

Ross turned his eyes to Casey's mother at the end of the long table. Her head was bowed and she was sleeping with a bottle of Moxie in front of her. He reached towards her and touched her and said, "Isn't that what you want, Marianne?"

Casey put a quilt over her mother's shoulders. She stood behind her, looking down at her silver hair. "So then, by your theory, when do we start wanting to go back?—because I don't want to go back at all."

He said he didn't think it had anything to do with age but depended upon disappointment. "Once you reach a point where you can't hold a dream out ahead of you, or maybe once you can look around and say, this is it, nothing changes from here on, this is the way my life will turn out, then you start longing to go back."

"I might be one of the people who never wants to go back," she argued.

"Maybe."

"You're always so certain about these things. Where do you get your theories anyway?"

He shook his head. "No," he said, "I'm not certain about anything. I'm just trying to figure it out."

At dusk the next day word went around the point that the bluefish were running. They carried their rods to south beach and stood in the sand casting over the waves. The big fish hit hard and pulled them into the surf. Jack sat alone in the dunes, his arms around his knees, his dark hair blowing. Ross yelled to him to join them but he just sat there. When Casey turned and looked back at him she saw something on his face, some look of sadness and anger. It struck her that Jack knew something and he was keeping it to himself. Ross finally coaxed him to join them.

When Jack was standing next to Casey she saw that his expression had not changed. She knew that if she pushed Jack hard enough he would tell her what was on his mind. But for the moment she didn't want to know what was making him so sad.

When they went back to the cottage Casey took her mother up to her room. She heard the chimes ringing softly on the porch. She and Ross had made them from silver forks and knives Jack stole from the hotel one afternoon when they went there for lunch. She had thought nothing about it then, this small theft, but now she felt guilty. She felt that somehow she would be made to pay for all the times they had broken the rules in order to have things their way this summer. In Ross's company they seemed to have had a license to live life differently. Now the chimes seemed to signal that this had passed. The time for sitting out on porches was ending. The nights were starting earlier. She was entering a new season, unprepared. She wanted to be excited about this new season, but the things they had gotten away with, the past they had outrun for a while, all that they had escaped and created, now began to ache inside her.

"*Summer is not the best judge. . . . Happiness comes too easily, and we can leave our manners far behind.*" Lines from one of Ross's poems. That night she told Ross that they should have laughed more. He turned to her and propped himself up on an elbow in their bed. "That must be the answer," he said with relish. "Once people stop laughing that's when they start looking back."

She put her legs around him. More than that, she thought. "There must be a life first, something beautiful to turn back to."

He said they were both right. He pulled her close, kissed her. She thought to herself that these were not the best times for laughter, this half-year she had known him. But a fine time for being taken away. He had taken her away. She would be twenty-two years old this winter. She wanted to believe that her life was ahead of her. Outside the windows, beyond the harbor, across the Bay, there was something waiting.

"Ross," she whispered, "we should go overseas, all of us. Could we maybe sell the car and go travel for a while?"

"We'll wear beads around our necks and make love in Paris," he said.

It sounded like another one of his fantastic promises. "We can take baths in the public fountains. They have fountains in Paris, don't they?"

"And Rome," he said. "Don't forget Rome. We'll get down on our hands and knees in front of your pope, and he'll tell you that I never really made that shot on the tenth hole." He lifted one leg out from under the blanket, raised it in the air and the moonlight struck it. "The General was taking a leak and I just threw the ball out of the woods. It rolled right in. I felt guilty for an hour or so, but he's got plenty of other cars. I planned to drive the convertible back to the Club our last day here. Just park it in the driveway with the keys in the ignition."

"Will you?"

"I don't know. It's yours anyway. I got it for you."

"Well, I might not give it back to him then. I wish though that you hadn't cheated him out of it."

He told her not to worry, that he would have won the car sooner or later, that the general couldn't putt worth a damn.

Sometime that night while the chimes blew he told her he and Jack had spoken and Jack had told him he was lost.

"When it comes to girls, Jack doesn't know where he stands. It's driving him crazy. I've got to think of something to do for him."

"I'll take care of Jack," she said. She turned away and knew he was looking at her. When she looked back, he seemed troubled. She wondered if he would be jealous of her if she were to make love to Jack. A part of her wanted to make him jealous. Once this summer she and Ross had met a handsome bellhop from the hotel out on the beach. He was just a teenager but he had flirted with her and she had thought of staying out all night and then fabricating some story to make Ross jealous. She had thought this might prove something. If she gave Ross a reason to leave her and he stayed instead, it might prove his affection. But she didn't have it in her to betray him that way. And of course she couldn't risk discovering that he wasn't jealous.

"Maybe there's a girl for Jack in Paris," she said smiling.

"Maybe."

"Or maybe he'll be lucky, maybe he won't need anyone. Maybe he'll find his own way."

They had a hundred old tennis balls to get rid of. Jack and Casey took them to the abandoned baseball field and pitched them to each other until the last had been hit over the fence. Then they walked back to the cottage. That August Sunday morning Ross stood in the sunlight. His legs were as bony as a boy's. Up top he was wearing only his leather jacket. He had scissors in one hand, in the other a mirror. She saw him standing in his curls.

"Does it look that bad?" he asked her.

"You'll lose all your power," she said. And she thought,

wouldn't it be nice if he could love me and fill me and save me but have no power over me.

He kissed her. "I have to get some things in town," he said.

They waited for him to come back. They walked the beach in the rain. They kept on walking for hours. The ocean was as calm as a pond.

When they got back to the cottage Casey wrapped herself in a sleeping bag and waited out on the porch. It was getting dark when Jack came out for firewood. "I'll get a fire started," he said.

"Don't you have something to tell me?" she asked.

He didn't look at her. "Come inside," he said. "It's freezing out here."

The fire was blazing when Jack reached out to her and told her Ross was gone. "His papers came in July. The Army."

When he stopped she looked at his face for some clue. He said, "He left all kinds of money for us, a drawer full of money in my room."

"I don't believe you," she said. She tried to stand up and walk away. She told Jack to look at her and tell her it wasn't true. When he didn't look up at her she yelled at him. "He didn't leave. You look at me and *tell* me, tell me it isn't true."

He telephoned her once from a train station in Connecticut. "I'm asking what every soldier asks. Please wait for me," he said.

By Labor Day he was at Fort Bragg, North Carolina. He sent more money. "All the colonels here are lousy golfers," he wrote.

When he called again he said his leave had fallen through and he was shipping out for Vietnam. "I'll write every day once I get settled," he said.

By the time the first of these letters arrived, Casey and Jack had already seen the *New York Times* article listing the names of the pilots and crew members shot down in a raid over North Vietnam. Ross was one of them. He was listed officially as missing in action. Casey held the newspaper and traced her fingers over his name, over the small black letters which made him seem as remote as her father had appeared on the television screen that afternoon at President Kennedy's funeral. This was in early November when there was blood and fire in the trees along the road through northern Vermont, the road to Canada, where you had to go in those days to escape the war or to get an abortion. She wouldn't let Jack come along with her. He had taken up with a group of seminary students in Boston, and they had made the arrangements for her through an underground organization in the Episcopal Church.

First Jack had tried to persuade her not to go through with it. "You could have this kid, I'll help you. There'll be lots of people for help," he said.

"It'll be a boy," she told him. "A son, and he'll come out looking exactly like him. Every time I look at him for the rest of my life I'll be reminded of his father." She paused and shut her eyes for a few seconds. "Where was his defiance in the end? Why couldn't he have just told the Army to go to hell? He didn't have to get on their damn train. He could have stayed with us."

On her way back from Canada she stopped at Hancock Point. She looked in the windows of the cottage at a life

—124

that seemed never to have belonged to her. When she saw his aviator's jacket draped over his bag of golf clubs the breath ran out of her. She leaned against the window sill.

When she looked up she saw where they had stood taking their showers after coming back from the beach. She thought about how nice a shower would feel. The insides of her thighs were crusted with dried blood. She walked over to the shower and turned one handle already knowing the water had been shut off by now. She thought about the nurse handing her the gauze pads to press between her legs. Finally she broke a windowpane and climbed inside and took the jacket with her.

She walked down to the water and stood in the sand with his coat over her shoulders. She knelt down and let the water wash over her legs. She put her questions to the sea, and like the summer people who had come here for years, she discovered it was true what Ross had told her and had written about the sea—to all questions we carry to the sea, the sea gives the same answer, but it is always enough. To all questions about love, loss, betrayal, injustice, pain, and suffering, the sea throws back the same response. But it doesn't ever say the same thing to any two people on earth.

Chapter Twelve

All winter they wrote letters to Ross. They had been instructed to address them to an office at the Pentagon which would forward them to another office in Saigon. Casey pictured her letters lying inside the drawer of someone's desk.

She spent Ross's money to lease a small house on the coast of southern Connecticut. She moved her mother there and by March it was warm enough for them to sit out on the porch looking at a different harbor where sailors arrived on weekends to ready their boats for summer. Another summer. More sailors. There were times sitting on this porch when Casey felt her life was no more than a series of scenes played in front of her, scenes varying only slightly and always attached to the past, scenes which she could only observe.

They were out on the porch the afternoon Martin Luther King was shot. All Casey could think of when the news came over the television was the black boy smashing in the car windows that day in Boston, his pure defiance, the way he swung his stick so hard that his feet lifted off the pavement as it struck.

Jack drifted back into the streets of Boston. After the assassination, the civil rights issue became his new cause. He was soon caught up again in a life resembling their old life, and he wrote Casey long letters which referred to the time *they* had in that city. Once he sent her a long meditation on his life. It included a puzzling and sad section about a laundromat:

"... *In the laundromat I use now the door doesn't stay shut and the wind blows dirt through the place. When the sun is out you can watch pinpricks of dust flying in the yellow rays of light. You remember those old days (they seem like old days now to me) when we all used laundromats. During the hectic camaraderie of our brief college days. In those days when we had escaped our parents' rule, I noticed nothing disheartening about laundromats, and except for the occasional and innocent robbery by way of mechanical malfunctions I hold no unpleasant memories. In fact, I recall there were often momentary but wonderful romances that sprang up while hunting for change or stray socks.*

"In those days we were trying to make sense of our lives. And now in this laundromat I think about our good expectations and the things that didn't work out for us. Many people I know in the city now have grown up and they live expansive lives with children and houses and heavy appliances to anchor them. And yet I seem still to be perched for flight. This is also true of my lonely companions in this laundromat. All of us seem puzzled by life now, as if we did not ever expect to still be doing our wash in a stranger's machines.

"I watch the people here as we sit among the shuddering washers and the racketing lint trays. I watch the unmarried

—127

mothers holding their tired children. Perhaps these ladies once owned gleaming white Kenmores, before the problems began. Perhaps they wonder if they'll ever have machines of their own again. And what of the elderly men who bring their laundry in paper bags from the grocery store? I watch their old faces and their eyes squinting against the fluorescent lighting. I wonder if there is a man among them who has never been chided for failing to separate the colors from the whites, and if he doesn't yearn from time to time to hear, once more, the voice that chided him.

"There seems to be something rootless and transient about us regulars here. Beyond waiting for the cycles to change we are all waiting for repose and renewal, or another chance.

"One night in the laundromat I listened to an old woman reading to a little girl who had climbed up onto her lap. Each time the woman paused, the little girl asked eagerly, 'And then what happened?' Tugging at the old woman's arm, she asked again and again, 'And then what happens, Nanny?'

"It struck me that the little girl had come upon your old question, Casey, the question each of us was asking secretly. Wasn't she asking the one question we had asked a hundred times and will probably ask forever? Don't we all want to know what will happen next and how things will turn out? For all of us alone in this laundromat, no question matters more these days."

What he wrote struck Casey as being true. Everything he said to her was true. He wrote her frequently, telling her they must never give up on Ross. But she had already begun to believe they would never see him again. She

—128

wrote Jack, "I wonder, has anyone's future ever been more uncertain than ours?"

One morning in April, a package arrived from the nursing home. It contained an Easter card from Sister Tamara, a pair of slippers, and two back issues of *Church World* Casey's mother had left behind at the nursing home. At the bottom of the box there was another, smaller package wrapped in brown paper and neatly addressed to Casey's mother. Casey turned the package over in her hands. There was no name or return address. She opened it carefully and found an old hardcover book which she recognized right away as the book she had seen on her mother's dresser when she was a little girl. She hadn't seen the book in years but she recalled its dark-gray cover. Opening it, she discovered it wasn't a book at all but a journal her mother had kept. The first page was dated December 20, 1945.

To my first child, from your mother, with love.

It has been a beautiful time for you to grow inside me. I went to the beach almost every day, collecting sand dollars and sitting in the sun. I feel you rolling over. I finished knitting you a green sweater yesterday. Your father has decided that you will be a girl. I wish I knew. I wish I knew what to call you. But I am putting this book together for you so you will have it when you are older.

First of all I want to tell you about how your father and I met. It was the beginning of summer and I was walking on the beach. I was looking for sand dollars. I'm always looking. He was sitting on the beach reading and I could

—129

tell he kept looking up from his book, looking up at me. Finally he came walking towards me. He said hello and I said hello to him. He said he wanted to apologize for staring at me, and he hoped he hadn't offended me. Well, I said no, that's okay, and I kept walking. He started asking me questions about what I was doing. Well, I said I had to get back to work and he told me his name. He said, "I'm Paul." I told him mine and then I left. Well, as you can see I didn't really want anything to do with him. To tell the truth I hoped he wouldn't bump into me again. He was only a boy. When I walked away from him that first day, he called out to me, something I couldn't hear. I was too far away. I thought I'd never see him again. But as it turned out he was visiting the house where I was working.

Dec. 24, 1945

Dear—
I really have had a wonderful pregnancy. I felt great the whole time and was so excited the whole time. I have prayed for you to be healthy many times a day. I've been waiting all my life to have you. You must remember this—I started wanting you twenty years ago when I was young—You would have had a pretty, young mother then. I hope you won't mind. One thing you've done to me is give me back the freckles on my face that I had when I was a girl. Until I got pregnant I hadn't had freckles on my face for thirty years.

Your father came by last night with a book of poems by Emily Dickinson. He laid his head on my belly and read to you, and all the time he was reading you never moved.

January 10, 1946

I went into St. Mary's church today to say my special prayer for you. You are coming soon.

Jan. 21, 1946

Just for the record, I think you shall be a girl and we will give you the name Casey. Your mother is sleeping next to me this morning. Last night I heard her talking to you in a voice that I hadn't ever heard before anywhere on this earth. She will teach you all the simple, true things about life. You'll hunt for sand dollars with her. I shall be the one who trys to teach you to turn life upside down hunting for its mysteries, to resist the urge to be like everyone else, and to dare to go your own way for the purpose of giving the world new thoughts and ideas.

Whoever you are, I will teach you how to sail. I thank God that you have been sent to spend some time with me in this life, this place. I think I am ready for you. Forgive me please for the ways I will let you down. And remember me for the good things I tried to do.

Love,
your father

February 2, 1946

It all began at 5:30 a.m. I woke with a cramp. I quickly thought this may be the real thing. Especially when I felt the second one. Your father called me but I didn't say anything to him about it, I wanted to wait and make sure. Sure enough I spent the whole day keeping track of contractions. Your father came over at noon and began writing down the times and lengths of the contractions. At 7:30 p.m. we went to the hospital. I was feeling fine really. After fourteen hours of early labor I felt this would be a lot easier than I had always thought. We checked in, they broke my water, and we waited. It got a bit harder as we got towards 9:30. Your father was with me for a while. He hid in the closet in the room so the nurses couldn't shoo him away. He held my hand. Then he had to leave. They took me away to the delivery room. I pushed very hard three times and you just popped out of me. You were as anxious as I was to get this part over with. And you were perfect. I couldn't stop crying. You were beautiful, strong, and healthy. You, little Casey, were born at last.

February 4

Yesterday and today, dear Casey, I couldn't sleep. I kept you in my room at the hospital and just lay there staring at you for hours. You are sleeping all the time or else making faces or noises. Your father is so happy with you. I'm so glad and happy in my heart that I could give him a daughter. I know he was hoping for a girl. We love you. God bless you always! XOXO,

Love Mommy.

Feb. 4, 1946

Dear Flowerpot, here are some headlines from the New York Times *for February 2, 1946, the day you were born.*
Love, Daddy.

RUSSIANS HAVE SPLIT ATOM. . . . Foreign missions in the Soviet Union, including the United States embassy, have reported to their governments that Soviet scientists have achieved an important step toward the production of an atomic bomb—the spontaneous splitting of the uranium atom.

MYSTERIOUS DARK STAR REVEALED. . . . A dark star similar to the sun but heretofore hidden by the brilliant globular cluster of Ophiuchus, a northern constellation that Greek fable describes as representing Hercules killing the serpent, has been discovered by a special technique in astronomical photography, it was announced yesterday.

UNO COMMITTEE PICKS SITE. . . . A rural area about forty-two square miles extending from Westchester County into Fairfield County, Conn., was officially recommended yesterday as first choice for the permanent headquarters of the United Nations Organization.

2 ACTS OF 'BOHEME' LED BY TOSCANINI. . . . Two acts of Puccini's "La Boheme" received such a performance by Arturo Toscanini yesterday afternoon in Radio City as critics had never heard before.

DINGHY RACES POSTPONED. . . . Larchmont, N.Y. A heavy northwest wind, which churned up the waters of Long Island Sound, forced officials to call off the dinghy regatta at the Larchmont Yacht Club today.

February 5

Well, you and I would both like to go home now. You were such a good girl for the nurses. You wanted to sleep with me tonight instead of in the nursery. You were fed at

—133

9:30 till 10. Then at 11 the nurse brought you to me and said you were a hungry baby. I didn't mind. I held you and fed you and kept you with me for over an hour. Then I brought you back to the nursery. Your face is so bright and red at night and you look so beautiful. You had your big green eyes wide open.

I couldn't get back to sleep because I wanted us all to be home. I wrote a letter to your daddy, then fell asleep. I love you. Good night and God bless you Casey. XOXO.

February 6

Today, Casey, was a special day for us. We got to take you home.

February 9

Today you were very happy all day. But you didn't want to sleep in your carriage (that was your bed because the crib looked too cold and big for you yet) so you slept all day in our bed. You liked the striped sheets a lot. We both took naps all afternoon. You slept five hours, then we took a walk back and forth across the living room.

February 13

It got warmer today and so I fed you and bundled you up and took you outside to get some fresh air. Your first walk outside. I walked with you two blocks and back. You looked so beautiful. We sat on the front porch until I saw your daddy coming around the corner and we walked to meet him. You didn't wake up at all. Then Daddy made me supper and he held you while we ate. He loves you so much and keeps telling you how sweet and beautiful you are. We love you. XOXO

Feb. 18, 1946

You are learning to keep your food down now. You love to suck and get too excited sometimes. You have been eating every four hours. Lots of smiles today for us. We love you so much.

Feb. 19

Casey, you know I love to hold you. When your daddy brings you to me at 2 a.m. you look so beautiful. You are a very good baby . . . so peaceful, healthy and strong. Everyone loves to look at you when we go out walking. They stop the carriage just to peek at your face. Your green eyes sparkle.

February 23

I wonder how much you will grow in your first year of life. It seems to me already that you are twice as big as you were when they first laid you on my chest after you were born. I hope you grow slowly. They told me I would never be able to have a baby, but they were wrong, weren't they?

February 27, 1946

Today we got to watch your daddy play basketball. You seem to love being outside, just like me. I hope you always love the outdoors.

March 8, 1946

Dear Casey,

In our first days together I have learned a few of your tricks. You prefer sleeping with company rather than alone. You have an orchestra of noises, most coming from instruments which play a great variety of grunts and groans in your belly. We love you more each day and cannot believe how fast you are growing. Your fingers look full-grown to me today. You and your mom are learning the fine art of eating milk without spitting it back up.

As I write this to you I am wondering what the world will be like when you are old enough to read and understand it. Someday you will be old enough to see your father's faults and failings. The world may be completely mad by then. But I cannot think of that. I'd rather think of dreams, the dreams I hold for you and for us as a family. I hope we get to spend every summer of your life by the sea.

I will never forget how you first looked at me, your green eyes wide open. They say all babies are born with blue eyes—not true. The look on your face was one of great surprise. This is a fine world despite the greed and hatred and ignorance. There is love waiting for you, Casey. The love of a boy. Children of your own to love. The love of a family. The great richness of friendship. I wish you all of these things. And as I write this I should tell you that you and your mother and I have been blessed these days. We have love and health and strength, and freedom. And we have time to live each day. Surely there is nothing more we could ask for. Sleep tight, little pocono.

Love forever, Daddy.

April 1

My dear Casey,

Today you cried your first real tear. You swallowed too much milk and you couldn't spit it up because you were sucking too hard on your pacifier and so it came out your nose. You didn't like this. Poor little thing.

I just can't believe how wonderful you are to hold in the night. I like to sleep and need lots of sleep but I really don't mind being up with you. You are such a joy to us. You make lots of noise and grunts and groans. It's just your way of talking, I tell your father. You kept him up most of the night tonight. Love and God bless. . . . Mommy

April 4, 1946. Rainy and cold.

You had a good night's sleep. You woke up every four hours to eat, then went quickly off to dreamland. You had your first bath and you really loved it. You look so chubby to us. I think you are getting a lot bigger and in only a few weeks. And you look a lot like your daddy today. I love you.

Friday. Rainy again.

Another good night's sleep for us all. You are so special to me. It is so nice to hold you. You love to be held and when you cry you want us to pick you up. I have been reading that it is best to let a baby cry for a little while, but how can I do this? You had a doctor's appointment today. You left the hospital weighing 7 lbs. 13 oz. Now you weigh 9 lbs., 1 oz. Also you grew one inch in length. You are strong and in great shape, says your doctor. His name is Doctor Wallace. You are a very pretty baby, the nurse told me. You are a joy. You are asleep now. I love you.

April 9

We watched your daddy play tennis today. I think you are going to be athletic like him. Your father says you'll be a gabber like I am. I just hope you are a happy, friendly, and content little girl. We love you so much more every day. I can't wait to take you shopping for some summer dresses.

April 10

Dear Little Casey,

Today a funny thing happened. As you and I were out in the sunshine talking to Daddy as he was hanging out the laundry, a bird flew by and pooped on your head. You just looked at me. I don't think you noticed or even felt it. We laughed, you looked so silly. I think the bird was saying hello to you. So many people want to meet you. Love you. Mom.

April 11

It is spring today in Pennsylvania. Someday I will teach you how to spell the name of this state where you were born. Your father talks about moving near the ocean if he can find a different job. Wouldn't that be wonderful, Casey? You know it will always be so clear in my mind the wonderful moment I first saw you. I'll never be able to forget your big green eyes staring right at me.

P.S. Right now you are lying in your crib and I love you every minute.

May 2

Dear Little Casey,

I am getting to know you better each day. You had two smiles for me today. You seem so happy! You are so much fun to be with. You held your rattle today but I don't think you knew it was in your hand. I love you. XOXO.

May 7

Your father calls you a real character. He loves to hold you and kiss you, and you know him so well by now. You turn your head to follow his voice when he's in the room with you. He loves you too.

May 12, 1946

Dear Pocono,

Because it was as good as a summer day here yesterday we pushed you to the park, and while I hit tennis balls around with a friend I carried you under my left arm like a football. You didn't seem to mind.

I want you to have great friends. Friendship is a special thing, Casey. I've always had the most wonderful friends, friends from my boyhood with whom I was very close. I mean real friends, people you can talk with about the important things you don't share with anyone else. You will have friends like this. But let me tell you what I have learned. That the world is complicated and life takes many strange turns, and it is not easy to hold close to these friends. You start out believing that you will just naturally stay close; you believe that no matter what happens, you will be different from the people who lost their friends. But there are concessions you must make, and many accommodations and even sacrifices in order to keep these friendships vital and meaningful. I would say that it is jobs, money and children which place the most pressure on your friendships. You may find this is not true. What I hope is that early in life you will make a few friends and that when your life is nearing an end that you will be as close as possible. And that you will always live nearby these friends so that you do not spend a lot of time longing to be with them, to talk with them again. I have one friend like this, Casey. You will meet Jack Kennedy and you will get to know him. Life would be so lonely without him for a friend. I hear you grunting in your crib.

Papa.

May 17

Dear Little Casey,

You are so beautiful I could just sit and stare at you all day long. And I do! A lot! Papa too. Your hands are so soft and chubby they look like little starfish. They are so perfect. You are losing your hair now more and more, and I tell your father it is going to come back in and be red. It is the Irish in you. Whatever color, it will be beautiful and I will let you grow it long so I can braid it for you. We love you.

Mommy.

May 20

I am sitting here beside your crib waiting for you to go to sleep so I can too. You laughed tonight, twice. It was the funniest thing. You are so much fun to watch. The past few days you have been pretty fussy in the evenings. Evening colic, your daddy calls it. But I think you just want to be held and fed all evening so that's what I do. You are a great baby.

June 4

I gave you a taste of ice cream today. You loved it on your tongue. I found a way to make you smile. I rub your head and you just smile for me, Casey. Lately I have been rock-

ing you to sleep at night. Sometimes it takes three or four hours because when I lay you down you want to be rocked some more. I think I am going to have to just let you fall asleep by yourself. I never see Daddy at night anymore. He is fast asleep when I get you asleep and come in. I love to hold you but you keep yourself awake at night just to be with me and you get so tired. We love you so much.

July 2, 1946

Dear Miss Casey,

There will come a time, perhaps even several decades from the time that I am writing this letter, when you wonder what you were like as a baby and what your parents were like. If you ask your mother and father, they will say that you were the most beautiful and happy baby ever. Both, your mother and your father, will say this to you with absolute loving conviction. I am writing this letter to you to say, as witness to some of the hours of your first months of life, that though your mother and father of course are biased in their opinion, they are also completely correct. You are, in fact, the most beautiful and happy baby ever born. You have hundreds of expressions. Your little hands grasp and throw things now. You move with perfect baby grace. Your hair is a brassy swirl on the top of your head, and you have eyes so green and clear and wondrous that I am struck dumb when I look into them.

You should know that your parents' love for you is so joyous and beautiful that people are drawn to the three of you, to feel human love at its fullest.

God bless you, Casey.

Jack Kennedy

July 4, 1946

Dear Peach Pie, please forgive me for not writing in your book for such a long time. First we were going to move to Florida when your daddy thought he got a new job. But this didn't work out. I woke up this morning to the sounds of you in your crib. You are beginning to make sounds that seem like you want to talk to me. You now have a bad cough. It is your first cold and I hope it goes away quick. I love you.

July 7

Dear little Casey,

You are the best baby a mother could ever have. I keep telling this to your daddy and he thinks I am exaggerating, but I have spent a lot of time around other people's babies and I know. Today your papa got a letter from a friend who is in Ireland. He sent a picture for you with a beautiful Irish girl standing up on a hilltop. I have stood the picture up in your crib so you can see it. I love you so much.
Mommy.

August 1, 1946

Dear Casey,

How can it be that you have changed so much, and grown so fast right before our eyes. We want you to stay small. We already feel the force of nature pulling you from our arms. But what a joy you are. Your slow, wide smiles showing us your gums. Your belly laughs. And yesterday you began a new trick, singing for your milk. You sound like an opera star who swallowed a spoon.

Some of these days I have not been there for you and your mother. There is a great heavy pain in my heart and it pulls me down some days and I can't do anything to stop it. But your mother will always be there for you and she will remind you that when I am away, I will return in a day or in an hour and my love for you will never be diminished.

Love,
your father

September 23, 1946

Dear little Casey,

It has been so long since I have written to you. The leaves are falling. I promise not to give up on this book to you. You will see over the years that I'm not very organized, that is compared to your father. You weigh 18 pounds now Casey. Not at all a shrimp like I had feared. I was a very tiny baby. I will tell you someday how I won a five-dollar gold piece when I was two years old. My mother took me to the fair, and Tom Thumb was there with his little miniature house. And they said they would pay anyone a five-dollar gold piece who could walk through the rooms of his house. You see, they must have thought that by the time a child was old enough to walk she would be too big to fit. But I was so small, I won the gold piece. I wonder what ever happened to it. It was the only thing I ever won. Yesterday I went shopping and bought some bottles to feed you with. I have not been feeling so well and I don't think there's enough milk for you. I got ten bottles on sale for twenty cents each! You will never know how happy you make me. XOXO

December 12, 1946

Dear sweetheart,

We must always be proud of your daddy. He tries so hard for us.

December 23, 1946

Oh Casey, I have such wonderful news to tell you. Your daddy might get a job in New Jersey, close enough to the ocean so we can hear it from our windows, he says! I am so happy for him. I know he will feel better if we can be near the ocean! We can walk on the beach together.

Casey sat on the porch that night reading her mother's journal, completely absorbed by her mother's past, by this sketchy picture of an old life which had contained hope and promise and love, things that were gone by the time Casey knew her. The moon was yellow and round. Across the road a teenage couple stood smoking cigarettes under a tree. The boy leaned the girl against the tree, and as he touched her she lay her head down on his shoulder. For Casey it was as if he had touched *her*. She didn't even know their names but she had seen them coming and going. They seemed so young to her, so much younger than she had ever been. She thought about Ross, how he had touched her, the places they had been when he touched her.

In the morning she took the journal to the library and checked the *New York Times* from February 2, 1946, the day of her birth. There was no headline about the dinghy races; it was just as she had suspected: her father had taken this headline from a later paper. He had deceived her in order to try to influence her, maybe to try to make her a sailor. She thought that this was the sort of thing fathers might do, and that with most fathers it would be innocent enough. But not with her father. She thought to herself—Well, I caught you in your first lie to me.

On April 12 that spring of 1968 Casey buried her mother in the cemetery behind the Catholic church in the seaside town where they were living. The train tracks ran just beyond the cemetery, and years of vibration had caused many of the old headstones to crack and topple off their granite footings. Standing here for the first time amidst the cracked marble and the faded inscriptions on ruined stone, Casey felt as if she had transcended time and was standing in a miniature coliseum in Rome or Athens. She spent much of the spring going back and forth to the cemetery to pray for her mother's soul. She prayed without really believing. One morning in June while she ran the beads of her mother's rosary through her fingers, she heard a train whistle and she felt the earth move beneath her. At first it was only a faint pulsing under the soles of her feet, but then it grew. The pulsing rose up her shins and ran through her arms. When she opened her eyes it was because the train seemed to be moving very slowly. She looked up. Out across an apple orchard, on the far side of a meadow she saw the last car of the train draped with bunting, an American flag flying at all four corners. Through the budding trees it looked unreal, like something in a dream. A man in a pickup truck, part of the cemetery crew that dug new graves, told her the train was carrying the body of Robert Kennedy. It was moving slowly, reverently through the new green countryside.

She thought back to her father singing with Bobby's brother, back to her mother watching Jack's funeral on television. She watched the last car disappear down the tracks, thinking, *There is this man riding on this train to Arlington Cemetery.* For the longest time she could feel the train receding down her arms, her shins, draining from her, back into the ground under her feet.

Chapter Thirteen

Two years passed. It was 1970, a new decade. Casey had been living in New York City, trying to forget. Jack had visited her often. He was forever talking about time, about how time would pass and how they would move ahead with things. He told her that everything, in time, assumed a logic of its own, that they only had to be patient and to have faith.

"It's you who have the faith," she said to him. He seemed to her to be growing up, getting over things. He was talking about going back to school.

"Well," he said, "no matter how much time it takes, I'm going to believe we'll see him again."

"Your hope, Jack," she said. "Your exquisite hope."

In the big, outrageous city, men came into Casey's life. She tried to be happy for a while with each of them. Then, before too long she began to need more time alone than they were willing to give her. She found one man, or boy, after another, and lost them as if they were only ideas. Because she wanted to see if she could forget Ross, she tagged along with a punctual stockbroker and then a pugnacious sculptor who had once been commissioned to do a bust of Ted Williams. She tried her best to explain herself, to give them the answers they wanted. Doors were slammed as she went on explaining. They said she had tricked them.

"I'm fine at the beginning," she told Jack. "You remember how we drove the Cadillac in the rain? When we went real fast how it seemed that we weren't getting wet? Well, it never works now; I can't fool myself about anything anymore."

The only man she allowed to touch her was an auburn-haired medical student doing his internship at the hospital in the Bronx where she worked. He was married and already had two small children, a son and a daughter. He showed her their photographs in his wallet. He was going to become a surgeon; he would be wealthy one day and live in a big house, but first he wanted to spend some time in Africa or Asia working for the needy. "We'll do it as soon as I finish my residency, before we settle down," he told Casey. He said that every man has certain things he feels he must do to test himself. "We have to go into the heart of darkness at least once to find out what we're made of."

He could have been answering her question about Ross.

The time the young doctor told her this they were alone in a windowless room, drinking coffee at three in the morning. She asked him about his children, whether there was any difference between raising a boy and a girl.

"It's too soon to tell," he said. "So far it's all diapers and trying to get everybody to sleep."

"Yes, I guess so," Casey said. "I always thought girls would be harder though. You know, boys just go out and play ball, but girls stay in their rooms and cry. Still, I wouldn't have given up trying until I had at least one girl."

"You talk as if it's in the past tense. You're young, anything can happen."

His words, she thought, were meant to reassure her. "Maybe," she said. "But I have something to tell you. I want to tell you something I've never told anyone but my closest friend. I want to tell you about my father."

She told him everything and when she had finished, he asked if he could hold her. He walked up to her and put his arms around her. She took his hands then and put them on her breasts. "The things we do in a moment of weakness," she said. Then she asked him if it mattered, if he thought differently of her after what she'd told him.

He said no. But when she touched him, he backed away and said he was sorry. "It's not very romantic of me, I know."

"I'm not looking for romance," she said.

"I mean I can't do anything. It's the guilt. I'd feel too guilty." He shook his head. Once more he said he was sorry.

"Don't be sorry," she said. "I know all about guilt." She tried to smile at him, to lighten the mood. "You're an honorable man."

"For once," he said smiling.

"I bet you'll always be an honorable man."

He looked down at the floor shyly. "I'll tell you something though, those things that happened to you—you know, with your father—you shouldn't feel guilty about that. That wasn't your fault."

She listened to him say this and thought, Of course, I've always *known* that. But then she acknowledged that

—149

there was new sin, sin more recent than that, sin of the abortion, a sin against nature.

"My father," he said.

And his words startled her. She thought he was going to pray for her. "What?" she asked.

"Oh, I was just going to tell you about my father. He's one of those Irish men, very private, always talking under his breath, never saying what he thinks about anything."

She asked, "What in God's name is it about Irish fathers? What are they all so sad about?"

"I don't know. Maybe it's just that they have too many kids. There were six of us and I swear there were times my father would come into the living room and see all of us there and he'd get this look on his face, a look of shock, like he was saying to himself, 'Who *are* all these people and where'd they come from?'

"I don't know what he wanted to be in his life, but he must have had some vision of himself just like your father might have had, and if you never get to see yourself that way you just curl up and stew about it, and make other people wonder what you're thinking about all your life."

Casey listened and thought to herself that if she ever saw Ross alive again she would tell him that both of them, in whatever lives they ended up living, had somehow to set their own children free so they wouldn't feel like they owed anyone anything.

It was October of 1971 when she rode a train to Boston to meet Jack and a soldier who had telephoned him in response to a newspaper advertisement Jack had published about Ross. It was a fine Indian-summer day. They drove to Amherst, Massachusetts. The sun swept low over the foothills of the Berkshire Mountains and the smouldering trees threw a reddish glow across the sky. They drove without daring to say anything and then they waited on the same side of a booth at the Fox Run Restaurant until just after noon when the soldier walked in through the doors straight to their table as if he had met them here a hundred times before.

He wore tan trousers and a matching shirt, a uniform of sorts. And the shine on his boots had been worked at. He spoke Casey's name as he sat down across from them in the booth. His face was thin and all but the palest trace of blue had been washed from his eyes, but his long blond hair made him look young.

"Do you know what happened to him?" Casey asked first. "What can you tell me?"

"I said I knew him," he answered in a clipped baritone voice. "We were together for a while."

"Yes, but you were with him when he was shot down?" Jack asked hopefully.

"I never said that. That was later. Look, I want some salad now."

He left the table. When he came back he sat down behind a large wooden bowl he had filled with green olives. "I love olives," he muttered as if speaking to himself. "My mom used to send them to me in Nam."

He raised one olive to his lips and sucked out the red pimiento center. Because at that instant he looked like a little boy to her, Casey said, "Your mother must be glad to have you back safely."

He wiped his mouth on the sleeve of his shirt. "I came home for her funeral," he said.

She told him she was sorry about his mother and when he said he didn't feel like sitting inside any longer, Jack suggested they drive to Amherst College. "We can sit outdoors someplace."

"We have to find out everything you know," Casey said.

"You can follow us," Jack told him.

"We'll take my car," the soldier said. He put several dollar bills down on the table and jerked himself to his feet. He took the bowl of olives outside with him.

He drove his big car very fast, accelerating around curves so that they were thrown back against the seat. He maneuvered the car with one wrist resting on top of the steering wheel. He shot through traffic lights as they were changing from amber to red, and soon they were out on the Massachusetts Turnpike speeding east.

Finally Jack leaned towards him and said, "What's the story, mister?"

He grimaced. The rear of the automobile lurched violently to the right and bits of gravel racketed against the floorboards before he managed to steer them back onto the highway with four fingers. "Don't worry," he said. "Don't worry about me, I'm a nice guy."

"Good, that's good," Jack said. "Then you tell us—"

"Jack," Casey said. She took hold of his arm. She felt his anger and fear running through him. She looked at his face and thought how his faith had increased his expectations beyond hers. He looked like he was about to explode. She gently pulled him back in the seat.

They drove on in silence as the countryside split down its middle over the big hood of the car and then flew past the windows. He exited at the town of Haverhill and drove by many huge abandoned factories. They drove several more miles and at the end of a dirt road he stopped the

—152

car and shut off the engine. He got out slowly, motioned for them to follow, then led them up the side of a grassless hill.

"I buried her here," he said. He stared dully at the ground. "This is her land. Mine now, I guess."

They stood for several minutes over a patch of new brown earth. Dark clouds shouldered over the hillside. He put his hands deep into his pockets. Finally he turned his pale eyes to them and spoke again. "She didn't want me to go, she saved the money for me to go to college. Isn't that a joke? I was flunking the damn commercial course in high school, and she thought some college would want me." He laughed a tense, irrelevant laugh. "All my life she talked about college like it could save my life."

Suddenly Jack leapt at him and grabbed him with both hands, shaking him violently and yelling, "We don't care about that! We don't care about your mother, goddamn you!"

Casey was looking into the soldier's eyes when he said to her, "Get him off me, ma'am."

Jack fell into her arms like an exhausted child.

They followed the soldier back to the car then. He told Jack to drive, and after he had helped Casey into the back seat he reached up and unscrewed the rearview mirror. He balanced it on his knees and from a small jar he poured a thin, white line of powder across the tinted glass. He lowered his head and with the quickness of a magician's trick inhaled the powder into his nostrils. All the way back to Amherst he kept his eyes closed.

At the restaurant parking lot he opened the glove compartment and took out a paper bag. "Here's your letters, ma'am," he said as he handed the bag to Casey. "The guys over there always read the letters. They looked

—153

for sex. But I kept yours safe. I read the first ones and then kept the rest safe. They haven't even been opened. You can see that for yourself."

Casey looked down at the bundle and then up at his colorless face. "Did you know him at all?" she asked.

He shook his head. "We never met. I just wanted to see what you would be like. I gotta go now."

When they were out of the car, he slid across the front seat, rolled down the window, and sped away with the radio blaring.

Jack often rode the train to New York City to see her. On one of these visits, after dinner at a small restaurant on Third Avenue, they ended up in front of the stereo on the hardwood floor of Casey's apartment. It was late and the noise of the city was muted at the windows.

"It's never easy for me to think of you here," Jack said.

"It's not much to look at, is it?"

"I don't mean the apartment, though when they're this small they should call them *com*partments. I mean the city."

"From the space of New England to the fuss and jumble of New York," she said. "But I like the commotion at times."

She paused and held her head so that her eyes seemed to draw in all the light from the room around them. "Do you remember the radio, that big contraption of a radio? The lights went on and there were those two little birds, each carrying a blue note in its beak."

"Yes," he said.

"Were they blue, the notes?"

He told her they were gold.

"You're right. You remember everything, don't you, Jack?"

"It's my great failing, a faultless memory. The radiator in my first apartment was Nesbit. The john was American Standard."

She laughed with him. "I love your memory. Can you remember, what was it he saw in me?"

Jack let the question pass between them. It seemed to clarify itself and gather some purpose. "Everything," he replied.

"Except all my questions," she said. She lay back on the floor and looked up at the white ceiling.

Jack looked at her doubtfully. "You're really asking?"

"Yes."

"You really don't know?"

"No," she said. "But if I give you long enough you'll come up with something wonderful." She laughed. "I know, it was my tits."

Jack played along. "That's it," he said. "You took the words right out of my mouth."

"Well, tough luck, they're already starting to sag. The accordian lessons are catching up with me."

He laughed. "No. You have a certain way. He wanted to protect you, take care of you. He was one of those men—"

She interrupted. "*Men*?"

"Well—"

"I think of you both as boys. But you're right, *men*. He was as determined as any man."

"He could have taken better care of you," Jack said hesitantly.

"I was as much to blame."

"I didn't mean blame."

—155

"No, but I could have done something. I wouldn't use the pill then. I had this idea there was something promiscuous about it. I've had the fear I think, that it ran in the blood, that I'd turn out to have the same poison my father had. Something in the genes."

She told him about the young doctor at the hospital and then said, "Wouldn't it have been nice if Ross and I could have pulled it off and left it at that. I think he ruined me for anyone else. It's the way this country's been ruined by Jack Kennedy. No one else will ever measure up. It took his death to establish him as a romantic figure. Maybe Ross went off to war for the same reason." She stopped and thought how people like Ross come into your life and when they're gone you spend a lot of time, maybe a lifetime, thinking about them.

Jack waited. "It's nothing we can do anything about," he said.

She told Jack he was right. "But I've thought a lot about what kind of father he would have been. I've read my mother's journal over and over, and it's strange, but those passages my father wrote, they've softened me up. Not towards my father, but towards Ross. Can you imagine the wonderful things he would have written."

She spoke about how she sometimes tried to picture Ross as a father of her children. "He would have been one of the fathers who organizes a workbench in the basement, using the little Gerber baby—food jars to keep screws and nails in. Hanging them by their lids, trying to get his things organized before the kids start walking and getting into everything. And then the years would go by and only the lids would be left hanging."

"That's perfect," Jack said.

"But he had this idea of himself as a father. It was right from Thomas Wolfe, where he described this big man, a husband and father who comes home at the end of the day and fills the table with provisions and hauls in firewood to keep the house warm. That's what Ross was, or wanted to be. The consummate protector, a man with the strength to be a protector. That was the way he wanted to see himself."

"Well, he could have had that if he'd wanted it," Jack said. "He could have had it with you. You could have both gone to Canada."

She looked at him with a wistful expression and thought, It's a long life, we can't be sure what will happen. "I wonder though, Jack, are we always going to sit around analyzing everything about the past, talking in the past tense? If you would just come into my bed and let me make love to you tonight, if we could just *do* something instead of talking."

When they were finished they lay in each others' arms talking again.

"That was crazy," Jack said.

"Worse," she said. "Now that you've made love with a sinful woman, your slate's no longer clean."

"I'll take my chances," he said.

She became very serious. She began thinking again about the abortion. She turned away from him and reached under the bed for something. "Here, I've been reading your Bible lately. It says something about sin. It says, 'For nothing is hid that shall not be made manifest, nor anything secret that shall not be known and come to light.' Do you know that passage?"

—157

"Luke," Jack said. He looked over and saw how Casey had marked the place in the Bible with the back of a book of matches advertising a career in palm reading.

"Yes, and I hope Luke is wrong," she said. "But this past tense business, this waiting, Jack, I think it's going to kill me."

Nothing changed for a long time. Three more years vanished without either of them knowing where on earth the time had gone. It was 1974, in April, when she wrote Jack a letter telling him she was going to marry a man named Kingsley Pierce, a man ten years older than she who had been left to raise three daughters alone after his wife died of cancer.

"The best thing about this," she wrote, "is that King has his law practice in Boston, so you'll have us for neighbors."

She tried to make Jack believe she was filled with optimism about this. She imagined this man's daughters in time might feel comfortable calling her Mom, and that soon enough the five of them would assemble at the dining room table, each of them aware that a nourishing affection and a restful equilibrium had come to settle beneath their roof. She wanted Jack to see that this was a chance for her to have a life. She went to meet him in Boston to show him what her letter couldn't convey.

Jack was in his last year of seminary and was planning to take a church in Framingham. As he showed her around the parsonage, she held his hand as they went from room to room. "You have it, Jack," she said. "A whole new life beginning for you, a life in the suburbs." She smiled at him and told him that King was big on church. "We'll bring the girls out every week. You can preach to us, you can show us the way."

They walked through the sanctuary and into the children's Sunday-school room. They stood there for a while, surrounded by the miniature chairs. Casey sat down in one of them and said, "We start out so small, don't we?" She looked up at Jack and his silence conveyed what she thought was skepticism about her plans to marry King. "Tell me," she said.

"Tell you what?"

She shook her head slowly. She held out one arm and traced her fingers along the veins. She said she had thought about it and now she knew. "When the past fills you with poison, you go around trying to flush it out. Maybe you've got the answer now, maybe religion is the cure for you. But I remember some of the old days, the days on the streets when you thought Shep could heal the poison. And then I thought Ross could heal mine. People with that great defiance, they seem to have a way out for people like us."

Jack was still silent. She told him she didn't mind running away from the past but she didn't want to run out of time. "I didn't want to just drift through the rest of my life, and King found me at the right time after so much drifting around. And he has the girls, you wait till you see them. You know how I've always talked about having children, and here I have an instant family. And while we're on the subject of children, I want you to know that King's done a lot of thinking and so have I. This is going to be *it* as far as children go. King's had one of those operations so there won't be any more kids, and that's fine with me, Jack, because I couldn't risk having my own anyway, not after everything that's happened. The risk would be too great. Not the risk to me, but to the babies. I've run up a bad record with all this poison in my veins. Too many sins, too many wounds. I could never be sure your God wouldn't punish me through my babies. Birth defects, something horrible like that, something to get even with me."

"Is that how it works?" Jack asked.

She looked away. When she turned back she was smiling, smiling at herself. "That sounded a little neurotic," she said.

She stood up, looked back down at the miniature chair, then walked to his side. "It's been almost seven years, he isn't coming back. That's an old story."

He looked at her. "So, will you be happy? I mean getting married and—"

"Oh what a question Jack. I'm getting such a late start. But must I convince you?"

"Have you convinced King, and yourself?"

"Yes," she said. "I'm sure I have."

—160

BOOK TWO

Chapter Fourteen

There were times during the first year of Casey and King's marriage when Jack was confident that they were doing well. Having a picnic supper on the patio overlooking King's fine backyard, or sitting between them on the front seat of King's car as they hurried into the city for the symphony, Jack was able to believe what he had said to Casey long ago, that in time their lives would assume a logic of their own, that things would fall into place after all.

Then there were times when it seemed to Jack that a web was building around their lives; times when he believed in his soul that this web had started to form long before any of them were born, long before he had found his life tied to Casey's and Ross's. It seemed that he, out of the millions of others, had been fated to walk right into the center of the web, to spend his life trying to free them from it.

It was 1975 and everyone was coming home. In early December, sixteen months after Casey and King were married, eight years and three months after he had gone

—163

off to his war, Ross came home. Jack was alone in the parsonage watching the TV news when he saw him standing in a row of soldiers on an airport runway. He dropped to his knees in front of the television screen. The report said these POWs were heading to Fort Meade outside Washington, D.C.

These were his first words to Ross when he reached him by telephone at Fort Meade. "Thing's have changed, everything's changed."

Ross's words paralyzed him. "Just tell me, how are they, Jack?"

"I'm coming down to see you," Jack said. "When will they let you go?"

"Oh no," Ross exclaimed, "I can't let her see me like this. I have to get some meat on my bones first."

"Well I want to see you. I'll bring down some of my fish sticks." Jack's eyes filled with tears when he said this.

There was a long silence. Then Ross asked, "Can you put Casey on the phone? Is she there?"

Somehow Ross must have assumed they were still together, that nothing was different. "I'm coming down," Jack said again.

"Alone?"

"Yes," Jack said, his voice lifting as if to invest even this word with some particle of hope or possibility. "She got married, Ross. I'm coming to you."

Jack packed a bag and left within the hour. He was prepared to tell Ross everything he wanted to know, to answer all his questions. At Fort Meade he was informed that Ross had been transferred to the Valley Forge Army Hospital in Pennsylvania. It was snowing when Jack found him.

They sat across a formica counter in the kitchen of a bleak apartment two blocks from the hospital's psychiatric wing. Ross was under observation but he expected to be discharged soon. There were deep brackets at the corners of his mouth. He was terribly thin. His neck turned within the circle of his shirt collar. Jack thought he looked something like a figure from a Modigliani portrait. He was smoking heavily, breaking off the filters with a snap and smoking the cigarettes down to his knuckles. Flecks of tobacco caught on his lips. He wore black motorcycle boots and a white T-shirt with the pack of cigarettes rolled up in one sleeve like a James Dean affectation. He seemed to be full of the old defiance Jack remembered.

"How long will they keep you here?" Jack asked.

"Oh, I don't know," Ross answered. "It doesn't make a lot of difference to me now." Then his eyes strayed from Jack. He looked past him, out the window above the sink to a length of clothesline strung across the porch. There were half a dozen clothespins clipped to the line. A breeze picked up, causing the pins to tilt and lift in unison. This brought a faint smile to Ross's face. "What do they remind you of?" He asked Jack.

Jack tried to think of something, tried to follow along once more. This time it wasn't a man on a train, but clothespins. "I'm helpless," Jack said. "I don't have much of an imagination."

Ross waited, then pointed to the window, at the clothespins, and said, "The Rockettes. You know, the Rockettes."

Jack smiled, and hoping to keep Ross's mind above their circumstances, he asked if he kept a baseball bat or some golf clubs around the place. Ross said there was nothing. "You ever think about how we spend our whole

—165

lives in rows?" he asked. "Right from the minute we're born, when they line us up in the hospital. We live in rows of houses, sit in rows of desks in school, work in rows of offices, eat in rows of tables in restaurants, march in rows, get buried in rows. Everybody's got to keep in line. Keep in line."

When he spoke again his voice seemed to be coming from very far off. "I have to tell you, I was scared shitless over there. I had a friend. They put two rats in a bowl and strapped it to his stomach. The rats ate a hole right through him. He just kept screaming." Ross's eyes were glassy and cold.

Jack reached across the counter and put his hand on Ross's wrist.

"That was years ago," Ross said.

"Yes," Jack said.

Then Ross cast his eyes to the ceiling with a look of incredulity that so much time had passed. He told Jack he had been reading Kerouac and that he felt like getting away. "I may hit the road for a while," he said without enthusiasm.

"Why don't you come stay with me, take it easy for a while?" Jack asked.

Ross shook his head. He said he was against taking it easy. He got up and dug around in a drawer for a note he'd written down with a quote from Saint Exupery. "Listen to this," he said. " 'You who built your peace by blocking every cranny through which light would pierce, making a wall of genteel security in routine, stifling conventions. Raising a modest rampart against the winds and tides and stars, having trouble enough to forget your fate as man. You are not the dweller on an errant planet and you don't ask yourself questions to which there are no answers. You are a petty bourgeois. Now the clay has dried and naught within you will ever awaken the sleeping musician, the poet-astronomer, that possibly inhabited you in the beginning.' "

Ross folded the piece of paper and slipped it in his shirt pocket. Then he said, "You, Jack, you're like Falstaff, feeling the pain for all of us."

Jack said nothing. He thought they had all had their share of pain.

"What was ever in it for you anyway?" Ross asked.

"The two of you."

Ross laughed cynically. "You weren't after some version of the American dream though. You were the smart one, just taking what came along."

Jack shrugged and looked away.

Ross went on speaking about how feckless life was for most people in America. He talked about people spending their lives squatting on a few hundred square feet of shag carpeting and linoleum, living out miserable lives, clinging to meager rituals. "Everyone's waiting for everything to add up. Not me, not now."

He took hold of Jack's arm and gave it a powerful squeeze. "Someone has to dismantle the myth before we all drown it its juices," he said angrily.

Listening to Ross talk, Jack had the impression that he really didn't believe in his own defiance. Below the surface, beneath the words there was something timid and weary about him. He seemed to be barely holding on to his ideas now, ideas propped up by some picture he held of the past. In his eyes there was a look of absolute exhaustion.

At one point, at the sound of footsteps outside the door, Ross pulled Jack down onto the kitchen floor, out of view of the window. He was afraid it was the Seventh Day Adventists coming back for more money. He said he had already given them every cent he had. "I can't turn the vultures away," he said.

Jack finally went to the door. There were two children standing there, a boy about six or seven years old holding the hand of his younger sister. They had dirty faces, orphan faces. Ross, still down on his knees, motioned them to come to him and then took them in his arms. He kissed the tops of their heads, then went to the desk and came back with the gift they had come for. It was a beautiful, egg-shaped glass paperweight, the kind that sends a blizzard down upon a miniature town when it's shaken. The children were delighted. They turned it over and over in their hands and then he sent them along.

Ross turned to Jack. "I pictured our kid this tall by now."

"I'm sorry."

"When I left I knew she was pregnant. It kept me alive over there."

"I know."

Ross looked into his eyes. "Abortion. Christ, a little soul floating around out there." He grimaced, then took a deep breath. While he was lighting another cigarette he said, "Why didn't *you* marry her, for Christsake? For *my* sake."

Jack told him. "I wouldn't have been able to make things right for her that way." He knew Ross already knew this. "What a crazy thing to say," Jack said.

In a cafeteria, surrounded by young but old-looking men in bathrobes and paper slippers, they sat with dinner on plastic trays. Ross wanted to know what Jack was doing.

"I finished seminary," Jack told him without looking up. "I have my own church."

"You could have married us then. You could have baptized the kid," Ross said. Then he just turned away. Neither of them could eat.

After a while Jack said, "You should go see her. You should just forget all your other ideas about everything and go see her, talk with her." He was thinking that once Ross saw it was over he could get on with his life.

After a little while Ross looked up. "Are you hungry?" he asked.

"Not really. You should eat though, eat something."

"Why?" He pushed the tray away and leaned back in his chair.

Jack waited. He looked around the cafeteria at the other men. Most of them were boys and there was nothing about the way they looked to make Jack think of them as soldiers. Except for the empty shirt sleeves, the missing limbs, the crutches and bandages, these boys looked remarkably like the boys Jack had never gotten to know in high school, the boys who drifted through the corridors with a bored, superior expression on their faces, bored because they had passed too quickly from adolescence to disillusionment, superior because they already knew about girls and car engines. In the presence of boys like this, Jack's impulse had always been to get as far away from them as possible. Now he wanted to get Ross away from them as well. He dreaded that one of them might turn to him at any moment and ask why he hadn't fought in the war.

Jack watched Ross light a cigarette and give it to a boy whose jaw was wired shut and held in place by an iron brace. The boy could barely part his lips wide enough to inhale it. Ross tapped his shoulder and gestured to Jack. "This was a friend of mine before the war," he said. The boy raised his right hand slowly and saluted Jack. "We used to hang out together," Ross said. He raked his fingers through the boy's hair, then turned back to Jack. "Fucking-A, man, if you leave now I don't think I'm going to make it."

"I'm not going to leave," Jack said.

"Well, you've got to leave sometime, I know that, but maybe you could just spend the night here."

They walked out into the darkness. Ross went ahead a few steps, kicking up snow with his boots as they passed rows of barracks, identical one-story rectangular buildings with narrow lighted windows. "I want to show you something," Ross said.

Jack followed him through the snow to a building at the far end of the base. They entered through a side door and came up to a nurse sitting behind a desk. She smiled at them. "Back to see the Major?" she said pleasantly.

"Yeah," Ross said.

"That's nice," she said. "That's real nice."

Ross opened the door to the sound of applause. It was a game show playing on a television set. A row of wicker baskets faced the television, shallow, round baskets no more than three feet in diameter. There were twelve baskets in all, and in each basket you could make out a man's head. Jack stared in disbelief. All that was left of each of the soldiers was just the head and torso. Ross walked over to one of the men. He called out, "Major, I'm back. Tell me your story."

Immediately one of the men in the baskets began talk-

—170

ing. "We were in the first assault wave. We hit the beach at o-nine hundred hours. Christ, we were coming in like gangbusters. Oh shit we had 'em, we had 'em, we had 'em, we had 'em."

"You had them," Ross said.

The voice started in again, sonorous and angry. Jack looked down into the basket. The man had a long, white beard which fell down over the blanket covering his chest. There was something odd about his face. It took Jack a few minutes to realize that there were no wrinkles on the face. Though the beard was completely white and the eyes looked like the eyes of a very old man, the skin on the face was like that of a young boy.

"They pinned us down. They ripped into us with those . . ." The voice suddenly trailed off.

"Major, I'm back," Ross yelled. "Tell me your story."

The major started in again precisely like before. "We were in the first assault wave. We hit the beach at o-nine hundred hours. Christ, we were coming in as gangbusters." A smile lit his face.

"You were coming in like gangbusters," Ross said. He turned to Jack. "Let's go."

All the other heads turned to watch them. The Major was still talking when they closed the door behind them. Outside in the snow Jack started throwing up. Ross took him by the arm and led him behind the barracks. Jack tried to concentrate on his voice. "I had a dog when I was five years old," Ross said. "It slept in a bed just like the Major's, a basket just like his. Did you see the handles on the side, the nurses just pick them up and carry them around. They've had them living in fucking dog baskets since 1945."

—171

He paused, struck a match, and cupped it in one hand. Then he lit a cigarette. "You alright?"

"Better," Jack said. He looked up and watched Ross lean back against the barracks wall. A jeep rolled past, its headlights sweeping across his face.

"So," he said, "you became a priest."

"Not a priest, but—"

"Do you believe it though? The whole deal, do you buy it?"

Jack started to say something, then just shook his head. "I believe things, yes," he said. He waited, expecting Ross to question him. A jet took off; its engines filled the darkness with thunder and seemed to shake the snow out of the sky. A terrified look came over Ross's face.

"What's he like?" he asked. "The guy she married."

Jack hesitated, then started describing King. He was conscious of trying to win Ross's sympathy by telling him how King had lost his first wife, how he was raising three daughters alone. Once he had mentioned King's name, Jack began to feel better about everything. He thought to himself that getting these things out into the open was a big step, the step he had to take for Ross's sake so that Ross would begin to see things as they really were.

"I was thinking," Ross said laconically. "They owe me about twenty thousand dollars in back pay. We ought to pack up some things and head out of here. What kind of car are you driving?"

"Ford station wagon."

Ross thought for a minute. "Maybe I'll buy us a better car, something fast, and we'll swing up to Boston and get Cascy, then just head out west or something."

Ross sounded so hopeful when he said this that Jack

—172

couldn't help thinking back to their summer, back to the afternoons they had spent driving the big Cadillac across the meadow. With Ross driving, Jack had felt protected and secure. But those old summer scenes belonged to another lifetime, and Jack was caught between wanting to protect Ross's feelings and wanting to tell him that nothing was the same, that everything had changed.

He didn't say anything. He looked over at Ross gazing up into the pale sky. Then Ross said, "No. You can't fight City Hall anyway." He pushed himself away from the building and started walking.

"Wait a second," Jack called to him. He was thinking he had never heard Ross say anything more stupid. He wanted to tell him that this was 1975 and people didn't say, "You can't fight City Hall." That attitude was out of date. It was something Ross could have said and gotten away with in the old days; Jack would have accepted it then. But now it was sad and annoying to hear Ross relying on dumb lines that no one would believe. "If you want me to think you've given up why don't you just come out and tell me?" Jack said.

Ross turned to him for a second. On his face there was a puzzled look. "What do you expect?" he said.

There was silence. Jack said he didn't expect anything. He could suddenly see the great difference between them; for him there had been eight summers since their summer together, but for Ross that was the *last* summer. For Ross, life had stopped with that summer, and now he hoped life would just start up again.

Somewhere on the way back to his flat they stopped at a garage where Ross paid a sergeant some money for a bag of hash. Ross said something as he handed him the money and the sergeant laughed and said, "Shit, this shit is great shit, man."

They were sitting in the kitchen of his apartment, the bag of hash on the table between them when Ross asked what it was like the day he left Hancock Point. "When you told her, what did she say?"

"I don't think she really believed me. She just kept waiting. She stayed out on the porch waiting." Jack was looking at Ross and thinking how he had looked on the television news, standing on the airport runway while the Marine band played. All the POWs looked the same on TV, just like all their names had looked the same in the *New York Times* when they were first listed as missing in action. At the airport they were trying to stand up straight, but while the band played some of them hung their heads. Jack was down on his hands and knees in front of the TV screen when he saw Ross turn to watch a soldier whose wife and children came running out to greet him. That must have been the reunion scene he had imagined even as he was leaving them at the cottage.

"You want some of this?" Ross asked, gesturing to the hash.

"No," Jack said.

"Me neither." Ross threw it onto the counter then walked to the refrigerator. He stood there with his back to Jack. "The bus went down Route 1 through all the hick towns in Maine. Guys kept getting on, kids heading to boot camp just like me. It was depressing. Each time another kid got on it was like there was a little less oxygen in the bus. I was going crazy. I couldn't breathe by the time we got to Portland. They stopped for a few minutes and I got off and ran. I ran right through the center of town and when I got back on Route 1, I started hitching rides. I got hung up most of the night outside some town, no one would stop."

He stopped and opened a quart bottle of beer. He swallowed some. Jack thought maybe he was finished talking, but then he started in again in a clear, steady voice. "I slept in a ditch on the side of the road. When the sun came up I jumped up and started walking. North, I mean. I was going to get back there if I had to walk the rest of the way. But it wasn't any good, it was a fucked-up idea, totally fucked-up. I turned around."

He sat down at the table and drank his beer. After a while he said he was going to take a shower. He went into the next room and got undressed. Jack saw how terribly thin he was. There was nothing left on his bones.

The shower ran a long time. Finally Jack went in to see if he was alright. He called to him.

"Yeah," Ross said. He reached out from behind the curtain for a cigarette he had left burning on the windowsill.

Jack wiped the steam from the mirror and looked at his face. All this thinking and talking about the past made him want to remember how his face had looked eight years ago. He thought about what would happen from now on in his life. He had his work in the church, and he was beginning to love it. It made him feel needed. That was a good feeling; it was the feeling he had now, and the feeling he had always had around Casey and Ross. Their needs had overshadowed his own and had given him a purpose.

"You shouldn't have left it up to me to try and explain things," Jack said. He wasn't sure Ross could hear him. "You should have come back."

"I tried. I just finished telling you I tried to hitchhike back."

—175

Again Jack didn't know how much he should say, how forceful he should be.

"That next morning," he said, "that's when she told me."

"About being pregnant?" Ross said quickly.

"Yes."

"She knew? She already knew then?"

"She wasn't certain. We went to the hospital. They called and told us that afternoon. I guess I thought the same thing you did. I thought somehow we'd get through it. We'd wait for you."

"The three of you?"

"Yes."

"Yes."

He sounded hopeful again, almost as if he believed this was still possible.

"If I'd known you were coming home," Jack said, "I would have been there at the airport. Someone should have been there."

"A family," Ross said. He stepped out of the shower. He wrapped a towel around his waist then stood at the mirror leaning against the sink, staring blankly at his face. He made an effort to comb his hair, but gave up, turned to Jack, and started weeping.

In the first light of morning they stood in the parking lot. Jack made him promise to call if there was anything he needed.

"What a trick," Ross said. "I thought I'd be gone a year, I'd get something out of my system and then come back and we'd go on. But look at you, Jack, you bounced back all right, didn't you?"

"I'm not so sure," Jack said. "But you know, they give me a place to live, I mean I get a house to live in right next to the church. And there's room for you. Let me write it down for you, and the phone number in case—"

"In case I crack up?"

"No. I meant, if you're in town or something."

Ross thanked him then turned and looked into his eyes. "If I'd run away," he said, "gone to Canada. Well, I couldn't have done that. I couldn't run away."

Chapter Fifteen

Perhaps it was the season that put the lie to Ross's intention, or perhaps he had known all along that he would go to her, that it was only a matter of time. Everything, it seemed to him, was a matter of time. It was Christmas Eve when he came into Boston in the last slanting light of afternoon. He came by train into South Station, where he stood among weary travelers, where he had stood with Casey years ago. A large clock near the entrance doors was still catching the winter light on its face.

Ross stood beyond the revolving glass doors, struck by the great difference between himself and those around him who had people waiting for them. They all looked busy, so purposeful and legitimate. To be without an occupation, he thought, is the first step toward misery.

At the moment he had a plan to occupy himself, and he had to hurry. The Christmas lights were on in Cambridge, shining like jewels. He walked below them, going in and out of shops where he bought toys. Many toys, and batteries. He thought of going into one of the men's stores and trying on clothes, but then, considering the time, he decided against this. He heard the sound of his boots striking the pavement. A sound from the past, a sound that had once carried the cadence of his life.

His fingers were blue with cold.

On Avon Street in a shop sparkling with tinsel he chose a dozen stuffed animals. A girl in a red smock-dress wrapped them while he waited, first laying each inside a shoe box. She looked up at him and their eyes caught momentarily. "How old are your children?" she asked him merrily.

He said he had no children and she began to hurry through the wrapping and to look a little wary of him as he stood silently beside her cash register.

She turned away to hand a polar bear to a Catholic nun.

Ross asked her, "Do you think I could leave these here with you for a while?" He glanced down at the packages. "I have some other things to pick up and then I'll be back."

She hesitated, then told him they would be open for only another hour.

He walked back out into the street and joined the thinning procession of shoppers. He felt marked as a transient. He looked up at the dark sky as he walked. He thought about how this would be the last Christmas of his twenties. This meant that he was still in possession of certain powers, the power to surprise, to create or to re-create, the power to be pardoned and to be accepted. He was still young.

The cold of the city began to penetrate the streets. Finally he went back for his packages, then filled the trunk of a taxi with them. The trunk and half of the back seat as well. The driver, a garrulous man, informed him happily that his shift would be over by ten o'clock. He was going straight home to assemble a bicycle for his grandson. He spoke proudly of this, as if he was about to put the finishing touches on a painting that would escape mortality. "The way that kid tears around, I give him two days with the training wheels, then he'll be flying!" said the driver. He fiddled with the radio until he found a station playing "Silent Night."

Ross leaned back against the seat. In one pocket he had a copy of his honorable discharge from the Army. In a small brown envelope he had just over seventeen thousand dollars in back pay. He thought of it as Monopoly money. There was something ironic about the way it had accrued to him while he was missing in action and assumed dead.

They drove past an elegant hotel where tables were being set for dinner. Waiters in red jackets glided past the broad windows. In the Commons a crowd stood before the manger. An old man walking by on the sidewalk stopped to give a quick salute to one of the Wise Men. Ross thought of priests preparing for mass. He thought of Jack.

Jack had encouraged him to make this trip, saying it was a chance for reconciliation, a settling of the old score. For Ross it was something he had to do, could not live without doing. From the moment he had left her, he had waited to be with her again. This desire, more than an instinctive will to survive, had kept him alive through unspeakable horrors.

He cast his eyes upon a vendor in a parking lot trying to get rid of a few sickly spruce trees he had left to sell. Ross wondered who it was that waited until Christmas Eve to buy a tree. Someone wanting a bargain maybe, or someone who had planned to skip a tree this year but then had given in to the season. Maybe someone expecting to be alone and forgotten this Christmas had received a call from a friend or a daughter or son and now would buy a tree and hope to convey a certain appearance of well-being. Ross thought, so long as there exists the possibility, however remote or unlikely, that the telephone will ring, that a visitor will appear, there is reason enough to hope that things will get better. Hope, then expectation.

As for him, he was trying not to expect anything. He wondered if he would suffer all his life because of his expectations. He had left a girl he loved, expecting that a child would keep her. He had expected that this was how love worked. Only now was he beginning to see how unrealistic his expectations were. They were constructed around beliefs distorted by a highly romanticized view of life. A view that did not take into account the great and sustained disappointments of life.

He had questions to ask her. He needed to make certain she had abandoned him out of fear; this was something he could accept. He could help her overcome her fear.

The taxi lurched and swerved. It dawned on Ross that he was traveling toward an unknown region where all his thinking and planning counted for nothing. His breath froze on the car window.

"Lord, that grandson of mine is growing up," the cab driver exclaimed. He put a cigarette between his lips. "One day he's gonna step in front of me and I ain't even gonna know who he is anymore." He brought a blue flame to the cigarette and said, "Know what I mean?"

"I know what you mean," Ross replied. He answered as a courtesy, but began to sense that this stranger had stumbled upon the precise reason he had made this trip. There has to be a reconciliation, Jack had said to him.

—181

But that was not true; much in life goes unreconciled. We have to let go of our anger, Jack had told him. Not always, Ross thought.

No, the reason Ross had come to Boston to see Casey was because, like the cab driver, he feared they would be lost to one another in the passage of time, that a time would come when they might pass on the street no longer recognizing each other.

At the hospital Ross unloaded his packages onto the sidewalk. It took three trips to carry them all inside. He put everything onto an elevator, then drifted up to the fifth floor, where a nurse greeted him.

"I thought you weren't coming after all," she said, smiling at him.

"This is kind of you," he said.

"It's the closest I've ever been to Saint Nick." She laughed or smiled, and when she assured him that the last of the children were asleep, they distributed the gifts throughout the ward, placing them at the foot of their beds.

"I'd like to stay around for a while," Ross told her when they had returned to her desk in the center of the ward.

"I'm only on until eleven," she said. "But you can stay as long as you like."

"Someone's coming to meet me here," Ross said and she seemed a bit disappointed. She glanced at one of the children's charts, made a quick notation with a pen, and then said she wished she were going to be around in the morning to see their expressions when they woke up.

"When you first called," she said, "I thought maybe it was some kind of prank."

"I once brought a dog up here," he said.

—182

"Against the rules," she said.
"We always broke the rules," he said.

For a moment Ross felt bouyant and appreciated. But after an hour passed with no sign of Casey, he began to feel like an idiot. The nurses changed at eleven o'clock. The first girl waved to him as she headed down the glossy corridor, oblivious to the fact that he sat waiting for a woman to leave her husband on Christmas Eve. He had actually believed that this would happen, that a few lines on a piece of paper would achieve this. He had counted upon the power and force of memory to conquer time and space and all uncertainty.

If she came at all, she would see he was pale and undernourished. Nomadic and rootless. He thought quickly of how he might countervale these appearances to make a better impression. He wouldn't tell her that the only clothes he owned at the moment were on his back. He would tell her he had rented a locker at the train station. Luggage—he should have some nice suitcases. Good luggage lends a certain legitimacy to one's travels, as if stating publicly that you are a person with a plan and a purpose, a person worthy of distinction among the masses in perpetual flight from poverty and disorder.

He would try to convey a sense of well-being and good health despite his appearance, for he was certain that her old love for him had been born in her belief that he possessed a certain strength and self-assurance.

How he had lied to her. Under this impression he had concealed his own fear, the fear of losing her. Looking back now, it all made perfect sense to him. He had taken her to bed for the first time, telling her that preposterous line of his—that every man wants to be a woman's first love, and every woman wants to be his last. He had believed in the power and authority of being first. He had fulfilled her in bed and then whenever his fears had begun to erode his authority or when he couldn't answer her questions, he took her back to bed. Their times in bed had renewed him and fortified his chances of keeping her.

He remembered vividly what she had been like in his bed. There were times when this memory made him ache across the surface of his skin.

That summer at the cottage in Maine he believed that a child between them would define their future and extinguish his weaknesses, that this child would mean *they* would flourish no matter how crazy the world around them became.

And, honestly, he had known no other way to keep her. He would try to make her see this. They would talk about this at last, one word at a time, and then in full, meaningful sentences that would answer all the questions she had ever asked him, finally leading them to a point of perfect silence where there would be nothing more to ask or say.

If she came at all, he would perform for her as he had in the past. He would draw back his shoulders and lift his eyes to her. An honest performance, as all the others had been. A performance designed to conceal the confusion running through him. It had always come down to this with him; the self-deceptions, the vanities and the extravagant performances of his life had sprung from the confusion he was forever trying to outrun.

Now he felt himself to be at the center of something, where he would be held for a little while longer in anticipation, and then would be released to a new life of acts which would be purer, easier to define. There were maybe five or six times like this in an entire life, when you knew for certain that something was about to happen that would change you, that would change forever the way you saw yourself, that would make the old illusions of youth impossible to abide.

Maybe it was only an illusion, his belief that Casey would come at all. To believe is to make real, he had been told. That is what his savior often told him, the woman who took him from the orphanage and raised him. She was a wise lady. She baked pies and did people's washing and ironing for money to feed him. There were always grains of sugar under her fingernails, streaks of flour in her hair. She was a woman so well connected to the natural world that she could tell when it was about to rain. A shift in the wind direction did not elude her. About girls, she had told him this, "Love one with all you have." He was sixteen when she died. He was alone again. Her death seemed to establish a precedent—people he came close to would always leave him. Or he would try to push them out of his life in order to see how devoted to him they really were.

He was aware of the time passing, the night growing later. He thought about Jack and wished he were here. Jack was the only person on earth who knew enough about what they had been through to understand why so much was still at stake. Ross thought how quickly the rest of the world would dismiss what he and Casey had shared: they were young, they were only together a short time. Christ, he thought, not much more than an adolescent romance. And maybe that was part of the reason he was here waiting to see her again. They were adults now and if they still felt as they once had, then this would make what they once had legitimate and meaningful.

He thought again of luggage, of the impression a

matching set of suitcases would make. And of his clothes. When he knew Casey they dressed in the careless fashion of their day, like happy bohemians.

The elevator down the hallway sighed and clicked. He lit a cigarette and the nurse waved to him to put it out. She didn't make a sound, but waved dramatically. The last thing she wanted was to awaken one of the children. It was Christmas Eve and in the morning she would feel righteous for having worked this shift. Of course there was no smoking. There was even a sign above his head. There was also a sign in red pointing the way to an EXIT. A way out. He thought about leaving, then decided he would spend the night here waiting for her rather than leave. If he left he would never be certain about anything.

He put his head back. He thought of the children slipping away in their medicated sleep. Despite everything, he fell asleep.

When he opened his eyes again Casey was sitting across from him. It was hard to believe. He was confused and instantly troubled when he noticed she was holding her head in a way he had never seen before. Her eyes were averted, as if she was impatient.

"How long have you been here?" he asked. He was staring at her, trying to bring her into focus, or to match her with the picture he had of her.

"Just a few minutes," she replied. There wasn't any melody in her voice.

"You should have said something."

She raised her head in a curious way. He realized then that he was already telling her what to do.

He noticed how odd her hands appeared in leather gloves. All his memories of her were set in summer scenes. The gloves, the leather handbag, the tweed overcoat. She looked older; she had begun to develop a style.

He said, "I wasn't sure you'd come."

"Really?"

"I really wasn't." He looked down at the tiled floor. "What time is it, do you have any idea?"

"After midnight," she said. "I had to wait until the girls were sleeping."

He had forgotten there were children, another man's children. "Do any of them still believe in Christmas?" He tried to smile.

She smiled back at him and said no. "The nurse told me you arrived by sleigh though."

"Oh?"

"You've brought your share of cheer to this ward," she said, and she seemed to hold this observation at a distance, as if she had not yet decided what it meant.

"And so have you."

"I quit my job here. I left them high and dry."

"That was my idea, my fault," he said quickly.

She looked at him. "Why? I'm the one who quit." She made a little gesture, almost a gesture of resignation.

Her legs to him looked very thin. "Have you become a runner?" he asked.

"Why do you ask?"

"You look thin, I mean beautiful but very thin."

"I don't run, no," she said. Then she told him she was much thinner a few years ago and when she said this he wondered if she was blaming *him* for that.

"You're the one who's thin," she said. "My God, are you all right, are you well?" Her voice was softer.

"I didn't have the right to ask you to come," he said. "No, I'm fine—it's good to see you."

"Do you mean that, or are you just saying it for me to deny?"

He was lost. "What?"

"That you didn't have the right."

"Oh, yes, no." He leaned forward in his chair. "I had no right, Casey." The sound of her name had the effect of someone else entering the scene. He looked away and then back to her hands. There was the impression of rings beneath her gloves.

She went on slowly. "When Jack told me you were back, there was just no way I could . . . you know . . . get down to—"

"Oh, I know. I didn't expect—"

"I wonder though, did you get a hero's welcome?"

"This," he said, and he opened his hands. "This is my welcome."

"I thought you were dead."

"What you heard, they souped it up. We weren't heroes, we were just stuck there."

"Nixon's a bum," she said just above a whisper. When he didn't understand, she told him about her mother marching the kids from school, chanting for Kennedy. "She gathered us all together after lunch each day and marched us back to school with our little signs. We were yelling, 'Nixon's a bum,' Jack and I. She wore those wonderful stockings. The seams I remember, seams up the back. When you're small, and that close to the ground you notice things."

"Yes, I'm sorry."

She looked at him. "Jack told you my mother's dead?" There was silence. Then she said, "But what am I supposed to say to you?"

"Whatever you want to say."

"What I feel like," she started, then stopped. "Coming here like this, sneaking away to see you—I feel like it confirms something about me that you want to be sure of."

"That you care."

"No, more than that. It sort of grants you immunity, or a pardon. I don't know if you should look at it that way."

He folded his hands and looked away. She sat waiting, continually piling up her hair with one hand and then letting it fall down onto her shoulders. There was a faint, lustrous tone to her cheeks.

"Maybe we could take a walk," he suggested.

But she hadn't heard him. "My coming here like this is a risk for me. It's like opening up one of those big road maps, not knowing if you'll ever be able to fold it back the right way."

"I don't want to make things hard for you."

"It's a little late for that," she said, and for the first time she looked directly into his eyes. Her voice became steady. "For a while after you left I spent a lot of time standing in front of mirrors. I found myself just looking into the glass. I don't know what I was looking for, but it was as if I had to figure out what was wrong, what part of me was missing. It was like trying to face your own death. I tried for a long time to get a picture of what life was going to be like." She paused, then asked him, "Why would you do this to me?"

"I was afraid—"

"No," she shook her head. "I don't mean *that*. I mean *this*. Why didn't you just walk up to our house and tip your hat to me and meet King? Just a normal scene? Why didn't you just accept things the way they are."

"I couldn't have faced that."

"That's the thing. It's always what *you* can't face. Everything has to be arranged around your . . . preferences."

"I'd prefer that you had no husband," he said.

This stopped her for a moment.

"Well," she said, "I have one. I have a house with children in it. I would have invited you inside though, I would have fed you a meal and we all could have sat around in chairs talking like normal human beings."

"But we wouldn't have talked about the things that matter."

"Oh Ross, don't you know? People never talk about the things that drive them apart. Why couldn't you have just come into my house like a friend, and we could have done what normal people do. We could have talked about things—"

"Things that don't exist," he said, cutting her off.

She let his words hang over them as if to ratify them, as if admitting with her silence that he was telling the truth about something. She said to herself, Things that *don't* exist, not things that *didn't* exist before.

"Are you talking about my life now, or some other life?" she asked.

"I don't know anything about your life now," he said.

She went on as if she hadn't heard him: "When things don't exist, you can still wait for them. You can hope they will exist one day."

She looked dissatisfied, and he wondered if her dissatisfaction had nothing to do with him. "Maybe," he said. "Before *you* existed, I knew exactly what you would be like. It wasn't anything I could describe, but I knew. Then, when I met you, well, I began to believe in my visionary powers." He smiled to show some diffidence. "I mean, there you were, exactly as fine as I'd imagined."

She told him she thought he was exaggerating. They were both standing there on the tiled floor, neither of them moving.

"I don't think I'm exaggerating," he said.

"You have to preserve your romantic picture," she said.

He shifted his weight from foot to foot. "I wanted to keep us going," he told her.

"Do you hear me?" she asked.

"Do *you* hear *me*?"

"Yes," she said. "That's exactly what I'm trying to do—keep going."

"Well, I just wonder what it is you're doing now."

She averted her head again with the same look of impatience. "I'm trying to go on, I just told you. And to give something to someone else." She glanced down at her purse as if to pull out something. Immediately he thought she was going to show him pictures of her husband's children.

"You don't know what it was like for me," she went on. She laughed nervously, then shrugged her shoulders and changed her mind about whatever it was she was going to tell him. "Do you know what I've been reading? Emma Goldman. That should please you. She makes some sense to me now. I don't care much for her views of anarchy, but about women she's very good. She wanted women to have choices, the same choices men have. She said since it was a woman's greatest misfortune to be looked upon as either an angel or a devil, her salvation existed in being considered human and subject to all human mistakes. You thought of me as some sort of angel, and it wasn't true, it was just that I treated you well. And I loved you with everything I had. You didn't see that I was capable of these great mistakes."

"The abortion?"

"I mean letting you do that to me—control me that way."

She stopped. She seemed to have no more to say. He

thought for a moment that she might be thinking about turning to leave, and he came up with something to say in order to keep her there a little longer.

"There was a kid in my unit you would have liked. He had this inner peace about life—he couldn't be shaken. He never should have been there. He came from the coal mines of Pennsylvania, from a mining family, and he told me something I'll never forget. He said we were all much closer to each other than we realized, people from different nations, different continents. He thought of us as being connected. He used to tell me that the stars we saw were the same ones you were seeing back here. He told me about this great fault in the earth. It begins in northern Spain in the Basque region, then goes far underground and comes up in Wales, where you can see it in the coal mines. Then it goes under the Atlantic Ocean and comes back up in Pennsylvania. The fault creates the identical face in the coal, and a miner in Pennsylvania sees exactly the same configuration in the mine as a miner in Spain or Wales sees. The whole idea is that we're bound together by nature and we can't be divided."

"Bound together by a fault," she said.

He looked down at his shoes, then up at her face.

"Was he killed?" she asked.

"No."

"Oh, I thought you were going to tell me a sad story."

"No. I used to tell him that no matter what happened, no matter how long it took me to get home, or even if I came back with a leg shot off, you would be there for me. I was sure. We were connected too, by something."

"The angel waiting with the child in her arms? That's what John Wayne would expect."

"Why diminish what you were to me?" he asked. He took a half-step away from her. "I remember we were

—192

going to live our lives. We were going to live life all the way to the end."

When he said this she took a deep breath. He could almost feel her trying to steady herself.

"Why don't we walk?" she said.

They passed the children's rooms, and she looked in at the boxes. "That's the thing about children—" she said, "they don't question the reasons behind gestures."

They went down to the street. Outside, the wind was slanting off the river. They said nothing to each other as they walked along. He waited for her to stop, to turn around. He wondered if he should stop her with a hand on her shoulder. Maybe she was waiting for him to make the first move of real reconciliation.

She walked to the trunk of her car.

"Is this a precedent?" she asked at last. "Are you going to turn up again and again like this?"

"No."

"So, I should go on with things?"

"With whatever you want."

She searched her pocket for keys and asked, "Where will you go?"

He said he wasn't sure. "I've got my things back at the train station," he lied.

She looked at him with a faint smile, then turned back to her keys. "Why don't you come to the house? You can stay the night. It's Christmas Eve."

"Well."

"Well, here, take this anyway." She took his aviator's jacket from the trunk of the car and handed it to him. "It's cold," she said.

He held it between them. Then she pressed against him and put one arm around his waist.

"You feel good to me," he said.

"You're all right, aren't you?"

"Yes."

She pulled away gently and walked to the car door, and he asked if he would ever see her again. "I mean," he said, "before we're old."

"I could see you in the morning if you'd take my offer."

"Well, maybe then, maybe I'll show up in the morning."

Then she started the car.

He called to her. "That woman, that woman Jack told us about, the one who came back to visit his father after all those years, do you remember?"

"Yes."

"Will you come back that way?"

She looked at his face and answered him, "God help me if I do."

She waved and drove away before he could tell her the one other thing he wanted her to believe, that he was sorry about everything.

That night she fell asleep in a chair with the Christmas tree lights coloring her face. He walked the streets of Boston aware of the presence of the Charles River, black and brooding, waiting to freeze. He heard a church bell toll like a buoy at sea. He recalled how Hemingway had written of Paris at night, old men roasting chestnuts on the corners, the evening crowd strolling the boulevards, offering a pleasant distraction to the lonely with time to kill. This city was deserted. He gave money to a beggar, then thought of giving him all seventeen thousand dollars. I can change your life but not my own, Ross thought.

In the train station rain ticked against the glass panels

high overhead. He sat on a bench across from a college girl in blue jeans who was eating from a quart container of ice cream. She seemed not to be afraid of anything. She had a backpack stuffed for travel and there was a look of pure contentment about her.

"If it gets just a little colder it'll turn to snow," she remarked as if making him a promise.

He felt the end of a year upon him. The end of a life perhaps.

"Where are you headed?" he asked.

"Maine," she said. She was smiling at him. "Like the song says—'Destination, Bangor, Maine.' "

Chapter Sixteen

Life went on then. For Casey it was a married life. A year passed and she stood at the kitchen sink slicing carrots one afternoon. Jack was joining them for dinner. She always looked forward to his visits. He was completely wrapped up in his work at the church now, and though they lived only a few miles apart sometimes weeks would go by and she would only see him during the Sunday service or driving through town on the way to somewhere. Her life was moving very fast. Sometimes after she had been with Jack, to talk with him alone for fifteen minutes or an hour, she would look back on this time with him and it would be as if her life had finally slowed down, even paused, for that short while. Things would be in focus, not blurred by the momentum of time passing.

A station wagon pulled up the driveway and stopped just at the end of the brick walkway. It was Meg Parker, a neighbor, bringing the girls home from swimming practice. Hannah was running ahead as usual, Wendy, the oldest, was next, then came redheaded Catherine. Hannah was always running, trying her best to interest her older sisters in things they had outgrown. Wendy was fourteen and in love, it was said, with a boy from just down the road who wanted to be a professional disc jockey. "He's got tapes and records and everything," the girls said. Catherine was a tomboy. On Saturdays she played as King's mixed-doubles partner at the club. She had freckles on her nose that turned to little red coals when she was angry. Catherine was twelve now and Hannah seven.

They yelled hello and asked about dinner and whether their daddy was home yet. Then they scattered like birds. Casey followed their voices through the house. They were King's daughters, but she loved them and was proud of herself for having been patient these first two years while their affection for her grew. It happened gradually, and now it was a familiar affection and they could ignore her from time to time just as they would their real mother.

Casey watched the Parker's station wagon stop at the end of the long, gravel driveway before turning back onto the main road. Meg Parker hadn't come inside to say hello, and this at once surprised and comforted Casey; parents were forever supplying rides these days and if each stop required a social call, it would soon get sticky.

But Casey couldn't take her eyes off the station wagon as it slid past the pines and the two elms that somehow had managed to escape disease. Meg Parker's husband, Frank, had been the father in the town of Dedham who persuaded the Little League Commission to make room for girls. He and Casey had worked together campaigning for this. He had two daughters and how pleased he was when his oldest came of age last summer. And then how sad it was that by then Meg had to drive him to the games at Furrow Street Field. This same station wagon was pulled up to the fence next to the bleachers and the back door was swung open and there was Frank Parker on his stomach, his head propped to one side on a pillow. He had seemed all right, and then in February he went in for some kind of tests and suddenly he was dying from rectal cancer, and only by lying prostrate could he escape the excruciating pain. But he was a loyal fan, and when his daughter's team scored a run he would call to Meg to beep the horn and flash the headlights. His illness got people talking again about how you had to make the most of each day. It was the accidents you had to watch out for in this life, the things that come without warning to take the wind out of your sails. And so, secretly, the parents of Dedham, Massachusetts, those who went to watch the Little League games last summer, wondered which lopsided and hopelessly protracted game would be Frank Parker's last. He died in August. Jack conducted the funeral service. And now Meg's life was going on under the momentum of time passing. She had confided in Casey near the end of her husband's life. She told her she had thought about getting a gun and ending his life on one of those nights when his pain was so great that even the morphine wouldn't kill it, when he howled through the night like a wounded animal.

After Meg told her this, for several nights after that, Casey wouldn't let King go to sleep until they had made love. And then, when they were finished, she lie there thinking about the first time they had made love, how King had said to her, "This is the point of everything under the sun." Casey had fallen asleep that time, and when King woke her the sun had already begun to rise and he had taken his shower and shaved, and without saying anything he wrapped her naked in a blanket and brought her to the bedroom window with him where they knelt down and with his soft face against hers he prayed out loud.

As he held her close to him at the window he said, "We can't ever forget to do this, to keep this close."

But they had forgotten. Very soon they stopped kneeling at the window, and frequently they let weeks go by without making love. Neither of them could say why, and perhaps for fear of making things even worse, neither of them asked why—why they no longer undressed each other, why when they did make love they were just lying naked in bed as if waiting for some ritual to start. You couldn't put your finger on an exact time or incident, but you could be sure that things had changed. You could be sure, the same way you might wake up in the middle of the night and know for certain that the first snowfall of winter had come. You know it has begun to snow, though you cannot say *how* you know. And then King began asking her if she was going to come. That night after Meg Parker had told her about her husband's pain, right in the middle of making love with King he had said, "Are you coming, Mommy?"

"It's all right," she said.

"No, tell me. I want to make you come."

She had wanted to say, for Christ's sake, King, just hold me. But she pretended for him because that was the simplest way for them to stop. And when it was over she wondered if making love with Ross or anyone else would eventually turn out to be like this.

Tonight over dinner they talked about the school play that was coming and the new spring L.L. Bean catalogue. King had always been an admirer of L.L. Bean. "I love the descriptions," he said to Jack. The catalogue was opened just to the left of his plate. "Listen to this. The Baxter

State Parka. A versatile, wind-resistant, water-repellent shell with a tough outer fabric of tightly woven, breathable and abrasion-resistant sixty percent, two-ply cotton and forty percent nylon. Isn't that great?" He helped himself to more meat and then passed some to Jack. "What if everything in life was listed in the Bean Catalogue? I mean what if right here on page thirty-seven you had the L.L. Bean commonly envied, consistently masculine, utterly dependable father of three with flannel-lined pockets? Hunh?"

"Daddy!" Catherine shouted with delight.

"Hunh? Or try this. The L.L. Bean usually hazardous, rock-strewn, pothole-ridden, sixty percent sweat, forty percent guts, road to success. What do you think of that, Jack?"

King liked to entertain his family and guests. He was always best when everyone was laughing.

"I think you've got something there, King," Jack said, laughing. "A great summing up of life." He turned to look at Casey. There was something on his mind, she could tell.

Night came on. The light of early evening reddened the white clapboards on the houses across the street. Casey used to tell the girls that this was the time of evening when night was on its knees, not yet fallen. And they always smiled to think of it that way. Tonight as she prepared dessert, she thought again of this expression. Every time she had said it to the girls, she vaguely recalled her own father telling her this when she was a girl. But tonight as she looked out at the darkening sky it struck her that it might not have been her father who had said this. It might have been Ross. She leaned against the kitchen counter and tried to bring into focus some scene from the past,

—200

some point in time which would settle this question. Nothing. But Jack would know. After the dishes were done, the girls were off to bed, and King was in front of the TV, she would be alone with Jack in her room on the third floor, her little glassed-in room where she went to read and think, and she would ask him.

"No," Jack said, "it wasn't him."

"Then it must have been my father." She sat in a Boston rocker, looking over at Jack and past him to the bookshelf, where, in a gold frame, stood the photograph of Ross's poet, Sylvia Plath, as a young college girl. Casey kept the picture because something in the poet's eyes fascinated her, something she had never been able to define.

"How unfair to him, Ross I mean, to confuse him with my father," she said. "I wonder how many times I've done that."

She watched Jack look away from her. He stood up and walked to the windows. "You can see all the way to St. John's from here. There's the steeple. I never realized you could see so far."

"Just until spring," she said. "Once the leaves come out."

Jack picked up the photograph of Sylvia Plath. Casey watched him turn it in his hands, the glass casting light onto his face. "Haunted," he said. "Is that it?"

Jack nodded and set the photograph down. "I remember him reading me a poem where she says we only have so many trips to the beach in our lives and then that's it."

"What a dismal thought," Casey said.

Jack looked up at her and apologized. "I know. I've been depressed lately—too many funerals, not enough weddings or baptisms. The strangest things have been happening. Monday night, the day the bridge gave way in Hollis, Edna Sullivan called me. She told me if she hadn't been out sick from work with the flu she would have been driving over the bridge exactly at the time it fell into the river. She said she would have been killed and she wanted me to tell her why God had spared her."

"What did you say?"

"Wait, it gets worse. The next morning a tractor-trailer was going down Route 134 when one of its wheels came off and rolled into a restaurant and into the kitchen where it killed a woman. The woman who was taking Edna Sullivan's place while she was out sick. So she calls me back and says, 'Father, it happened again, what does God have in store for me?' "

"So what did you tell her?"

"Oh, I told her . . . you know, I just told her she was special, her life was a gift. That sort of thing."

"And the woman who was working in her place, the one who died—her life wasn't?"

"She didn't ask me that. But I knew you would." He looked at her with a helpless expression.

She just smiled at him. "No, Jack, I don't need an answer. I just said the first thing that came into my mind."

He thanked her. "I could tell that story to the whole congregation. I mean I could use it for a sermon and you'd be the only one who wouldn't swallow it whole. Everyone else would settle for the simplest explanation."

She knew Jack was right. She knew King would be one of them who would settle for less. "In the old days," she said, "I would have pressed you for an answer."

They talked a while longer about the girls and King and the coming of spring. Then as Jack stood up and put his coat on, he muttered, "In the old days."

—202

"What about them?" she asked.

"Well anyway, here," he said. He handed her an envelope. "Here, take this. I'll leave you with this."

He left her with seven typed pages. She could still hear his feet on the stairs when she began reading.

I have begun to take a hard look at the summer that has just passed. I spent it in a house at Hancock Point, Maine, a secluded promontory of land that drowses under bright sunshine and watches the light drift out over Frenchman's Bay. The house was one of those great, weathered cottages that seem to go on and on, and scarcely a day went by without me asking, "Now where does that door go?"

The days were restful, long and warm. I had plenty of time for reading. I picked the season's wild berries, I took thoughtful walks along the shore, and with an inexhaustible curiosity I watched the residents of this seaside colony, the summer people.

I have always watched the summer people. As a boy I had gone to Hancock Point one summer and worked at the Inn, where the summer people spent fifty dollars a day for their room and meals. Many of them stayed the whole season. My summer there I was quarantined at first in the windowless kitchen scrubbing pots and pans as part of my rite of passage into the dining room, where I was finally promoted to the position of busboy and had my first brush with the Inn's guests. Late one evening while on my hands and knees buffing the dining room floor, I discovered a man's tie clasp under a corner table. I handed it over to the night clerk and thought nothing more of it until the following afternoon, when the manager summoned me to his office to meet a dignified old man who wanted to speak with me. He was dressed impeccably with a white shirt,

—203

brick-red trousers, and a navy-blue blazer with some sort of emblem sewn in gold threads on the breast pocket. With a shaky but baronial voice he identified himself and thanked me for recovering his clasp. I stood across from him, nervously shifting my weight from foot to foot as he looked me over. Then he suddenly drew his shoulders back and gave me his right hand, which was knotted in a tight fist. As if passing a secret message behind enemy lines, he pressed two folded bills into my hand and quickly closed my fingers around them.

After he left I opened my hand and found that the reward for my vigilance was two one-hundred-dollar bills. I rushed to find the old gentleman, certain he had made some mistake. No mistake, he told me. The tie clasp had once belonged to a classmate at Princeton in 1921. Its sentimental value was inestimable.

This sort of experience caused me to pay great attention to the dining room floor and to the ways of the summer people. I learned that many of them were descendents of families who had been coming to this place for years. They were well-to-do. I learned that there was very often a precocious self-assurance about the children of these people. And often a recklessness. One afternoon I observed two teenage boys racing their fathers' giant sloops out in the crowded harbor, seeing who could come closer to the pier without bashing into it.

At the Inn I first discovered that a grown man would spend an entire day reading newspapers out on a porch, moving with a courtly negligence from chair to chair as the sun moved across the sky, while someone brought him coffee all morning and tea all afternoon.

The ways of the summer people were of amazing interest to me then because I was young and trying very hard on my own to figure out how the world worked.

The world seemed to work against me from time to time in those days. One week I worked for extra money as a caretaker for Mrs. Alexander Chadbourn, a dowager in her late eighties who resided in one of the largest cottages on the Point. I did everything for her and she appeared to be very fond of me. Sometimes she would call out to me to come inside for lemonade, hollering out across her shaded lawn as she must have done once for her own sons. She liked to call me Scotty (I never found out why), and when she pronounced that name she hit very hard on both T's. Her husky voice was accented with violent gasps that gave dramatic weight to even the most mundane declarations.

One morning she called to me: "Scotty, I must get a weather report for tomorrow. The Blanchards have invited me sailing and I'm much too old to go blowing off in a hellish gale. Go and find me a newspaper with a reliable forecast."

Off I went later that day, riding my bicycle to the market and back with a newspaper folded under one arm. As I was heading towards Mrs. Chadbourn's place I spotted her out on a neighbor's lawn with several dozen gayly dressed people who had gathered for cocktails. I parked my bicycle and walked across the lawn as inconspicuously as I could. Mrs. Chadbourn had her back to me, and someone who watched me approach motioned to her with a hand that held a highball glass. She turned slowly. "I've got the paper for you," I shouted triumphantly.

Mrs. Chadbourn said nothing at first, and I will never forget the look of disappointment that swept over her face. Her eyes narrowed, her mouth opened, and she said, "No, no, no, no, no, no, no. This is not the right place for that." She hammered all three T's. I wanted to sink into the fabulous lawn. That afternoon I learned my place among the summer people. It was a place I held and a place that suited me for a long time when I became a restive, ornery young man. But that summer my politics were different and my feelings were hurt. That summer I had met Miss Winslow, a widow close to a hundred years old, whose room in the third floor annex was especially reserved for her. That was the very room where she had spent the first night of her honeymoon eighty years earlier. And I was there in that room when she reopened the door for the first time.

I was nearby when Miss Winslow died that summer alone. I took her breakfast (one four-minute boiled egg, one piece of unbuttered whole wheat toast cut diagonally, and a glass of apricot juice served on a silver tray) on one of the last mornings of her life. That day she called to me to set the tray down on the bureau, then she motioned for me to come to the side of the bed. She looked longingly at me for a few seconds before, at last, she said, "Do you know the world is for the young. Because you have time, and time is everything."

I look back over this past summer just as I have always looked back. For as long as I can remember, I have searched my past for the chronological hinges on which the stages of my life have swung. I have wanted to be able to say exactly when certain changes in my life took place. Was there an event that marked the last afternoon of my childhood? Did my adolescence begin with the inning of a baseball game, or the arrival of a letter in one day's mail?

I wonder about these things, and what it means that I have spent my first season as one of the summer people. This summer I lived among them and paid my own way.

I often thought back to my first summer here when the summer people seemed to me to be so unspeakably old and odd. If, in certain ways, I have started to become like them, then surely I am approaching that time when I will no longer be called a young man, when the umbrella of youth's resilience is lifted and I will not be pardoned for squandering energy and time.

Ross Peterson.

Casey read his name on the last page. She thought back to the day she and Jack had read his name in the *New York Times* in the list of American soldiers captured and missing in action. She wondered why he had sent this. Was it to show Jack and her that *he* had found his way back to a place and a time he knew they couldn't forget? Or did he just want to keep in touch with them? And if keeping in touch was what he had in mind, then why not a letter, a decent letter? But when she thought about this she realized that what he had written was more telling than a letter could have been.

For a long time she sat alone trying to figure out what this meant, if it meant anything at all. Then she decided she would try not to make too much of it. Ross had gone back, and he had written them about it. That was all.

She folded the pages in half, and then folded them a second time and slid them behind the cardboard backing on the frame of Sylvia Plath's photograph. She turned off the lights and went out, closing the door behind her.

Chapter Seventeen

Three years later Casey was trying to keep them straight in her head, all the names: Haldeman, Erlichman, Mitchell, Colson, Dean. The Watergate characters in the book by the two reporters from the *Washington Post*. It was 1979, the hostages were in the news, and Watergate was an old story by now. Nixon had been out of office almost five years, the wars in Vietnam and Cambodia seemed at times to have never really happened at all. But Casey couldn't let go. She had absorbed all the news stories and read book after book which revealed the astonishing immorality of Richard Nixon, and still she hungered for more facts, more details. She was trying to complete her history, to educate herself fully. In some ways she was trying to make up for her ignorance. People now were talking with reverence about the 1960s as a time of extreme awareness. But she remembered a time of extreme selfishness, a time when she had thought mainly about herself and her satisfaction. She wanted to atone for this. Nixon and Kissinger had exploited her ignorance; she, in her indifference, had sanctioned their monstrous sins. Their sins were so vast, so hideous, their guilt so irredeemable—maybe she dwelled on their guilt in order to escape her own. Or maybe the defiance she felt over this made her feel alive again.

Or maybe it was something else. She recalled her conversation with Jack long ago when he had visited her in New York and she had spoken to him about how they were always examining their lives in the past tense. So much time had passed since then, but she was still looking back. She was married now to a man who didn't look back and who wouldn't understand why she couldn't let go of a memory that had covered such a brief period of time. It wasn't as if she and Ross had spent *years* together, or had devoted themselves to an endless struggle for a cause of some profound importance. She realized that, like King, the average person on the street would never understand why her past mattered so much to her. These days she wondered if the resonance of her past could be explained not in the events of the past but in her own brokenness. Maybe the wounds her father had inflicted on her had left her susceptible to everything that followed and to a lifetime of looking back.

She walked across the patio with a glass of iced tea in one hand and *All the President's Men* in the other. She looked down to where blades of grass were growing up between the bricks. The sky was effortless blue but for one small cloud in the west. Some wind was trapped overhead in the tall pines. The air smelled like wine. She waited for this time of day, these mid-afternoon hours, as people might wait for something they've lost to turn up again. They wait but never acknowledge waiting.

She thought about that for a moment and said out loud, "What are you waiting for?" What on earth *was* she waiting for? For things to get better perhaps. Or worse.

In any case, for things to change, for something to move her from inertia.

She recalled an old fairy tale, the one about the girl who awakens in the middle of the night and being very thirsty starts to climb out of bed to go for a glass of water. But then the girl stops to think, what if she does go for a glass of water, what if she goes downstairs and just as she is holding her glass under the spigot there is a knock at the door, and what if there is a handsome man there knocking, and what if she lets him in and what if he falls in love with her and she falls in love with him, and what if they have a grand wedding and then one morning he is struck down by lightning and dies. The prospect of such unutterable grief is too much for her to contemplate, and so she lies thirsty in her bed. The risk is just too great.

Casey set her glass down on the bricks. She drew her knees up on the chaise lounge and ran her palms down her thighs and calves. At least she had stayed in good shape. That weight on her bottom was long gone. It was something to be glad about. Not long ago she stood behind a fat neighbor when the woman bent over to pick something off the carpet. A fat, lumbering woman she was, and looking up her dress Casey saw an alarming assortment of straps, pads, catches and snaps. All *that* to conceal the fat. Poor dear soul, people had probably bothered her all her life about being fat. Why, Casey wondered. Why must weight always be an issue for women. She wondered, what if *she* got up night after night while her husband slept, and what if she went down to the kitchen and mixed up a container of dip and what if she just sat right down and ate the whole thing with a quart of root beer and a family-sized bag of chips and what if her husband left her because *she* eventually got as big as a barn. Then what?

Then she would be out in the cold, cut loose, banished, on her own, liberated, emancipated, free as a bird, stranded. Would she be any happier? Who could say.

Well, the world was full of disappointed women, and the idea of being among their ranks bored Casey. It didn't do any good to complain. You couldn't sit around wondering what might have happened. What if, what if. You just don't ask what if. You just get up and go on, go on, go on. And if you think about trying to go back and change things, if you actually get up in the middle of the night and go downstairs and sit by the window thinking maybe you might change things, then you're in for trouble. Why, the entire world knows this.

King was home from the office. "Hello, Mommy," he called out to her.

"Out back, Baby," she replied.

He had begun calling her Mommy soon after the girls started, and Casey used the word Baby much of the time now. It bothered her that they seldom used real names. But somehow it made the distance between them less sad. The sense of loss was almost vicarious this way. Baby and Mommy could easily be anyone else.

King was bad with names anyway. He was forever calling her friends by wrong names. And so, when someone had asked her the other week which law firm her husband was with, she answered, "Something, Something, Something, and Something."

This had brought a nervous laugh. But she knew it hurt King. Why did she need to hurt him in horrible little ways now? Well, everyone in Dedham was a lawyer, weren't they? There were far too many of them everywhere. Sometimes she wondered if there were still men left who did not practice law, who did not go back and forth to an

—211

office, who did not jog, who did not rap their college rings against the kitchen counter, who did not do push-ups on the floor before getting into bed—straining and grunting like that. (Soon after they were married King began doing his push-ups down on the floor next to the bed, and she had shocked him one night when she called to him, "My God, King, I thought you were jerking off down there."

Anyway, it did bother her that King forgot her friends' names.

She went into the kitchen to answer the telephone. King got there first. She held the receiver up to his ear while he undid his necktie. "Okay, Paul," he said. "Look, you have your girl call my girl in the morning. We'll settle it tomorrow. Right, so long."

"They're not really girls," Casey said. She hung up the phone for him. "You always call them girls."

"Hey," he said, "where *are* the girls anyway?"

"They went with the Jamisons," she said. She watched him nod his head and then stick it into the refrigerator.

King wandered off into the dining room calling back to her, "I'm going out for a few miles. Be right back."

He had put that stuff in his hair again. The brochure spoke about the product in solemn, tortuous prose. King ordered it through the Cornell University Alumni Magazine. She had never said a word about it, but she could always smell it. It was supposed to clean and restore the roots. And his newest thing was a set of headphones he wore jogging and when he sat on the john.

When King appeared again he had the headphones on and was dressed in a brightly colored jogging outfit, and Casey thought honestly there were times when she didn't know him at all. Often she felt like she was lying on a dock reaching for a line of rope that hung from the bow of a boat. The currents would tease the rope, bringing it closer and then moving it away. There was only so much time, there were only so many chances to grab at the line before the tide would carry it far out of reach and the boat would drift off.

"Those doggone Japs are clever," King called out, standing at the kitchen door. "It's all in the microchip. Doggone microchips." He had told her this before. He had said that word, *microchip*, with absolute rapture. Holding his finger in the air when he said it, as if he had just stumbled upon a new word, the single word that held the cure to greed and cancer and global instability.

Soon King was out the door and gone. He was a mover, she thought; he could lose a wife and bounce back.

There were joggers up and down Stimpson Road. A few years ago you would have wondered where all those people were going in their shorts. The husbands often took along golden retrievers. The wives ran in old Harvard and Yale T-shirts. King liked to watch them bounce up and down, and when their nipples were showing, he would say they had their headlights on.

One night after the girls were asleep she was sitting in their bedroom with her book when King came up behind her. He covered her eyes with his hands and said, "Surprise!"

He waited and then said, "Come on, Mommy, guess."

"What is it?"

King saw the book in her hand and said, "God, the stuff you read. Come on, *guess*."

Finally he dropped his hands and popped out in front

—213

of her. As he stood there in his pinstripe pajamas, his wet hair slicked back in a Valentino style, at first she almost missed it.

"Oh, *that*," she said. "Well, it's pretty sharp, isn't it?"

"Sharp? Hey, is that all?"

"It's one of the best," she added.

It was a necktie. Another silk necktie. "Look at this," he sang gleefully as he danced over to the closet. He swung open the door. "That makes ninety-six, no ninety-seven. And not a loser in the whole bunch. Aren't they something, Mommy. Jay Gatsby had his silk shirts but they were nothing compared to these babies."

Suddenly King was putting on an act for her. He spoke into his hand as if his fist were a microphone. "Yes, Mr. Cronkite, it *is* amazing. What you're looking at here is not, contrary to popular perception, a collection of neckties. No sir, no indeed. Before you is a highly sophisticated, technically flawless, individually calibrated, wondrously synthetic, large intestine. When properly connected from end to end there is ample organ here to accommodate one alumnus from each of the Ivy League schools. Let me just show—"

"Enough," Casey said, laughing. "Enough."

"Did you like that one?"

"It was more than worth the price of admission," she said.

King turned to the closet and caught her face in the mirror mounted to the door. "I love your eyes when you laugh," he told her.

She could tell by his eyes that he had had too much gin. Not only by his eyes, but by one corner of his mouth, which drooped slightly.

"I'm going down to the kitchen, you want anything?" he asked her.

She said no. He wasn't only going to the kitchen, but to the dining room and to the mahogany hutch where she would hear the tinkling of bottles. She knew his habits. She knew that if he spent more than three or four minutes downstairs he would be drinking a shot straight, before he poured the second shot into the glass with tonic which he would then bring back upstairs with him. The extra shot he drank when he planned to make love to her. Booze the aphrodisiac, the stimulant, the emancipator, the bromide, the wonder drug. Booze the solver of problems, the prince of peace.

Down the hallway Hannah was crying. Casey started to her feet but King called out that he would go check on her.

In a few minutes Casey followed down the hallway, walking quietly, tracing the nail of her thumb along the textured wallpaper.

"Do you want me to sing for you like I used to?" she heard King say.

He began singing and then Casey heard Hannah interrupt him and ask him about Moses.

"Oh, sweetie, Moses is in heaven," King said.

"I miss Moses."

"We all miss him, sugar. We sure do miss old Moses. But you want him to be happy, don't you, sweetie?"

"Yes."

"Well, right now Moses is up in heaven. Moses is in a special place in heaven just for dogs. Dogs that are black and kind like Moses was. Did I ever tell you about that special place?"

—215

"Nope."

"Well, it's very special. Green grass all around and when it gets windy each dog gets a nice blanket to wrap up in. And five, no six times a day who do you think comes in with a special bone for every dog?"

"Jesus?" Hannah said.

"That's right," King said.

When King went on downstairs, Casey went into the bathroom. She was thinking about how God seemed to have been replaced these days by Jesus. Everyone was talking about Jesus as if they knew him personally.

She looked at herself in the mirror and held her face with both hands. For an instant the face was unfamiliar to her, as remote as the face of Jesus himself. She shook her head from side to side, sending her hair in soft waves across her cheeks. Quickly she began to undress. She pulled on her nightgown except for the sleeves so she could take off her underclothes beneath the warmth of the flannel. There were tiny veins in her thighs that had broken and bled in thin blue lines. Looking down, she wondered if it was possible that her thighs would one day widen the way her fat neighbor's had. You can never be certain about such things.

King was soon down on the floor at the foot of the bed doing his push-ups. A glass of gin sat on the table next to the morris chair. She picked it up and wiped away the moisture and placed the drink back down on the cover of the *National Geographic*. King would never remember such things no matter how many times she reminded him. She turned on the radio by the bed.

"You count please," King called to her. "I'm only doing forty tonight. I'm whipped."

She didn't want to count for him. "I'm going to read,"

she said. "You go ahead." He had already begun. His joints cracked eerily. Soon he was through. He got to his feet and the blood drained slowly from his face. When he went to fiddle around in his closet, Casey walked over to the opened window. The breeze caught her nightgown and tucked the flannel in tight folds against her breasts. It was a cool breeze, and without looking around at King she asked, "Fall. Why do we call it fall?"

He answered right away as if he'd just been called upon in some class at Cornell. "Well, the leaves I suppose. That's what I always think of anyway. The leaves coming down around our ears. The temperature falling."

Our descent into winter, Casey thought. She began to speak as if she were talking only to herself. She was looking out over the darkened town to where Jack lived. "You can feel it in the air tonight. It comes on us so fast. I always feel like I've missed something. I mean when summer is through I feel like I didn't get close enough to it. Jack said to me once, we only have so many trips to the beach."

"God, what a thought. You're not going to be gloomy again?"

She reached her hand behind her back and gathered up her hair and held it in a knot over her head. "I remember spending whole days on the beach one summer of my life. My father quit his job and stayed out of work for a summer. We lived in a bungalow on the Jersey shore. I was the first one on the beach in the morning and then by noon the beach would be filled with people and I'd watch them all and wonder if there was another person in the crowd like me, and if any of them were as thrilled as I was to be there that summer. If you stayed long enough there was always a time late in the day, no matter how hot a day it had been, when for a few minutes you could almost feel the seasons changing right in front of you. I remember the feeling, the wind would back around off the water and the dune grass would bend away from the shore and it felt as if fall was right there for just those few minutes. It was always sad though."

She paused and looked over at King as if it had just dawned on her that he was in the room and that he was married to her and that he was the father of the children down the hallway and that he probably wouldn't understand at all what she was going to say next.

"My mother used to write notes all the time before she got sick," she went on. "She used to leave them around the house when I was growing up. Sometimes after we'd argue I would wake up the next morning and find a note by the bed: 'Casey, would you like to go do some shopping with me at three? Check YES or NO.' "

"She always put YES and NO with a box next to each. I remember that. And the time just after my tenth birthday when she came into my bedroom. She wasn't at all happy then. My father had been at her throat. But that night she sat down next to me on the bed and she had the notes with her. She wanted to show them to me. She had saved every one of them. I think she wanted to be able to point to something, some proof that we had been close and that once there had been some happiness, that she and I hadn't missed the chance to be close, or something.

"I looked at her that night and I thought of her as . . . it was hard to say, but I thought of her as *temporary*. She wasn't going to be with me much longer. I had this great regret that I hadn't known her as a young woman. I always wished I had known her when she was young."

It was the sound of King opening a drawer on his

bureau that reminded Casey she was not alone. Soon he began speaking, and she thought he must be speaking to her.

"That reminds me," he said with eagerness in his voice. "It reminds me of my freshman year at Cornell. The third floor of Connor Hall there were two guys who roomed together and everybody thought they were queer. They dressed alike and their room looked like one of those rooms in a *Better Homes and Gardens* magazine. They had vases and monogrammed books of matches, the works. They were the ones who always answered the telephone at the end of the hall. I mean with thirty people living on the floor no one ever bothered to get the phone because what were the chances it would be for you? So they answered it. They were considerate, but they weren't queer, I don't think. Just different from the rest of us.

"Anyway, there was a blackboard at one end of the floor and every morning I'd get up and go down and erase what had been written about them the night before while they were asleep. The worst kind of things. Every morning there was something there."

"You cared," Casey said softly.

"What?"

"I said you cared. That was nice of you."

"Well, I just didn't like it, the whole thing," he said.

King turned away from her and seemed to be deep in his thoughts. Casey was deep in thought too, the thought that she was married to a good man, a man whose faults and failings and sins did not match her own. She looked across the room at him, thinking to herself that in this world bad things often happened to good people and no one was to blame for it.

King changed the subject and told her they were expected to have dinner next week with Judge Bolivar Rideout and his wife. "They're counting on us for the game," he said enthusiastically.

"I'd like to skip it if we can," she said.

The game was a board game called RISK, which Judge Rideout had become notorious for. When you were invited to his house you were expected to come prepared for a long evening, for the game of RISK involved taking over the entire world and this, of course, could take some time. You were also expected to wear an appropriate costume which would embellish the character you were assigned by the Judge to play. The Judge was always Hitler and he wore black boots and sometimes he sketched on a moustache with his wife's mascara.

"I already told them we'd be coming," King said. "We're not going to look very good if we just back out. Besides, it'll be fun."

There was some sort of argument coming on and Casey could have stopped it dead in its tracks but she let it come closer, and she encouraged it because King was actually paying attention to her now that she had threatened to disrupt his plans.

"The Judge will be disappointed," King went on. "He's not the person we should let down, all things considered."

What he was really talking about, it seemed to her, was that it was unwise to tinker with the scheme of things. In many ways King had asked her not to tinker. Why not accept the flat, reliable truth that *she* had been rescued and given passage into a fine, new world, that Providence and chance and biology had conspired to make her comfortable as she turned thirty years old, that she was living in a privileged world. All that was required of her was acceptance. Equanimity over ambivalence. All she had to do was accept the marvelous order of things. Shut her eyes at night and open them in the morning to pour the orange juice and open the curtains and then get on with another day. One day after the other. The rest would take care of itself. There were trust funds and insurance policies and stock options to see to this. It was all so impossibly simple and neat. If you could just pour the orange juice and keep the dentist appointments straight and mail the right checks to the right places and get hold of the man who fixed the plumbing, then the gears and wheels of privilege would keep going. The machinery was perfect. It had been refined by social evolution. At the Houghtons and the Bishops and the Turners and the Cornwalls and the Pratts, the faultless machinery was moving along. They were all plugged into the same outlet. At night, beyond the hedges and stone walls there was a tiny, red pulsing light by the front door of every house, installed by the helpful, solicitous man in green khakis from the Honneywell Protection Team. And these tiny red eyes watched the dark streets and shadowed lawns for you while you slept to make sure that life went on as you had come to expect it should. Your self-assurance, your pride, and your confidence were easy to explain, for you were immured from all evil. You were guaranteed, actually wired right into a security system that would never let you down. Never.

"King," she said. "Please don't do that tonight."

King paced the bedroom to the music of his own voice. At times like this when they were caught in some disagreement he would pretend to be out on the tennis court, as if the discussion could be settled and won to his satisfaction with one quick forehand volley. He rocked on the balls of his feet and swung an invisible tennis racket indolently from side to side.

"What puzzles me is why you want to make this a federal issue," he said. "I'm only talking about a simple social courtesy."

"And is it an act of sedition to refuse to be at the beck and call of Adolph Hitler?" she said.

"Sedition? I don't think we have to be so derisive of the Judge."

"*We*? Why do you say '*we*' when you mean *me*? It's like the way the old biddies in the library used to talk when they came snooping around with a finger pressed to their lips—We must learn to be quiet in the library!"

"Why are we arguing about my grammar? I meant the editorial *we*."

"I'm not arguing."

"Good," King said and then he hit a swift shot down the line of his imaginary court, his eyes following the flight of the ball to the other end of the room. Casey asked him again to please put his racket away. He took one more swipe at the ball before settling into the chair where he clipped his toenails over a wicker wastebasket.

After a while he looked over at Casey. "Why don't you let me in?" he said, and his voice was suddenly contrite.

She waited, then said, "I was thinking of Cape Cod."

"What about Cape Cod?"

"Do you remember right after we met, you were driving me home one night and you said we were going to go to Cape Cod sometime before we were married? I remember exactly how you told me about it. You said you were going to drive and I was going to lay my head on your lap and sleep all the way down. And just when we got to the Bourne Bridge you were going to open all the windows and wake me with the scent of the ocean. You were going to sing to me."

"I remember, Mommy," he said.

"The perfect summer scene," she said.

"We've been to the Cape a dozen times," King said. He got down on his hands and knees, searching the carpet for a toenail paring that had missed the wastebasket.

"But never like that."

"Let's go down some night next week then. We can get Mrs. Collins to stay with the girls. I'll speak to her tomorrow if you want."

"No, that's all right."

"Well, what about the White Mountains then? For a few days at a country inn. The NIKE Road Race is going to be held in North Conway this year, along the Kancamagus Highway. It'll be great. I was thinking I might enter. I'm ready for it this year."

She didn't answer. She sat on her side of the bed and stretched out her legs. She gathered her hair in a single braid, pulled it over one shoulder and swept it across her breast. She felt her heart beating under her palm. King walked over to the bed and sat down next to her. He took the braid in his hand and pressed his knuckles against her nipple. She felt it begin to harden and she wondered if this involuntary reflex would encourage him. How unreasonable it was that her body could express a desire so completely opposite from the thought she had at that moment, the thought that she would have given almost anything to be left alone. She had an idea that solitude, no matter what its shape and temperment, would hold the answers to questions she did not dare ask. She longed for solitude, for the irony and consolation of it, for its uncertainty.

"What I want to do," King said, "is take you downstairs just for a little while. We can fix a drink and sit in front of the fire. I'll build a fire and then I'll touch you like this. Oh, Mommy, it'll be nice for both of us."

Soon they were in the living room and she found that she had brought along her book about the fall of Richard Nixon, and King said, "That story you keep reading about, I don't understand you. That was the saddest thing that ever happened to us and you want to dwell on it. It's the worst fall we ever took."

"*We?*"

"Our country, our president."

In a few minutes King was on his way into the dining room to get them what he said would be "just a tad more brandy." When he left the room Casey looked over at his shirt that was draped over the rocking chair. She thought of it as a shirt she had never seen before, a shirt belonging to a man she had never seen before. This was one of the possibilities of solitude.

When King came back into the unlighted living room she saw that he had taken off his pants and left them somewhere. He stood in his BVDs holding out a glass to her. She took it and when she saw he was hard and stiff in his underwear she said, "Forgive me."

He looked down at her. "For what, Mommy?"

"I'm not going to be able to do this," she said.

For a while he kissed her. He got her nightgown off, but then she moved away from him and silence fell. She thought of saying something that might break through this silence, but the words she imagined saying were pale and would have been lost in the darkness of the big room. So they slept on the floor like children while a fog crawled over the hills of Dedham, Massachusetts, and seeped through the woods behind their house. They slept through that part of autumn when the sky blazed with yellows and reds and the hills were the color of an old tweed coat, and out on the patio at night you could smell woodsmoke in the air. They slept through winter too. And then came spring, the first spring of a new decade.

Chapter Eighteen

By this time in his life, by the age of thirty, Jack had lost the ability to just lay down his head at night and fall asleep. He often spent nights the way many people spend them; unable to sleep, they start to figure things out, things they believed were taken care of a long time ago, but like rooted weeds had secretly flourished below the surface of neglect or indifference. There are certain things to fear about the darkness. At night, alone, people dwell on thoughts without the benefit of familiar objects to distract them. They lie vulnerable in their beds. There is often a face in the moon that appears to know too much about them. Sometimes the trees bend low in the woods as if in prayer. Only at night do the monsters of childhood dare return. How easily people can be deceived late at night when they can hear voices in creaking stairs and see the outline of a stranger where a coat hangs in the closet.

It was not uncommon for the people in Jack's congregation to call on him at night. In the parish ministry this is how it went. And Jack had developed a sense about their needs. His sympathy for them was so intense that he was often able to anticipate certain callers. He was drawn to their suffering; he had learned to tend his flock. It was true what the Bible said about the good shepherd—he will go searching for the one lamb that has wandered from the fold.

For a long time Casey was one of the callers. She came after the girls were in bed. She told Jack she just wanted someone to talk to. One night she made him agree that they would only discuss the future. "It'll help keep us young," she said. "We'll talk about space shuttles and test-tube babies, we'll be thoroughly modern, Jack. No looking back, no turning into old has-beens."

This agreement about the past held up pretty well for a while. Then there was the night when Jack called Casey asking her to come over. She found him in his study weeping like a child. He had just been notified by the police that a woman in his congregation had been brutally beaten by her husband. Jack told Casey *he* was to blame for this, that the woman had called him for help.

For a long time Casey just sat with him. Then when they talked, Jack said, "I was afraid to go over. I was afraid of the husband."

"What do they expect from you?" she asked.

"They don't expect me to be a coward."

Eventually Jack talked about the night the boys had come for him to paint his body green. He said there hadn't been a day in his life since then when he hadn't thought about that night. He told her how they turned him upside down and flushed his head in the toilet. "I can still feel the water in my nose, the feeling I would drown."

She tried to make him see this didn't make him a coward. Even while she was trying to console him she was thinking how neither of them had outrun the past, and now that Jack had spoken of the past that would be practically all they ever talked about.

One night when Casey went to see him, he was up late, sitting in his study. The trees were tossing out beyond his windows. A faint breeze rattled the screens. She began speaking about how she felt *diminished*. He listened to her tell him that her life was diminished. Diminished in the eyes of his God, in the eyes of people who knew her. She stood at his desk and said she felt she was no longer living her life. For a long time she had felt as if her life was going on outside her, beyond her reach. "Everything is moving past me," she said to him. "And then out of sight."

Jack wanted her to sit down. He asked her several times to sit, but she walked from one piece of furniture to another as if she doubted any of them could hold her weight. She looked as if she had misplaced something.

"Did you drive over?" he asked after a little while. "I didn't hear a car come up."

"No, I walked," she told him. "I've been out walking a long time. What time is it anyway?"

He told her it was almost one o'clock. Her eyes were glazed, remote. "Well, come sit down here," he said again. "I'll put on some water. There's tea in the kitchen."

"You always keep everything so neat," she said looking across his desk and bookshelves. "That's commendable."

"It's a sickness," he said smiling. "It's to belie the confusion inside."

"Oh?" she said with a surprised look. "My father's old trick." She waited a moment and then said, "I shouldn't ask, Jack, but have you got any liquor?"

—228

He told her there was some brandy and she seemed consoled by this, by the thought of a drink and by the knowledge that Jack would violate the prohibition against keeping it in the rectory.

"I'll get the bottle," he said. "But please, sit down."

When he came back with the brandy she had chosen the straight-backed chair by the window. The room was silent. A heavy, iron silence seemed to stand between them, and though he kept trying to say little things that might reassure her, his words were flattened against the silence and they slid away without any effect. When at last she looked up at him from her glass, she looked like a stranger to him.

"You came to tell me something," he said solicitously.

"Not to tell, to *ask*."

"Go ahead then, ask me. Ask me anything."

She craned her neck at some sound outside. "It seems to be getting light already," she said.

"There's a good moon. You see the birches there, how white they are? They're brighter under moonlight than when the sun is on them. I've always been surprised."

"Do you still know all the trees, Jack? I remember when you could name every tree."

He smiled and said, "Right from the Boy Scout handbook. Well, maybe I was meant for a different life. A little while ago I overheard two women talking. One of them was saying to the other that there were two kinds of men in the world. The first kind goes out on his porch at night before getting into bed and looks around and says, 'The wind has backed around to the east.' And the second kind of man goes out on the same porch at night before getting into his bed and *he* looks around and says, 'Over-the-counter trading was off today.' And the other woman said,

'Yeah, that's it, and we fall in love with the first kind and marry the second kind and spend the rest of our lives thinking about the first kind.' "

Casey put her head back and laughed with him for a moment.

"It's silly," Jack went on, "but it's the kind of thing you hear some women saying. And for me, I'd be the first kind, unmarried but unforgotten."

"Yes," she said. "There's no virtue in being married. But unforgotten—now there's something."

She turned slowly and walked across his room and stood looking down at his desk, touching his things. She was wearing a dark-blue skirt that fell below her knees, and a white blouse with the collar turned up and rounded at the corners, and one of those hand-sewn, woolen sweaters with dark-brown reindeer and gray snowflakes and buttons down the front. She pulled at the cuffs of her blouse. Jack watched her, thinking her body was the same as it had always been but there were new creases on her face. Still she looked even prettier than when she was a girl.

"You want to be chosen before you get old," she said. "If you're a girl you think about who will choose you. It's like once you're married you'll walk down the street and everyone will know *you've* been chosen. A childish thought."

She looked up into his eyes and a lopsided smile fell on her lips, ending there. "A child. How does it go? 'When I was a child I thought like a child, I spoke like a child.' "

" 'But I gave up my childish ways,' " Jack finished for her.

"Poor fellow," she said, "he shouldn't have. Except I suppose they get you in trouble, don't they? These childish ways, childish dreams. When you behave like a child, people have to forgive you."

A troubled look came over her face. She went back to the window and stood behind the chair. "I was thinking. A couple years ago I decided to get a bicycle. I wanted one of those old things, nothing with all the fancy gears like everyone has today. I was going to put a little seat on back and ride Hannah all around. And then I found the perfect one at a yard sale. I paid fifteen dollars for it, I painted it green, I was very proud of myself. One morning I asked King if he would pick up a reflector, one of those red plastic ones you screw onto the fender. He came home that night with a reflector powered by a generator. It cost forty-seven dollars. He told me it was worth the money, my safety and well-being were worth the expense. Now, Jack, how can I ever be forgiven for that?"

"For what?"

"For making him try so hard to please me."

Jack said nothing. He watched her pour herself more brandy.

"It's been a long time," she said to him. "It'll be six years soon since I saw Ross that night. Have I told you all about that night, everything I said to him?" When Jack gave her a hopeful look, she laughed lightly. "You're too kind to tell me I've told you a hundred times already. Am I turning into one of those women everybody has to pamper because she's becoming a little bit crazy?"

"Of course not."

"Maybe it *has* driven me crazy. The other day when I was alone in the house I went up to Catherine's room. I was looking around, looking at all her beautiful clothes, the things she looks so nice in. Then I tried on one of her miniskirts in front of the mirror. It was very sad. I mean there was something pathetic about it. I was surprised at myself for caring."

She turned her face away and paused.

"But what I want to ask you about is this, Jack. The vow 'Till death do us part'—what does it mean? Death of the body? Death of the spirit, death of love, death of understanding, death of respect? So many kinds of death. Don't they all count, don't they free you from the vow?"

She waited a moment. On her face there was an expression of satisfaction, as if she had just come upon an answer she had searched a long time for. "Looking at Catherine's clothes though, I thought how when you're young you struggle to have things, and then as soon as it's easy to have things, you begin to get old. When you struggle," she said with her eyes suddenly filled with light, "you're up on your toes, poised and looking around for signs, clues. We all want to know where we're going, where we'll be, what it will all be like for us in the end. And even more than that, what will happen when we die. Will we be able to look down on all this and see how things turned out? Because I'd like to look down into *his* life, Jack."

Jack walked to his desk and sat behind it and opened one of the drawers while she went on telling him how one day they would be sitting down and everything would be in place, the place they had come to, and they would have memorized the view from where they sat, and they would know when the clocks would strike and the plants would need watering, and nothing would change anymore.

"I've changed," Jack said. "I've been holding the line against certain things."

She looked at him carefully. "Well, it's your business, isn't it?" she said cheerfully. "I mean, you have to uphold certain rules. But you'll forgive me, won't you, because I don't want to just wait for the bad things to come along—sickness, and the loss of old friends. I can't sit here like some girl at a Town Hall dance, knowing the whole thing will be over soon and I'll still be sitting here in my good dress."

"You're asking—"

She answered this for him. "I'm asking what everyone's asking for—I'm asking to dance."

The room was silent again. She watched Jack as he took out an envelope and then several pages from inside it. Right away she recognized these typed pages. She held out her hand. "Another story. Has he sent another story?"

Jack put the pages down in front of her, as if he wanted it to be her responsibility to pick them up, her decision. "This came soon after the other, but I, well like I said, I've been holding the line," he confessed. "Only because I wanted to see you work out this new life of yours. I thought you all might be happy, and you could just go on."

"But it's not over yet," she said, picking up Ross's story.

Jack said maybe it wasn't. He told her Ross had sent this over three years ago. "I didn't want it to add to your—"

"Choices?" she said.

"Ambivalence," he said. "That's all."

She kissed him before she went back home. King's house surrounded her with stillness. Before she went upstairs to her room she stopped to see that everyone was sleeping. She was waiting for something holy to begin. She stood in the moonlight in each of their rooms and it struck her that she could say anything at all to them and they would not stir. She could say "Good-bye, I did my best."

She opened the pages and read what he had written.

ONE SUMMER WITH THE FAMILY
by Ross Peterson

That fall the rain went on day after day washing the colors from the trees and drilling the tin roof of our old house like thousands of buttons dropped from a jar, and I remember how this water music sent my father to sleep in his winged chair next to the window in the hallway. When something was bothering him he would sit in this chair out in the hallway as if no single room in our house was big enough to hold his discontent and his vexation. He sat there in the gray khaki trousers he wore to work the night shift at Thaxter's Mill, and the white undershirt that strained over his big, thick shoulders. His hair was the color of oats. He was an unbelievably handsome man.

There were eight of us living together then, but my father found ways of being alone. Alone in his winged chair he would sit reading biographies of Faulkner and Thomas Wolfe, maybe hoping to discover that they had once asked life the same questions he was asking secretly.

In the winter my father would sometimes bring hobos into our house to get them in out of the cold. My mother would turn the davenport downstairs into a bed, and my father would use electrical tape to mend the poor men's glasses. One of these hobos was the first person I remember who called my father Mister Harding. He said, "You kids got quite a daddy. They threw away the mold after they made Mister Harding."

My father could not keep a job for long in those days.

He never stayed long enough in a job to be rewarded with a Thanksgiving turkey or a paid holiday. Part of the trouble was we lived in rural Maine, out in the sticks, and my father kept having trouble with his bosses, bosses who did not possess his keen understanding of love and economics. I used to tell my friends at school that he was going to be president of the United States one day, and for a while this exaggeration held up. But that October of the rain I turned ten years old and I began to see what the rest of the world could already see on my father's face—the distant, anguished expression of a man who at age forty-six had figured out that if success was to come at all it would come too late for happiness.

One night that autumn my father didn't go to the mill. When I went to bed he was in his chair looking out at the rain. I remember the light from a streetlamp fell through the window, throwing a coin on his left arm and half a star on the back of his chair.

In the morning he was gone and my mother was standing at the window with tears streaming down her cheeks. I looked up at her and then turned and found a sheet of paper on the floor next to the chair. There was a lady sketched on the paper, a lady whose face I had never seen before, and she was standing on a beach. It would be years before I could see why it had made my mother so sad to have discovered that her husband had stayed up all night trying to draw the picture of a stranger, a woman out on the beach.

My mother had something to show me that morning. She took me into her bedroom, and while I sat close to her she placed a smooth glass paperweight no larger than an egg in my right hand. It contained a miniature town, a white church, four white houses with green wreathes on their front doors, a milk truck, and a store with an American flag hung over its striped awning. Water surrounded the scene. My mother told me to shake the egg. As I waved it back and forth the cottony, white flakes of snow blew up from the street and swirled through the water, then slowly blanketed the village. I shook the egg again and again, watching to see if any single snowflake ever landed in exactly the same place.

"Would you like to give this to your daddy for Christmas?" my mother wanted to know. "I got it for him."

I thought, then asked her if he was going to be happy at Christmas.

She pulled me closer to her. "Oh, yes, sweetheart," she said. She turned my face and looked into my eyes and finally she went on. "You see, we all have each other, you and your brothers and sisters. But your father doesn't have anyone but himself."

My father's happiness that Christmas had nothing to do with the rain that finally stopped or the glass egg that snowed with the shake of your hand. He had quit his job at Thaxter's Mill because of problems with the night-shift foreman, who was referred to around our house only as "the knucklehead." Two days before Christmas my father drove to a town outside Boston to meet a man named Haskell Cleaves. At first I knew little about this meeting except that it was so important my father had to use the Christmas savings to buy himself a stiff blue suit and black shoes that you could see yourself in if the light was right. "I can't show up at his office looking like a hick," my father said that morning while my mother stood at the kitchen counter making him his lunch. "This fellow Cleaves needs a man to take over the whole New England territory. He's not just talking sales now, no way. It's a lot more than that."

"Oh, I know it is," my mother said kindly.

"This is the chance to be my own boss." He walked slowly across the floor as if savoring the mental picture he had of himself as a boss. He came up behind my mother and hugged her. "And it's the break we need," he said. "For the new baby."

My father spent Christmas Eve and most of Christmas Day out in the hallway where the persuasive voice of Haskell Cleaves resonated from the tape-recorded message he'd given my father to bring home and study. "Sales tools," my father said casually as if we all should have known.

These sales tools were recorded messages that my father would purchase for fifteen dollars each. There would be thirty in all, and they would arrive in the mail every Tuesday. The machine these messages were played on cost my father another forty dollars, which he would pay off in ten-dollar installments to Mr. Cleaves. The idea was that my father would take Mr. Cleaves's sales course and at the end he would be invited to take an exam which was allegedly being given to thousands of candidates throughout the country. "If I place in the top ten percent, I'll get all of New England," my father explained hopefully.

My mother showed him some enthusiasm and then asked, "What will you be selling in New England, Charles?"

"Lessons," he answered flatly. "Lessons in self-confidence. It's a nationally recognized course with books and tapes and everything. Of course in the next few months I'll have to be in Boston off and on."

And so, that Christmas the wise man who would save my father from the gloom of another night shift at another mill, spoke in the hallway of our house. His voice was as persistent as the rain that had preceded it. It was a pleasantly modulating voice, a rambunctious voice but also at times very graceful, like the voice of Walter Cronkite.

On one lesson the voice said, "Once an eager young chap asked me what I thought was the key to success as a salesman. I thought long and hard and then I looked that fellow right in the eye and I said, 'Friend, if you're going to sell and do it well, you've got to be at peace with yourself.' Peace on the inside is what I was trying to make that fellow see. I was thinking about the most famous salesman of all, Willie Loman. Now Willie's problem was that he hadn't found any inner peace. I mean there was a war going on inside his chest and his head. He was at war with himself. Why? Because his expectations were all out of whack. And that brings me to the point of this lesson—expectations!"

By summer mother was big and round and her skin tasted salty when you kissed her. One Saturday all eight of us drove to Bay Ledge for a picnic. It was a bright, sunny day. The sun burned, and big boats top-heavy with sails creased the ocean. Along the beach people by the hundreds lay with the white soles of their feet pointing out to sea as if something as powerful as the tide had dragged them onto shore and left them there.

"You deserve an afternoon off," my mother said pleasantly.

Father sat at one corner of our blanket with his legs crossed. He listened to the tape recorder through a plastic cord that ran into his ear. With the big toe of one foot he drew circles and boxes in the sand, then smeared them out with his heel.

She motioned for me to come to her side. "Put your hand right here," she said. "That's it. Now press down a little. Can you feel?"

I had my hand on her belly and I could feel a faint pulsing. And then something kicking at my hand. I stared at her belly and in my mind I began to think again of the world inside the glass paperweight.

I was still thinking about this when my father raised a finger in the air and, looking out across the sea like a man waiting to be rescued, said, "Discipline." He came down hard on each syllable. A thin, ironic smile fell on his lips then, and he repeated the word several times as if this single word held the promise but also the illusion of prosperity and permanence.

For two weeks in July we moved all the furniture around the house preparing for the arrival of the baby. Then one Sunday afternoon we all watched my father and mother drive away to the hospital. "Be good," my mother had called out to us. "I love you all."

I do not know why my mother and my brother died. I was never told. I remember only the brooding commotion that followed as neighbors brought all kinds of canned goods and casseroles to our house so we would not have to spend time in the kitchen, a room made bare and cold by my mother's absence.

I remember the cemetery was a large, artless piece of land on a shouldering hill that was burned and cracked from the summer heat. My brother's coffin seemed way too big. And when I leaned over to kiss my mother good-bye I remember being surprised that she did not smile up at me. After the service we stood around with my father while the workmen pushed heavy shovels of dirt into the graves and flattened the dirt down with the backs of their shovels like someone tamping tobacco into the bowl of a pipe. My father stood watching with his arms folded across his chest.

Soon after this my father gave up the sales course, and one day Mr. Cleaves dropped by our house. My father wasn't home and my sister and I stood looking at him on the porch. To my surprise he was a tiny, thin man with sorrowful brown eyes. He brought us some money, what he said was a "total refund." He tipped his hat to my sister and said, "Tell your daddy he can keep the tapes and the machine. It's all fine by me." He smiled and turned away.

It was years later, soon before I was about to leave my father's house when I awoke one night to the sound of the tape recorder playing out in the hallway. It seemed impossible that Haskell Cleaves's voice had returned to our house.

My sister was sitting in the winged chair and she was crying when I came up to her.

"What are you doing?" I asked.

"The world stinks," she said angrily. She looked up at me and then down at the machine. Then she reversed the tape a bit and started it again. On came the voice of a woman. All the voice said was this: "When you're done with that silly lesson, Charlie, come roll me in the sand and I'll give you a lesson of my own."

A light burned most of the night in Jack's study. He knew what he had given Casey. She would have the same questions Jack had had, questions of great urgency to her. Was he married? Did he have children? And was there the image of a girl on a beach which would lead him to leave his wife? Would he always suffer because of his expectations? And was he still expecting something from her?

Jack sat at his desk most of the night writing a sermon

on the subject of death. It was one of those sermons he wrote without even trying. He was always thrilled whenever this happened, when God or his muse visited him in his study and he worked straight through the sermon until it was finished.

Casey was right, he thought. And he wrote that there were many kinds of death, each in its own way making room for new life, new possibilities, new resolutions. Those words from Christ on the cross—"It is accomplished."

Death, an accomplishment.

When he was finished it was morning, a morning so bright it could not be faced without squinting. He walked to the church under the influence of a spiritual intoxication. He passed through the shadowed corridor into the room just off the altar, where he dressed in his robe and stood before the mirror adjusting his collar. The sanctuary filled with the dancing strings and the soaring horns of a Handel cantata. Jack could feel the paneled walls tremble under the current of bass and tenor. In the mirror mounted to the wall he saw an eagerness in his eyes, and a desire to get this right, to say what he had to tell them all.

He spoke from the pulpit. He spoke of birth and life and death and being born again and again in the newness of God's infinite love just as the town around them had been reborn this spring morning. And even as he was saying all this, it sounded terribly old and unsatisfactory to him. And then they were celebrating Holy Communion and suddenly there was Casey kneeling at the altar with those sea-green eyes looking straight into his. Jack first placed a disk of bread into King's hands and then into the opened hands of the three girls beside him. And then he stood before Casey and said, "This is the body of Christ which is broken for you."

Casey looked up at him and he couldn't look into her eyes. He could barely keep his balance, pausing there in front of her hands. Because what he saw was that she was counting on him and trusting that he would do something. When he reached to her with the bread it fell from his hands and landed on the carpeted floor with the silence of a moth.

BOOK THREE

Chapter Nineteen

She wore a tailored pink skirt that fell above her knees and a matching pink jacket trimmed with black felt around the cuffs and collar. On her head, a pink pill-box hat with a black net veil that swept across her eyes.

"Jesus," King had said to her when she was getting dressed. "You're just going to piss off the Judge, plus make me look like a fool. He wanted us to come as the Reagans."

"Screw the Reagans," Casey had said, "and the Judge—screw him too. I'm going as Jackie Kennedy."

She looked remarkably like Jackie had on the day of the assassination in Dallas.

Casey had threatened to pour catsup all over the front of her outfit, but King had pleaded with her, "You know the Judge is from Texas. Please—be kind."

"What no knickers? You promised knickers, King. Oh hell, you really let me down," Judge Bolivar Rideout cried out. King stood there in his ten-gallon hat and cowboy boots. "I tried," he said. "But, you know, a woman has a mind of her own these days, Judge."

"Well come on in anyway," the Judge insisted. "And hey, don't get me wrong. I like your wife no matter what she has on." He put a drink into King's hand and then walked past him and kissed Casey on her mouth. "Jackie, eat your heart out," he said.

Tonight, as usual, the Judge and his wife, Jan, would represent Germany in the RISK game. The Judge was dressed in black with his hair slicked down. Except for an extra hundred pounds he looked like Adolph Hitler. Al Davenport was dressed like Mussolini, his wife like an Italian mistress. Earl and Betty Speiss would use the red pieces on the board and would play the part of Stalin. It had been decreed long ago that the United States would not be represented by Roosevelt. The Judge had a particular contempt for FDR.

There was dinner first. Prime rib and vegetables. The Judge talked about sailing, one of his favorite topics. He steered the discussion as he steered his fiberglass boat, which was moored in summer months in Marblehead harbor. "If it wasn't for the wife," he said, "I probably never would have stuck my toe in this Atlantic Ocean of yours. I was as happy as a hound in a meathouse back in Houston until I met Jan." He called out into the kitchen for Jan to open another bottle of wine.

"Oh, I don't know about that, Bolivar," said Earl Speiss. "Seems to me you've got sailing in your blood. I don't think we could have kept you away from it forever."

The men flattered Judge Bolivar Rideout because they were all lawyers and he was a judge, and except for the cut in pay such a promotion would involve, they too wanted to be judges.

"Right you are," said Bolivar. "I remember the first time I came East. We were down in Atlantic City for a

—246

bar convention, and right off I felt some sort of—I don't know what you'd call it—an affinity, you know, an affinity for the sea. I took some sailing lessons then, just to get the fundamentals under my belt, and it wasn't long after that when the wife and I took our first cruise up the coast. Hell, they said we were crazy to go out alone like that, but we did all right."

"Smooth sailing then," said Al Davenport.

"Oh, yeah. Oh, it was great. Sailing becomes habituated in the central nervous system pretty quick if you've got some aptitude for it. Oh Jesus, we had quite a time on that cruise. All the way up the coast of Maine, up to Campobello. Let me tell you FDR had some spread up there. Hell, they jumped all over Nixon for Key Biscayne, but that was a *barracks* compared to the spread Roosevelt had up there in Campobello. All the privacy a man would ever need. You know, we saw the porch he was sitting on that morning when he came down with polio. They say he had taken a swim with his kids and he was out on the porch just reading his mail. He feels a chill, goes upstairs for a hot bath, then lies down. Well, he never got up again, not without those iron braces and somebody holding him by the arms."

Earl Speiss, who sat with his arm around his wife, said that perhaps Roosevelt's battle with illness had given him the mental toughness to pull the country out of the depression.

"I don't think you've thought that one through," the Judge said. "Don't forget, he sold us out to the Reds at Yalta."

Earl Speiss tried to hold his ground. "Maybe. But he had a lot of courage, personal courage."

"No, Earl. I think you're way off there. Just stop and

—247

examine the facts. You and I are paying up the yingyang for all the FDR programs. All the giveaways. Am I right? Who pays? *We* pay. It takes courage to cut that crap *down*, put the lid on those expenses the way this big fellow we got in the White House now is going to do. Am I right?"

"I'm with you on that," King said with enthusiasm.

"Course you are. That's why you're headed for a political career right here in Massachusetts. Maybe the governorship."

"Well," said King bashfully, "you'd better not let my wife hear about that."

"Why not?" said the Judge, laughing. "She doesn't have to wear knickers in the State House."

"No, when you put it that way, I guess I'm with you on FDR," recanted Earl Speiss.

"*Sure you are, Earl.* You know what hard work and restraint is all about. You're a goddamn German. You Germans aren't happy unless you're breaking your backs working night and day cranking out ballbearings or rubber tires for some great *Wehrmacht*. Right? Am I right on that?"

Bolivar stopped to light his cigar. "I'll tell you though, I like that big fellow we got on Pennsylvania Avenue now. He's not going to take any crap from anybody. He knows where to draw the line."

"I only hope it doesn't get us into a war," said Lindsay Davenport.

"I agree," said Betty Speiss. "I think this nuclear thing is immoral."

"I say we let the big man in the saddle take care of things," said the Judge. "He's got those big broad shoulders. Let's eat and get going here."

They ate a big meal. Throughout dinner Bolivar lectured on a variety of subjects which ranged from federally funded day-care centers to Western art, which he advised them to invest in. "Those Remingtons are worth their weight in gold," he told them. He spoke several times about the election coming up in Massachusetts, saying that King would be a good candidate for the governorship. Casey listened with incredulity, but began to see that King had been discussing this idea with the Judge.

"Old John Connolly got his start in the governor's chair back in Texas," said the Judge. Casey thought to herself that she could never under any circumstances live one day of her life in the state of Texas.

The table was cleared, the women were in the kitchen, and the men were seated around the RISK board when Bolivar looked over at King and resumed his monologue on the election. "You don't want to take this thing lightly," Casey heard him saying. "Maybe they're right, that Flynn can't be unseated this time around, but you'll be making progress for the future. And there's not just the party to think about. This will be a boon for your firm. You've got some law partners there who would give their left ones to see you in the race. Great exposure for the firm, just great. And you know how it works, the firm puts up a couple hundred thousand, right up front for the campaign. It's their contribution. And if you work it right, what they do, I mean for tax purposes, is they buy out your partnership for the couple hundred thou, and then after the election, if you lose you buy it back for a buck. That's the way it works best."

Soon the game was under way. There was hollering and clowning around and the women marveled at their husbands, at the way they deferred to Adolf Hitler, at the look of submission on their faces. They had been dragooned into the game by the mighty Judge, and they would be defeated by him.

When Earl Speiss tried to knock Al Davenport out of the Congo with the hope of winning the continent and thus receiving additional armies to defend his territory, Bolivar laughed at him. "Oh Christ, Earl, you never learn. You have to build up, build up, build up! You try to take all that land so soon and you'll lose it—you'll lose your ass."

The Judge had a theory how this game would be won consistently. He called it his blob theory. The idea, he said, was to move around the world, taking victories where they could be taken and winning victory cards that entitled you to cash them in for free armies. He would put all his new armies down on one remote country, just stacking them up until they numbered in the hundreds. Meanwhile, the other players would be fighting among themselves for territory which he would later sweep through with a giant force he called his Maximus Blobbus.

Casey had learned from past experience that it was best to drink heavily during these games. She was drinking white wine tonight and already her head was reeling. She stared at King in his cowboy boots and hat and thought how out of place he looked in the Judge's den with its richly paneled walls, its costly carpets, and the tall bookcases with leather-bound volumes of the classics. Who reads these books? she wondered. Has anyone in this house learned an atom of truth from these books? It was better not to be cynical, not to judge others too harshly. Cynicism led to malaise. She remembered the last president had been run out of office for talking that way. Strange. But she was cynical about the law. Just the other day she had argued with King about his legal practice. "What I hate about your law," she had told him, "is that it doesn't care about the truth, only the way things can be made to *seem* and *sound*. And look what it's done to you."

King had stood there, his hands raised in a gesture of reconciliation. He had pressed her for facts. Lawyers were quick to get at the facts, she thought, and then to twist them. Softly, King had said, "I deal in facts, Casey."

"Facts, I can give you all the facts you want. For one thing, it's turned you into a careful, timid, indoor person." She pointed out his skin creams and hair tonic. The facts were cold.

"You want me to train lions for a living?" he had said.

She complained about his office. Thousands and thousands of dollars had been spent on the interior design because in order to attract prosperous clients you had to make your office look very good. The profligate surroundings were meant to put the client at ease, to make him feel secure. Surely in such opulent quarters, wisdom must reside. What they were after—all the world knew this—was the look of a Victorian library in an English country house. What they got was something different. The designers and decorators of these law offices understood that the most successful interiors would be those which made the office look like a cocktail lounge in a Sheraton Inn.

She looked over at Al Davenport, a man who, no matter how carefully he dressed, appeared untidy in a way. This had probably kept him back in his profession. It was known that he did not bill as many hours as his partners and he was on thin ice at the firm. Even tonight he did not look relaxed. His white skin in contrast to his shock of jet-black hair gave him a severe look. Poor Al.

And Earl Speiss, who was said to have once been an all-American in football, had ballooned with weight packed on around his middle.

Better not to be cynical, because once you started, there was hardly anything one could not be cynical about. Casey looked into the faces of their wives and wondered if any one of them still practiced the little self-deceptions that kept a marriage safe from intruders. All of them had children. Were children somehow a part of this? You feel the promise of life sliding away from you and so you have children and make believe the promise exists *there* in the children, in *their* future. You make believe that they will amount to something different, something better. That they will be more self-reliant, less compromising. That they will stand up for what is right. But they become just like you. They're doomed to the same disillusionment. They'll wake up one day and see that they're just like everyone else. In time, they too will join the firm.

King put up a good fight in Egypt before finally falling to the advancing armies of Judge Rideout. He had managed once again to build up a powerful force in Madagascar where no one could get at him. Al Davenport was the first to reach across the table and shake the Judge's hand, congratulating him on another victory. Poor Al, a faint ring of Maalox on his lips, the deceitful practice of law had gotten to his stomach.

How many times had King said to her, "Now, Mommy, the law's been good to both of us." He had told her about the day he learned he had been accepted into law school. He was working a summer job and he took the day off and drove back up to Ithaca, New York. He went in town to a wine shop and bought the most expensive bottle of wine, one the proprietor assured him would be "exquisite" in ten years. Then he went back to his fraternity house at Cornell and up in the attic he hid the bottle in a corner where no one would find it. "I promised myself," King had told her, "in ten years when I came back for my reunion I was going to have a toast to life." He knew he would be coming back as an attorney, a successful man, a man with a wife and a family. "I was going to stand around with those guys and listen to everyone telling everyone how well they had done and I was going to know that no one on earth had it better than I had it."

What confidence in the future, Casey had thought. Who on earth these days would even be willing to place a bet that they would still be around in ten years. Better to buy the wine and drink it up right now before it was too late. By the time King drank his, his wife's cancer must have been spreading. Soon she would die. But why hadn't *he* become cynical? Casey watched him, his eyes darting around the RISK board under the brim of his foolish hat. He really was a remarkable person to have been through that and to have come out on the other side with his faith and his optimism intact. Well, he had said he had his daughters to keep him going. But many perish while the children are nearby. It had to have been more than that.

Casey did admire him. Even tonight in his silly costume. He was a man with an irrepressible faith in life itself. He had said to her, "I went through a rough time, a very rough time. But I always believed I would be happy again. I never doubted that. And then I met you and I felt blessed. Positively blessed."

Casey had come to feel the burden one may feel when one is the reason another person feels blessed. She felt the burden tonight.

—253

"I'll tell you what we ought to put our money into," the Judge was saying as he finished a bold sweep through Southeast Asia. "Hey, and I hope this doesn't offend the ladies present. But forget about plastics. Plastics had their day. The best investment today is this panty-shield business. No, I'm serious. You've got all these crazy brands: Light Days, Maxi, Mini, Carefree, Stayfree, New Freedom, Sure & Natural—you know the list. Well, what this country is ready for is a new pad that captures the new mood of the republic. Patriotism, nationalism. What about the new D-Day Pad? I can see it now. You're watching Dallas on TV and here comes the commercial with a gal, mighty pretty and mighty powerful, a take-charge sort of gal, and she says, "When one day is *the* day you've worked for and waited for, would you trust anything but D-Day? Absorbent, scented."

If only King would stand up and knock his teeth out, Casey thought.

Bolivar was still going strong when the doorbell rang and Jan ushered their nephew into the room. He was introduced as Billy Cameron. Billy was thin and bearded and had a handsome look in a disheveled way.

"Billy!" shouted the Judge, springing to his feet. "Well, well, how goes it? How goes the battle?" Chairs were pushed away from the table and hands were held out to be shaken while Bolivar led the introductions. "Gentlemen, you're looking at a boy who knows his way around a RISK table, and who bears the lamentable and ignominious distinction of losing to me in less than an hour. One hour. Billy, is that about right?"

He said shyly that this was right.

"Oh, that was a victory all right. And may I hasten to add that you were gracious in defeat, which is not necessarily a family trait. Now, come on, sit down. Take this chair right here. What are you drinking, son?"

He asked for some coffee.

"Jan," the Judge said, "get the boy some coffee and put a stick in it. Hey, we half expected you for din-din. Your aunt cooked half a steer."

"I'm sorry, I—"

"We went and killed the fatted calf, didn't we, gentlemen?"

"It was great," said King.

"Quite a feed," said Al.

"We could have used your help," said Earl.

"So, hey come on, sit down. Take this chair right here," said the Judge. Have you had any luck with Paul Findley?"

"Not yet," Billy replied.

"No? Well hell." The Judge turned to the men to explain that he was trying to get Billy hired on the staff of the *Boston Globe*. "Billy's a pretty good writer. I told him it just takes a few good connections."

Casey noticed that the Judge's nephew had turned to her and looked right into her eyes. Then he crossed his legs and uncrossed them and crossed them again in the other direction. "Actually," Billy said, "I'm pretty active in the Freeze movement. That's what I'd like to write about."

"Oh now, none of that doomsday stuff tonight," the Judge cried. He whistled through his teeth, then said, "Let's finish this contest of global avarice—what do you say gentlemen?"

While the game went on the women talked and it was clear to Casey that she and the young man were very much aware of each other's presence. It was a feeling that if one

—255

of them were to suddenly leave the room, the other would be disappointed. For an hour Casey listened while Billy was cross-examined. He tried to defend his work in the nuclear freeze campaign. He was modest and forebearing. He was defenseless among the lawyers. If he had no morals or no love in his heart, that would have been all right. But he had no job, and that was unforgivable to the lawyers.

Miraculously King came out of nowhere to deplete the Judge's forces in central Europe, and this meant the game would drag on for hours.

"I'd like to go home," Casey said to King.

"Okay," he said, moving his new armies into Greenland.

"I'll take you," offered Billy.

There was a disjointed search for coats and hats and then they said good-bye and were off. He opened the car door for her and when she was seated he bent over her and shut the door again to make sure it was closed.

He started up the car and put his right arm around the back of her seat as he turned his head to back out of the driveway. While he drove he asked her questions about herself.

"Do you have kids?" he asked.

She told him three, then explained they were her husband's children. "He doesn't want any more or we probably would have had a big family." She couldn't understand why she felt obliged to be so thoroughly honest with him.

"Funny, I would have guessed that was your idea—no more children I mean. These aren't the times to be bringing children into this world. You don't seem like the others," he told her. "I mean I've spent enough time in

—256

hostile crowds to know how to spot an ally." He smiled and then said, "We need all the allies we can get."

She smiled back.

At a stop sign she said, "You remind me of someone I once knew."

"Really?" he asked. "Whose side is *he* on these days?"

She didn't know how to answer.

When he pulled the car into her driveway she asked him if he wanted to come inside for coffee or tea. He said he couldn't.

She had her hand on the door handle and was about to get out when she stopped. "You know, I have to forgive my husband. He had to grow up too fast. If he's compromised himself it's because of his children. He had them to think about instead of our old ideals. I think maybe we get greedy once we have children. But tell me, the nuclear thing, do you really think things are hopeless?"

He was silent at first. "I can tell you it's only a matter of time," he said. "A short time. I'm absolutely certain. Go where you have to go, do what you have to do, and don't stop to shake the dust off your shoes."

She went to bed with Billy Cameron's words drumming in her head. In the morning she found King in her bed, fast asleep in his clothes, the ten-gallon hat on the pillow next to her.

As long as she lived she would wonder if what happened next was only coincidence. She had always suspected the events in her life were connected in some way, each small event paving the way for other, larger ones. At times she believed there were forces at work, and that each coincidence was actually a careful brush stroke on the canvas which would hold the portrait of her life.

For a month, ever since reading Ross's second story, Casey had the feeling that something was going to happen to change the direction of her life. She had waited and waited. And now coincidence came knocking at the front door. She went alone to the door and there was an elderly woman standing there already speaking through the screen, speaking with an Irish brogue. "I don't want to be botherin you, ma'am, but my sister, Maureen, she's fierce worried that the end is near, and I say praise the saints; the poor soul's suffered long enough already. But Maureen, she's been carin for him and all, and she says to me, 'We've got to go find his daughter before it's too late.' "

She paused and looked into Casey's eyes.

"I don't understand," Casey said.

"Why it's your father, child. He's at death's door."

"What are you saying?"

"Maureen's there with him now. Will you go see him?"

Chapter Twenty

Casey had been gone three weeks when Jack drove to meet her at her father's house on Cape Cod. He drove up onto the great Bourne Bridge and when he reached the crest he rolled down his window and felt the salt air rushing by his face. Then he came into the villages of white and green, clapboards and grass. He was inspired by the scene around him. There were churches everywhere on the Cape; they occupied the center of the quiet towns, their steeples pointing toward heaven as a reminder to the many who had retired here that there might be something else for them, something better, after this was over.

Jack gazed at the white steeples as he drove along. Death and life *were* at stake here. Casey had said to him before she left, "I may not live through this." He had taken her words to heart. Now she was waiting for her father to die. And she had told King that after it was over she wouldn't be coming back home to him. King had come to Jack for consolation. Sitting in a chair with his head bowed he had spoken about his life ending.

Jack had prayed for all of them. He prayed for an answer, for something he could tell Casey. And now he was coming to her with his plan. He had taken things into his own hands. He had made arrangements to rent the cottage at Hancock Point; he had written Ross. As Jack drove along he kept telling himself he was doing the right thing. Going back to Hancock Point would give them all the chance to see exactly what was left of their past. From the time Ross had come home Jack had believed they would have a life ahead of them if they could see that the past, regardless of what it had been, was behind them. He would try to make them see that.

But first came this trip to her father's house. What justice—poetic justice Casey had called it—that her father should be leaving behind a house on the ocean for her, a place to come to, at last a place of her own.

Jack found his way to the house. The front door was wide open. He walked in, surprised to see how cluttered and chaotic the place was. He stopped to straighten one of the carpets with the heel of his shoe. He noticed a scar on the arm of a chair where someone had forgotten their cigarette. Under the glass on the coffee table some kind of substance had run and hardened. Jack wondered what kind of life Casey's father had led here. An old man alone. He felt a terrible sorrow that this had fallen on Casey, this responsibility to help her father die. What else was there to do; he was her father.

What else is there to do, Jack said to himself. He had heard the words a hundred times in his work. "What else is there to do?" they asked him, shaking their heads. "What else is there to do?" they asked him, looking toward the door as if resigned that he could suggest nothing so they might as well be leaving. "What else is there to do?" they asked him after they had conceded that things would not get better and there was no choice. The X rays called for amputation—"What else is there to do?" The house must be sold—"What else is there to do?" There's been no word—"What else is there to do?" The question is asked and then a cigarette is lighted, a suitcase is packed, a document is signed, stairs are climbed, money is withdrawn from an account. What else is there to do? In the end it came down to no choice at all. He remembered Casey telling him about her mother's notes to her with the boxes for YES and NO to check. There's only yes or no, not much choice.

Jack walked to the foot of a stairway and called out her name, too softly for anyone to hear. At a window he heard the waves breaking. He craned his neck and looked beyond the gable of the next roof, down the beach toward the center of the village. If she was out there she would be walking, he thought. Until she came into his life in Boston and started taking him on walks, he had never been one to walk just for the sake of walking. He thought how many subtle ways they had influenced each other's lives.

Jack listened to the surf and had a momentary sense of dread. He rushed out the door and ran down to the beach. When he couldn't find her anywhere he cut through the dunes to a neighboring cottage. Then Casey called out to him from her porch. She came down the steps to greet him. Her cheeks had reddened. Her hair was tangled around her bare shoulders. She had never looked more beautiful, more awkward.

"I'm on my own," she said with a big smile, and she opened her arms to embrace him. "First time in years."

"Since you showed up at my door," he said.

"We've got each other," she said. Her cheerfulness surprised and encouraged Jack. She stood at the screen

—261

door and began telling him how she missed the girls, and how she had had them down to visit. "Wendy has her license now," she said. "Look out! But anyway, Jack, she drove down with her sisters and we had the best time here. We're always going to be close no matter what happens, because I think they trust me. Wendy came to me a few months ago and I took her to the doctor to be examined for a diaphragm. We didn't tell King—I mean it was between Wendy and me, that's the way she wanted it."

She smiled and reached for the door. "I keep thinking how I didn't know anything about sex at her age. The mystery is gone for this new generation, and that's a good thing, isn't it? They won't make the mistakes I made."

She apologized for the place being a mess. She led him inside and hurried around the kitchen opening doors, running water. She wanted him to have a glass of her iced tea. "I've learned to make it in the sun," she told him. And then she stopped and walked up to him and held him for a minute.

"You smell like summer," he said. She was so close to him he could feel the effect of his comment running through her. "I don't know what to say. I wish to God things were easier for you."

She shook her head. "We're all grown up now, aren't we?" She said she had thought about this, how when you die in your youth there has to be an explanation, people want to know why. But after you reach a certain age no one asks why. She recalled walking by her old elementary school with her mother. "She told me how she worried that the bomb would destroy life for us. But it doesn't take bombs, you can pretty much do it yourself, can't you."

He told her they all had a long way to go, that they were going to survive the bombs and themselves. "Not all of us," she said. "But can you imagine this? He kept track of me. He was covering his bets, Jack. He didn't want to end up alone."

They sat down at the kitchen table with their tea. Jack said he was worried about King. Casey traced the rim of her glass with one finger, drawing dozens of circles as if to let enough time pass so that Jack's observation would float away. At last she said, "Tell me, what can I do for him?" She waited for him to tell her something, and then she began to sob. She put her head down on the table. Jack knelt beside her. He brushed her hair back from her face. "My anger comes in stages," she said, almost calling out to him. She had been angry enough at times to ask what kind of God would have let her marry a man she didn't love enough, and then find out the only man she ever loved was alive and out there somewhere.

She lifted her head and cast her eyes to the ceiling above them. "My father had some woman here with him. It wasn't until after she had left and he'd gone into a coma that his nurse sent for me. That was probably *his* idea, I'm certain it was. So I've been waiting here for weeks, waiting for him to say something that will make sense. I'm still waiting for answers."

Eventually they went upstairs and found the nurse sleeping in a chair. At first there was no movement or sound in the room, but then the curtains blew full and gave the impression of sound and life.

This was, Jack thought, no man he had ever seen before. He couldn't connect this face with the face he had known as a boy. He said a short prayer under his breath.

—263

He touched her father's hand, and its dampness startled him.

Casey came to him with a book opened to a handwritten inscription in front: *"To My Son, I have found that there is considerable joy but also great danger in teaching a child to sail. For once he learns in his soul how fine a thing it is, he may grow up to trust far too much to Providence and the changing winds."*

"From his father to him," Casey said. "But it isn't signed, not even a name, only words on a page. God, when you think what passes for love in this world."

In the back of the book there was the photograph she had sent to her father that summer from Hancock Point. The picture of Ross and her in front of the Cadillac, she trying to look reckless and independent. It was mounted in a light-blue frame she had painted. Jack held it into the light. The photograph had captured precisely the mood of that afternoon in the meadow.

"That was the day he talked about how certain things happen in life and then they never happen again," Casey said.

"It's a good picture of you," Jack told her.

He looked at it, thinking how many generations of boys had been photographed like this, with one foot propped on a car. The automobile had symbolized everything a boy of nineteen or twenty hoped to possess in life—freedom, power, the ability to get someplace.

"It was when everything was so good," she told Jack. She had wanted her father to see that she had someone who loved her. She wanted him to see she had gone on with her life and was doing all right.

Jack looked down at her father, then back at her. She said, "I see him lying here like this and I want to think

—264

it's just part of some organic process. But I look at him and wonder if God is punishing him."

Jack told her it would all end, it would be over soon. "I've rented the cottage," he said. "I've written to Ross. We'll all go back."

She backed away from him a step and asked what made him think Ross would come back. Jack told her he *would* come, and this time she seemed to believe him.

"Just to be there again," she said. "How many people ever get to go back?"

They stood out on the front lawn. A sea gull floated overhead, the sunlight flashing against its white undercarriage. She turned to him. "Forgive me, Jack," she said. "You will, you always do." Then she was smiling at him again. "Maybe I'll put my hair up in braids for you when I come up to Maine."

He told her that would be nice. He watched her look up at the sky, following the flight of the sea gull. "And if there isn't anything there, if all of that was only just a dream, then I'll get some life started here. I'll begin all over again," she said.

When King arrived the next morning she was in her father's boat tied to the end of the dock. He was unexpected. He stood on the dock, then stepped onto the deck of the boat. He was shivering with cold. There was a heavy chop on the water, the boat was rolling from side to side.

"Will you take me sailing?" he asked her plaintively.

"You don't want to go out in this," she said.

"How would you know what I want?"

She could smell the liquor on his breath. "I'll make you some coffee," she said. She went down into the cabin. He started after her and tripped on the ladder and landed at her feet. He tore his trousers at the knee. When she had helped him to one of the bunks she wet a towel and bent down to clean the gash on his leg.

Even as it began she knew she would never be able to remember exactly how it happened. He sat up suddenly and grabbed hold of her. "Oh, don't do this," she said to him. "Please don't do this to me."

He pulled her blouse away under her sweater without saying a word.

With a hand on both her shoulders he pushed her to the floor. "You don't know what you're doing," she told him. His eyes were vacant. His movements were slow and ungainly. She barely struggled beneath him. From where she lay she looked up and beyond him. She looked out a porthole to the world of pointing, tilting masts, of clanking halyards and wandering clouds. Waves were slapping against the hull of the boat.

He took a pillow from the bunk and handed it to her. She thought he must mean for her to put it under her head, but then he pulled it back and asked her to put it over her face. "I don't want you to see me," he said.

"That's no way out," she said. "You'll still have to remember."

Finally he got off her. She heard him walking away down the dock.

Hours later, after he had left the cottage, he returned. He told her he just didn't want to go home. "I come across as the big dummy," he said. "I've done these crazy things, but it's not me."

She felt sorry for him. She let him spend the night. She showed him to a room upstairs where the scent of cedar boards was strong. She stood in the doorway looking at him. The bell was clanging in the harbor.

"Do you think when summer's over and all of this is done, you'll want to come home?" he asked her.

"Oh, King," she replied, "I can't talk about that right now. I can't talk about anything."

In the morning King woke to a stunningly bright day. The morning sun flared and slashed through his window. He had slept like a baby. Opening the door to his room he stood looking into another room. He walked to the threshold of this room, and the breath rushed out of his rib cage. He felt as if he was looking into a room in heaven. He gasped. He was looking into a white room, brilliantly white so that he could barely face it. The walls were white and the curtains at the windows white. And there was a woman standing next to the windows; she was dressed in white, a nurse. There was no color in her legs or arms. Her pale face was turned toward a large four-poster bed where there were white sheets neatly tucked in at the corners. The sheets covered the outline of a pair of legs and the body of a man whose face was cadaverous and white. He stared at the face, and then he saw that the posts of the bed had been turned into masts and there were winches and ropes draped from them, and across the foot of the bed a triangular white sheet fluttered in the breeze. A sail, he thought. The bed had been transformed into a boat. The figure in the bed was lifeless, and yet one of the ropes was wrapped around the fingers of his right hand. King did not dare take another step. From where he stood he could see that the bed had been pushed across the floor up to the windows so that the man faced the harbor.

Something touched King's arm and he felt his heart drop.

"It's all right," a voice said.

When he turned, he found that it was Casey. His relief was so profound he took hold of her as if she had saved him.

She backed away then, and led him over to the bed. "This is my father," she said. "His boat. I did this last night." She gestured to the apparatus of rope and sheets.

"He'd be grateful to you, dear," the nurse said.

Casey turned to King and said, "You see, we all do crazy things sometimes. God knows, I've done my share."

At night, standing at her father's window, Casey could see ships at sea, their red and green lights blinking, straying across the water. She thought about how her father deserved to die alone, how he had kept track of her and then sent for her to keep him company. He had beaten the odds. She thought about growing old. There would be no one to take care of her when she was old. Perhaps the abortion condemned her to this. No son or daughter to watch over her. A son would be patient with her; he would make room for her in his house. He would feed her, help her up and down stairs, hold her hand. A daughter would help her in the bathroom—"Are you ready, Ma? Are you alright in there?"—her voice calling gently. No nursing home for her, no surly nurses angry at life and taking it out on her, calling her by some nickname. Was this too much to ask? Shouldn't she be taken care of by a child of her own, someone who would remember what she had been like in better days? She thought of things like this while standing at her father's window. She was waiting for her father to die. She was waiting for answers.

Chapter Twenty-One

Ross stood in the doorway. He looked at the scene before him and felt that he had wandered onto a stage set, not one that had been abandoned by a play closing after poor reviews, but one thoughtfully arranged for a new play about to open. The furniture was much the same as it had been fourteen years ago. The summer sun fell in the windows and across the wide floors as it had always fallen. The breeze ran up from the harbor, rattling the same loose panes of glass. Ross suddenly had the feeling that his feet were jammed into shoes two sizes too small. His throat went dry. No one had instructed him what to do with his hands when he made this grand entrance. Was there someone offstage in the wings, someone who would prompt him with clever lines?

"Our sponsor for tonight's production," he said archly, "is Kraft, the makers of Velveeta." He took a second step, not the graceful, balanced step he had hoped for. He checked his watch, adjusted the navy-blue baseball cap on his head, then took it off and pushed his hair off to one side. Slowly his anxiety was replaced by a calm curiosity. He looked around from where he stood. "Jesus," he said in a whisper.

He walked over to the desk that was pushed up against the back of a long couch, the desk where he had sat in the middle of the night trying to write his first poems. He found the copy of *The Atlantic Monthly* he had found on the shelves here fourteen years ago. At the time he had thought of taking it with him. It was the May 1939 issue, it had a dull-orange cover and had sold for forty cents. He had read all the articles in it that summer, many of them he had read in bed with Casey. He picked it up and paged through it, looking mainly at the advertisements. The ad for Stetson hats—*"What do they think as they pass you by? Divine . . . Awfully nice looking . . . Very attractive."* That was an age when all the men wore hats. Then the ad for Brooks Brothers clothing that pictured three urbane men emerging from a sleek, black sedan. Ross thought of his old wardrobe, and how he had once mocked this ad. He could have been a parody for Brooks Brothers in those old days.

He passed the ad for Clemenceau's book, *Grandeur and Misery of Victory*. The publisher had written this ad: "Like a lovely Aubusson carpet among the grass rugs of contemporary fiction." Bullshit, Ross thought. There were ads on every page, and in a section titled EDUCATIONAL DIRECTORY a list of prestigious preparatory schools, all of them for boys. He wondered where the girls went in those days. Oh yes, here was the picture of Miss Porter's School where you could send your daughter to have the appropriate layer of polish applied. All the investment banking ads were discreetly placed at the end of the magazine, after the literature had been paid its due. Otis & Company. Starrett Securities boasting the construction of the Manhattan Company Building, "Wall Street's greatest skyscraper."

Then came the hotel ads, and then finally the advertisements for trains. He remembered the one for the Southern Pacific Railroad, featuring four great transcontinental routes. The picture showing a young man and his adoring wife on board a train. They were leaning back in a red seat while the countryside flew by their window. Wife? Well, in the 1930s you presumed it must be his wife. It was only an artist's sketch, but it captured such a scene of promise. A husband and his new bride, a sweet, devoted girl.

Ross moved suddenly and this movement started a pencil rolling across the top of the desk. He remembered making love to Casey here in this cottage, right above where he was standing now. He remembered the first time they made love, back in Boston, when she had said to him, "Well, now that the damage is done, let's do it again."

What would he tell her now that he had come back? He would tell her that he had fallen in love with her when she said that to him. That he had decided at that moment he would never want to live without her. What good would it do to tell her this? Instead, maybe he should confess his great deception. He should tell her he had tried to make her pregnant when they were here because he knew he would be going away and he believed that only a child would guarantee their future together. Even now, as he thought about that old scheme, it seemed like a pretty good plan. Except that it was irredeemably selfish. He should confess his selfishness.

He pushed the magazine aside. He thought back to that time when he was confused about everything, when he was afraid of losing everything he had. How many changes his life had been through. That summer, then the years in Vietnam, then the Christmas Eve he went to

Boston and saw her as a married woman. For a very long time it had seemed his life would end in misery. And then, out of the blue, another change. He was sitting one day at the lunch counter in a corner drugstore. Two old men sat next to him talking of a friend of theirs they had recently buried. One of the men said, "You've got to say this about Gil: Gil would give anybody the shirt off his back."

A common enough thing to say, but it struck Ross at the time as something that would never be said of him at the rate he was going. The man's words were an epiphany. Suddenly Ross saw that he was squandering his life, and he took a step toward turning things around; for four years he had been living with and ignoring and using the girl he'd met in South Station on Christmas Eve after he had last seen Casey. Her name was Carol. He had gone to Bangor, Maine, with her, and they had hung out together and she had refused to give up on him while he was taking his long fall. Now, after the experience in the drugstore, he went to Carol and asked her to marry him. He promised to think first of her and to try to give her a happy life.

When Jack's note arrived he read it to Carol: "I need you to come back to the Point. I've rented the cottage for us. Please make the greatest effort. Jack."

She understood how important it was to him to go back. She had always been understanding of his past. He had told her everything about Casey, and when he awoke in the night, often in a cold sweat, often dreaming of Casey and sometimes even calling out her name, his wife had consoled him.

So, Ross thought, I'm here because I care about these people. I loved them, and still do. But that's it, that's as far as it goes. Only a selfish man would come back here to *get* something. Or to be forgiven. Life is funny, he thought. You have this idea of the perfect person to marry, and after a while you compromise and marry someone else because you've become convinced that the perfect person won't ever come along. And then after you're married you walk into a hotel lobby one night and there she is, the whole package, everything you ever wanted. And she could be yours, if only for a night. And if you're selfish, you take her. And then you pay the price for betraying someone who loves you.

He spotted the Panama hat across the room, walked over to it, and held it out in front of him in a band of sunlight. He remembered how they pushed Casey's mother around the Point while she wore this hat to keep the sun out of her eyes. And Jack's crazy sunglasses. And Casey had taken a picture of him in this hat. He remembered posing for it with his foot up on the bumper of the Cadillac convertible. There had been many photographs taken that summer and he had never seen any of them. He had often wondered how he would appear to himself in those old pictures. A boy possessing a precocious grip on life? A boy hanging morally and spiritually by a thread? He often thought back to that selfish time in his life and imagined that love and friendship then were only parts of some elaborate structure made of matchsticks. He had misperceived everything important. He had been blind. He had been young. And yet he had to admit that he was still drawn to that time in his life. This made him wonder if he was still relying on the same flawed perceptions.

He remembered the wooden floor where he now stood, how that summer it was always tracked with sand from the beach. And the leaks in the old tin roof. When it rained hard and the ceilings leaked, they caught the rain drops in old tennis ball cans.

Ross heard footsteps behind him, out on the porch, then Jack's voice.

"I knew you'd make it," Jack said.

They shook hands then. Ross said. "God, look at you. The life of a minister must be good to you."

"Well, can you believe this?" Jack opened his arms.

"No, it's impossible."

"Casey's coming."

"I wasn't sure what—"

Jack finished for him. "I know, my letter didn't tell you much of anything. I'll explain though."

"Hey, where the hell's the radio?" Ross asked.

After so many years, they stood there talking about a radio, and then about the old black dog that used to come by the cottage fourteen summers ago. And then about the Red Sox.

"The Red Sox haven't gotten any better," Jack said.

"And the music," said Ross. "There's never been any real music since then."

"Plus the ads," Jack said. "I still listen to ball games on the radio, anything to avoid the damn TV ads."

"Be careful what you say," Ross said slyly. "Those ads butter my bread these days. I've been writing ad copy for two years. You know the one where the guy takes the scalpel and saws off the top of the Digell tablet? That's ours. The bra for the full-figured gals? Ours too. The great spurious debate between bulk and liquid laxatives? Yep, ours. And the stubborn tobacco stains on dentures." He finished with a quick laugh. "Well, we all have to grow up sooner or later."

—274

He walked to the fireplace where he took a small sailing trophy down from the mantle. Jack watched him weighing it in his palm. "You know, in an ad you just create a problem and then solve it right before the viewer's eyes. I was always making problems for everyone. You remember."

Jack said, "You're still writing then?"

"I'm a hack, but, yes, still writing. And getting paid a bit of cash money for which I'm very grateful. There was a long spell with no money at all. You know, I'd taken my vow of poverty, and I was going to write literature. What a laugh *that* turned out to be."

"The last story you sent, there was something special about it."

"Oh, it wasn't very good. It started up all right, but ended like a dirge. I wrote it—I don't even know *how* I wrote it. For a long time I thought I really would write something fine, but it was killing me, Jack. Nothing burns up a man like writing with an impassioned mind. Always looking back, day after day. You struggle because nothing seems more important than writing a perfect sentence, turning a good phrase, getting at the truth and passions of life."

"Yes," Jack said, "but that story. You had a reason for sending it, and there was passion there."

Ross shrugged his shoulders. "God, I was getting off-center for a while, I can tell you, Jack. I started thinking back, back to this place, to the time we had here. To Casey. I think I was just sort of calling out from the wilderness to see if there was anyone who would answer me." He set the trophy back on the mantle. "Tell me, Jack," he said, "how did she like the stories?"

Jack told him she admired them. "I didn't give her

—275

the second one for some time though. I thought it would just make things harder for her."

Ross nodded. "Well, but if she liked them. I mean, she drove a hard bargain. My poetry was really lousy in those days, I guess." He looked up from under a painful expression. "So there were two decent stories and that was the sum of my literary career. And now here I am mutilating Digell tablets to make a living. But it's kind of fun; you just learn not to take yourself so seriously. And no matter what anybody says about the ads on TV, they set the standard for advertising around the world. You go to Thailand someday and turn on the tube and you'll find two Thai ladies comparing their laundry to see whose is whiter."

Ross went on and on. He talked, raking his fingers through his hair, rambling on to the cadence of his hand motion. Jack could see that he had put on weight around his middle. But his eyes were still boyish and intense, his face lean and handsome. Jack stood there nodding earnestly, thinking how Ross's old propensity for making speeches had turned into a kind of pleasant babbling.

Ross didn't stop, and instead of slowing down, he picked up speed. He seemed to be just hitting his stride in a monologue that was unrehearsed and yet remarkably seamless and well constructed. He covered one subject exhaustively and then improvised a perfect transition onto the next subject no matter how disparate from the former. Jack had no room to say anything. He thought that perhaps the rigid requirements of having to compress his ideas into sixty-second time slots for television had frustrated Ross so that he jumped at the opportunity to speak without restrictions. Or maybe he knew that if he kept talking there wouldn't be any room for questions.

"Well, Jack," Ross went on, "we're both doing the same thing really. You write sermons, I write ad copy. We're both selling something."

He walked across the room and stood at the window, leaning against the sill and looking out to sea in a pose Jack recalled. "The whole time in Nam I thought about getting back here with Casey. I was out on patrol just getting a feel for the place. We came upon a village that had been badly bombed by our B-52s. The place was still smoldering, there were some Red Cross people there already, setting up makeshift operating rooms, and we were rounding up the bodies, picking up the pieces. I was walking around in a daze and I found this little girl. A gorgeous child. She was just coming into consciousness, just realizing her leg was gone, and I saw how hell poured over her face. There would never be any more happiness in her world, that was the end of happiness. I felt ugly for it."

He paused, rapping his knuckles lightly on a pane of glass. "I never saw much of the war. I was hit on my second mission. But I saw enough on that girl's face to know the whole thing was immoral. That's what I wanted, I guess. I wanted to see for myself.

"In the POW camps I wrote two whole novels in my head, novels about the war. But then when I tried to put them down on paper they didn't come. I wrote them in my head to try and keep my sanity. I wrote them out of a sense of guilt, extreme guilt, if you can understand that, Jack. For six years I had to listen to the bombs we were dropping day and night, and I had to think about that girl's face. I grew up there though. Or, I thought I did. But when I came home I fell right back into my old selfishness. I mean here I was expecting everything to be the

—277

same, expecting her to be waiting for me with a kid in her arms."

Jack said, "When we were here, I thought of you as already grown up. I wanted to be like you."

"Bad choice," he said. "Sometimes it scares me to think how much I didn't know then. I didn't know anything about anything. I thought I did. But it was, well, it scares me to think how much we all could have been hurt, how dangerous my youth was. I'm just glad to be through it. Life goes on. Sometimes I think to myself, damn it, it was all a crazy, mad time, and we were all crazy along with it. I mean the sixties. There won't ever be a time like that again for us. It's a wonder, a great wonder really, that we all made it through." He told Jack he was still sorry for a lot of things that happened.

"I'm sorry too," Jack said.

"Yeah, but when you say you're *sorry* it can mean everything or nothing. But I was sorry the day I left here. There I was on that train, after all my riddles about a man on a train. There I was, and I was crushed. And then I got back home thinking it would all be here for me. God, what kind of idiot was I?

"But now I think, damn it, we were *young*, weren't we? We were only doing the best we could. We didn't know what to do really."

He paused, then picked up again. "God, Jack, I'm really hogging the microphone here. I didn't mean to do that. But it feels terrific telling you these things. You know, for a while I was going downhill fast. People had disappeared out of my life and it got to me. You start believing everyone will vanish and you turn it into a self-fulfilling prophesy. I kept saying I wanted something that would last, but I was pushing people away from me when

—278

they got too close, when they started to figure out that I was scared to death on the inside. I guess I was testing them all, to see which ones really had the stuff to last with me. I was testing Casey.

"But when I saw you that afternoon, and then Christmas Eve with Casey, my mind was reeling. I kept thinking how she'd snuck away from her husband to see me. I just left. I met Carol in South Station and I went to Maine with her. We went up to Bangor, we lived in the streets for a while. There were some wild street people in Bangor, people with gnarled, twisted faces, women of amazing proportions living on garbage. Some of those people would have caught the eye of Mr. Dickens. Every now and then a dwarf would walk by. And Carol and I were living with them in the gutters, under the bridges. I had seventeen thousand dollars in back pay. I gave it away in about two weeks.

"There were a lot of down-and-out people in Bangor. Most of the city had been gutted and knocked down in the name of urban renewal, it was a wasteland. There was one nice restaurant where the high-rollers used to hang out. You know, a place that served desserts they set on fire at the tables. When it was very cold we hung around there, not for handouts but to lie down on the hoods of the big cars when the rich people had parked and gone inside to eat. There was enough heat from the engines to keep us warm for a while.

"We had a lady up there living in the city dump. She was a jazz pianist, a very special lady. A terrific musician really. Her name was Pearl. She was in her seventies. She was known all over the city, a real jazz virtuoso. She lived in a fantasy world of New Orleans jazz clubs and tours to faraway places in the tropics. Whenever it was snowing,

—279

which was every damn day, she would say to me, 'I'm about to leave for Tahiti. I like to play where I can swim.'

"Someone in the Shrine Temple there raised the money to open a shelter in the armory and they moved in an old broken-down piano. I remember one leg was missing and we propped it up with a golf club. Pearl would take off her layers of rag clothes and sit down and say, 'Tonight I'm going to play Gershwin, *Rhapsody in Blue*.' She would get the most beautiful music from that worthless piano. She would mesmerize everyone. She once said to me, 'Someone told me that the blues are the story of a woman's life. Each year you add a chorus.' Pearl was right."

Ross stopped talking then. He began to sing a chorus of his own in the living room closet and then another chorus in the basement. He sang in the pantry until he found what he was looking for. He emerged, smiling, with a mop in one hand. He leaned the mop against the kitchen table then stomped on it with one foot, breaking off the head. He assumed a batter's stance and swung away, one clean beautiful swing. The mop handle whistled through the air. "I gave up golf," he said. "An old man's game, like she said. But I play in a softball league at work."

He ordered Jack out to the car, threw the stick into the back, and drove off to the tennis courts, where he bribed the teaching pro to loan them his shopping cart filled with old practice balls. It took both of them to lift the thing into the trunk. When Ross settled back behind the steering wheel he clamped one hand down triumphantly on Jack's knee. "Need I say more?"

"I hope you know a good orthopedic surgeon," Jack said.

"Come on," Ross exclaimed, "oh man of little faith!"

The ball field had been abandoned sometime after they last hit balls there. The redwood-slatted fence still hung on beyond the outfield, but it sagged in places. The infield and the pitcher's mound were overgrown with wild blueberries. Down the rightfield line a flagpole had been bent cruelly in half and it hung against the sky like a fractured limb. There were huge mounds of sand off beyond the fence where the town road crews came to fill their trucks throughout the winter.

Ross handed Jack the mop handle, then pushed the shopping cart out to where he approximated the pitcher's mound had once been. "This is my wife's one, foolproof way of shutting my mouth," he yelled to Jack. "She puts a bat in my hand and she pitches to me high and outside, just where I like them, and I shut up. After a while my talking gets to be like some form of Chinese water torture, each sentence is another sledgehammer pounding against her forehead."

"You sound good to me," Jack called back to him.

"You're just trying to soften up the opposition with Christian charity. I know your tactics."

Jack laughed with him. He was trying to get a clear picture of this scene, one he would never forget: Two grown men with a mop handle for a bat and a shopping cart full of old tennis balls. The green grass, the blueberries, the red-slatted fence, the sun washing to gold, the sky washing to violet.

They hollered and laughed like old times. They had enough balls to play an entire nine-inning game without stopping to pick them up. And when they were through and exhausted, they dropped into the grass.

"I seem to remember when we used to hit them out of here with ease," Ross said. "Right over the fence."

"Not me, I never got a ball past the pitcher's mound. But you—"

"It's my timing—the timing's way off, my friend," Ross

—281

said. He put a blade of grass between his teeth and lay back, propping himself up on one elbow. The sunlight brought a wonderful complacency to the late afternoon. Soon there would be a plum-red sunset far out beyond left field and the sun would drop below the fence slowly enough so that they could watch it fall.

"I want you to know," Ross said, "when I went to see her I wanted to do the honorable thing for once in my life. I respected the fact that she was married. It had nothing to do with honor maybe. Maybe I just didn't want to lose her again by pushing myself on her. The timing though, the timing was all wrong. We should have had a lot more days here."

Night came on. Jack lighted a hurricane lamp and set it in the front window. "Maybe she'll follow the star to Bethlehem," he said. "I'm sure she'll be here, if not tonight, then tomorrow."

It was quiet when Ross started talking again. He spoke in a low, calm voice. "I listened one night to Pearl playing that broken-down piano in Bangor. I sat across the room, a room full of wanderers, and she sounded wonderful. When she had finished she said to me, 'Did you hear the grace note?' I didn't understand. She said, 'Oh, that's right, you're not a musician. But you're a writer, you should know about the grace note.'

"The grace note, Jack. A grace note in jazz is a special thing, a note just above the rhythm, a variation that makes all the difference but never disturbs the timing of the bar. We had that here, for a while we had the grace note."

He stopped and reached into his back pocket for his wallet. He handed Jack a photograph of a child in a sailor's outfit. "This is the grace note in my life now," he said.

—282

"She's mine, she'll be two next month. You ought to see the way she smiles at me. I turn around and she's just smiling up at me like I've done all the right things in my life."

He put the photograph away. "But I'll tell you something. I was someone who fell hook, line, and sinker for the American dream. And I paid a price. The price was high. I can see it all now, Jack. This dream—you spend all the years of your youth trying to get things, and then you spend the rest of your life just trying to hold on to them. I mean if I work my ass off from now until the day I die, I'll be able to keep what I've got. The dream isn't a dream, it's an American tragedy because you end up dying. And you end up forgotten. And that's where you fit in, Jack. You can promise them everlasting life, something to soften the blow."

He told Jack he had come back because when he was here with Casey the dream seemed whole. "I'm thirty-four years old now. Half my life is over. I didn't come back to try and recover something. I just want to see where something ended, and maybe figure out why."

When Casey arrived the next morning the flowers were in a riotous bloom. Through the woods, along the narrow paths leading to the tennis courts and the chapel there were blueberries by the millions fattening in the sun.

"I tried the braids," she said to Jack when he met her at the car, "but they made me look like Sitting Bull."

He held her. She had driven barefoot. It seemed to her as she looked at him that they had both spent their adult lives retreating from this place. She could tell that he was already wondering if she would be able to see beyond the darkness to this new, open world of blues and

—283

greens, the world they had all once believed in so passionately. Out beyond the cottages and the clusters of birch trees the sun was breaking on the water.

There were her things to be carried inside. "Load me up," he said, holding out his arms and smiling. She said she hadn't brought much. In the car there was only one suitcase on the back seat. Casey looked at him. It was the suitcase she had with her that first summer, the one with the leather handle missing. He recalled how she had gathered up her things in that suitcase their last day at the cottage, and how she had carried it out in front of her like a room-service tray.

"You look exhausted," she said.

"We were up most of the night, right here on the porch."

"Telling old stories?"

"Yes. And waiting for you. He went to town," Jack told her.

"Just the two of us again then?"

"He'll be right back," Jack said. He paused, then asked about her father.

"The nurse is there," she said. "He'll be gone soon." She looked away, then asked if they could go to the beach and take her things inside later.

"He'll be coming right back," Jack said again.

"But let's go right now," she said. "I was thinking all the way up, we could just sit on the beach and maybe we could talk about the way things used to be."

She walked out into the surf, her skirt hiked up to her knees. She leaned down and dug a scallop shell out of the sand. When the wind picked up as she was walking back toward him it filled her skirt and, just for a second, she looked down and then up at Jack and she knew he was wondering the same thing, how she would have looked pregnant.

We've come back to finish the story, she thought. We've returned to the scene of the crime. She stood off by herself drawing in the sand with her toes. She talked about that first afternoon she knew Ross was in love with her. They had been out on the beach having a great day. It was June, near the end of the month, and summer still seemed like it would go on forever. They came back to the cottage where Jack was taking a nap on the porch. Ross showered and when he came inside she was in the kitchen at the sink. She was stuffing mushrooms, Jack's favorite. "We decided we were going to cook for you. Lamb chops. You remember that meal?"

"The garlic salt," Jack said.

"I put in too much?"

"Never too much for me, no."

"That's what you said then. I thought you were just being kind. But anyway I was there in the kitchen and I had such a wonderful feeling, the feeling of being grown up, a grown-up woman, running the show in the kitchen. It's silly now. But I was at the counter with my back to him. I had on a lavender sun dress, just some simple thing. He came up behind me and said I was pretty. Ever since my father, I dreaded anyone telling me anything about the way I looked, but when he said that, it felt good. He told me he was going to buy me a hundred summer dresses. That was the future, Jack, the idea of going on together for so long. A whole closet full of dresses you could point to someday and say, *'There, I lived!'* "

They walked together down the beach. Two little girls in candy-colored bathing suits had been left in the care of a fat nanny. She sat looking out at the sea while the girls joyfully poured buckets of sand over her, trying to bury her legs. "Don't forget to cover my feet!" she called to them. "Don't go and forget my big feet."

A little farther on a father and his son walked toward the dock. The boy carried two oars, their long handles dragging behind him. The father was loaded down with canvas sail bags. "Ready about," the father said. "Hard alee!" the boy replied. They practiced those lines all the way to the dock.

Out behind the chapel Jack and Casey stopped to pick the season's berries. Jack took off his shirt and laid it in the grass so they would have something to carry the berries in.

They brought the berries into the kitchen. Ross was still not there. Jack watched Casey looking at things, pointing out things. She went upstairs to the second floor, to the bedroom under one of the gables on the west side of the cottage. At the window she stood looking out. "Those flowers down there," she began. "The rows of flowers. Like the ribbons on a soldier's jacket. Isn't that how he described them in one of his poems?"

Jack thought back to when he went to the Army hospital to see Ross and how Ross had spoken about rows, rows of beds, rows of graves.

They walked slowly through every room and when they came back downstairs she could see that Jack felt the same thing she was feeling. The joy, the pleasant nostalgia was fading. Walking through the rooms she had thought about the people who return after fires to walk through their burned-out homes. There was a sense of loss and disintegration.

Night came on. They waited on the porch for Ross. Jack thought about how they had waited for him before.

They were waiting for him again. He had changed, he had made compromises in his life, he had let them down, and yet they were still waiting for him. Whatever Ross might not amount to in his life, he would never be forgotten by them and that counted for something.

Casey leaned back against the rungs of the railing. "All those letters I wrote him were full of anger, but I never said what it was like, I never told anyone. They told me I couldn't cry out on the street or the doctor might be suspected. I had to exchange the money before I crossed the border into Canada. Seven hundred dollars for an abortion, Jack. It was a lot of money then. There was this big house on a hill, a stone house, like a castle in a children's book. Nice flowers in front and a long, white fence. I had to dress up, and I was told to just walk around the side of the house, out back to a wading pool, like I had come for tea or something. I kept wondering who used the pool. A part of me was hoping the doctor had children of his own and that he would change his mind and come out back and tell me I couldn't go through with it.

"Then this woman came out. Her hair was so thin you could see her white, papery scalp. She looked down at me and I knew I was supposed to stand up, but I couldn't.

" *'La mère?'* she asked. *'La mère?'* And that was so weird, Jack—asking for the *mother*, as if I had come to deliver the baby, not to *kill* it."

She stopped for a minute before going on. Then she talked about her anger, how she knew it began before Ross, and how she wanted to free King from it. "I don't want to pass it on to him and the girls. Innocent victims of my anger."

She paused and turned her head to look up at the stars as if the next thing she wanted to say could be found there.

"I've decided something. When he's dead the slate

—287

will be clean, Jack. I won't have to be running away from all of that anymore. And I'm going to let go of King. I'm going to start over again on my own."

She looked at Jack and asked him not to say anything. She wanted him to be happy for her, that she was going to be making her own way finally, making a future instead of running away. "I've always been running away, and looking for someone to light my darkness for me, but you have to take care of this yourself. I know that now. You depend on someone else to light your way, and then they let the light go dim for just a second and it seems as if the darkness has always been there. The light seems so real, like a way out, or a future maybe. And when it goes out, even for an instant, you're left stuck with who you are."

She told Jack she wanted to be alone for a while. He knew she was thinking Ross wouldn't show up, that he had disappeared again. He watched her walk away.

She walked down the old lanes, past the old cottages. On the porch of the Andrews place she saw a woman sitting alone, rocking. Off in the grass, in her garden a radio was playing softly. Casey stood in the lane for a while and watched her rocking back and forth. When she got up and walked across the porch, she stopped and steadied herself on the railing and stood looking over at her garden.

It was a strange moment. A woman alone, out on a porch, the house dark behind her, a radio playing in the garden. Casey thought about this woman. She thought how contented she looked, how she didn't seem to be waiting for anyone or anything. Casey thought how often *she* had been alone, but how she was always waiting for someone. She had spent too much time looking out her windows, waiting for something. . . . Out of our windows late at night we gape and watch the stars but do not see them really. The cars hissing by on wet streets mean everything to us. It is either sleep that calls us, or the arms and legs of a lover. A lover for one night, one hour, many years. Who has not wished the hours would compress and disappear. On the big clock in the hallway a black hand pounces deliberately from one moment to the next. When it matters, the time will not last. At night on dark streets, the houses stand dully animated by the light on silver screens. Someone waits for love, not sleep. No matter how hopeless, there is still the chance that love will come out of nowhere pressing a heart against your own. How many times Casey thought of this while staring at the photograph of the poet. Reading the poetry of Sylvia Plath, staring at the photograph. What was in that face, that young, unlined face? Something dangerous and strange, a listless despair, a lost look, a desolation? But wasn't even *she* happy for a little while when she was in England on her Fulbright fellowship, where she met the man she would marry? They must have taken walks together, drunk wine, played bridge perhaps. In the London snow when she laid down on her back and swept her arms above her head making an angel for him, was there the vision of death in her head? Casey wanted to imagine that on at least one sunny afternoon in England they shared a room where the breeze blew white curtains full. See him in his chair, smoking a cigarette, that mischievous expression. She sits on the bed, wan and frail. On a high bed and her feet hang above the floor. Oh what a pretty white dress, like the material the curtains are made from. He waits and watches and it is almost unbelievable that this pretty, young girl who slowly pulls her dress up for him, up over her smooth legs, over her glistening thighs, up to her belly where she will carry his children, will one day kill herself in a horrible way. Oh, but we never know, Casey thought. The lovers we have waited for and dreamed about, will they come at all? Will they kiss us in the morning when they leave our beds? Will they talk nervously of returning, and if they do talk like this is it only to spare us from a sordid scene, a harsh memory? Will they say anything meaningful, or will they dress in the half-light of early morning and leave without a trace?

Casey watched the woman out on her porch and she thought about Ross. About that photograph in the back of her father's book. Ross with his foot propped up defiantly on the bumper of that old car, the car with its fine sweeping fenders. Someday there would be no one left to remember how he looked that summer afternoon. That afternoon when the whole world was ahead of him. All the boys had once been photographed alongside cars. Cantankerous cars which they drove with a high sense of drama and purpose. Passionate boys. The boys were alike in many ways. Boys accused of idleness, suspected of having only one thing on their minds. One thing other than cars that is. It was a thing they had to *get*. One of many things.

Well, Casey said to herself, he got me.

In the morning she saw him. He was up before her, standing out on the porch when she came down the stairs into the living room. They didn't say much. He asked her if she wanted to take a walk with him. The wind was rising. Someone had hung brass chimes from a porch rafter.

Out in the harbor a gull bobbed on the swells, forward and back, forward and back, Ross pointed it out. "A rocking horse," he said. They walked down along the edge of the sea. The bright sunlight outlined her legs against the cotton dress. They stopped to regard the scene across the lane: out on a lawn a young man stood with a camera while his wife clapped her hands, gently coaxing a child into a photograph. A shirtless little boy walked toward his mother on wobbly legs, clutching a clothespin in each hand as if he believed he was holding on to something that would keep him from falling. Casey wondered, if this was the illusion in her life too?

They walked on farther. Casey wondered if anyone spotting them out walking would be able to tell what they had been through. Or would they be anonymous. Thirty miles north of one city another city is destroyed and this will not deter the one man in the southern city from worrying not about the loss of life above him but about the balance in his checkbook. That is life, she thought. People are too busy to think much about anyone but themselves.

At the dock she told him she was glad to see that he survived. Then she said, "I have a speech for you."

He smiled. "Go on then."

"I guess I always knew you were a survivor. I was thinking about this last night, waiting for you. Men like you and my father, it's so hard not to romanticize men like you. And a summer like we had here. But you emptied me. You both emptied me, you passed through my life like spirits."

She spoke of how her father made her rise up higher and higher. The more he took from her, the more she rose up to try and please him. He took from her and she rose up higher and higher, like a ship rising in the water as its cargo is taken from the hull, as it's emptied. He emptied her with his wonderful hands and his supreme indifference and discontent. He emptied her and so she went looking for someone to fill her again.

He listened, then told her he hadn't ever meant to *take* anything. "I was just scared to death."

"Of what?"

"People finding out how scared I was."

She believed him. "Maybe neither of us was capable of love," she said. "That *kind* of love I mean. Because maybe we both needed it too badly. We were both starved for affection and warmth."

It was late afternoon when they ended up alone in a room with a stamped tin ceiling and wainscoting running halfway up the walls. A room left behind from a former life. She had once memorized the pattern on the ceiling. It came back to her now. For the first time in hours he was quiet. There was nothing left to say.

"Come here," she said to him. She wanted to make sense of this, make peace with herself, make up for lost time, make love.

They make love. They make love in memory of love, in memory of themselves. For a few minutes it is better than the memory, more than she had imagined it could be. They both find a penetrating stillness at the circle's center, a stillness surrounded by light and color. They are dancing, holding on. His hands are all over her, her arms around him, tight around his back to show him that her feelings are current and real, not merely recollected.

Then a fine light came out of nowhere and flashed in his eyes. He lay still, looking at her face. Did he see Sylvia Plath's face in hers, she wondered. She thought how grand it would be if she would conceive a child with him. She could almost picture a little boy, a boy like the one down the lane this morning. A boy with golden curls. And those precious little feet so fat they look square, the feet coming to her bed in the middle of the night. He comes to tell her he can't sleep because there is a puppy in his room—a puppy of all things! She goes to the room, with him leading the way. She shows him the room is empty and safe. Down on the floor they crawl together, under the bed, behind the bureau, into the closet where one of his plastic confederate generals is lying in a sneaker. No puppy. Then she gives him what he wants, the feel of her skin next to his. She climbs into his bed and pulls him up after her, pulls him close to her, thinking to herself that *this* is the point of everything under the sun, that *this* is love.

Ross spoke to her. "What I regret," he said, "is all the time we wasted. I'd like to have some of that back."

"We were unfairly punished," she said. "And really, we never did anything really wrong, you and I."

"We did. I'm afraid we did."

"Well, don't tell me then, please."

She turned away. She could see out the window all the way to the harbor where a fishing boat was being followed by a swarm of sea gulls. She still knew him well enough to know what he was thinking about. He was trying to tell himself that he was just a soul in the world; he tells himself this to assuage his guilt. He is just a pinprick of motion in the constantly turning galaxy, and all of this is only part of some aimless journey. He cannot be blamed for following the journey. He cannot be held accountable. And what he has done he has done out of love. He betrayed Casey when she was a girl, but out of love. Now he has betrayed his wife for the same reason.

"It's all very strange," he said. "We all want the same thing. We all want love. And so many mistakes are made because we confuse the feeling of love with the feeling of wanting to *be* loved. Do you know what I mean?"

She didn't answer, and oddly he started talking about

John F. Kennedy, how he would always picture him entering a room with his right hand jammed into the pocket of his suit coat, the left hand gesturing. There must have been a time when John Kennedy looked into the mirror and saw it plain as day, his own potential for greatness. He must have found it in the eyes of people following him, a confirmation. It was a matter of having everything right, of having been dealt the right hand of cards and then having the ambition to play them. Didn't God love him? How else would you explain his greatness? And yet the women came and went through side doors and basement doors, their collars turned up to conceal their pretty faces. A succession of women. Young and buxom. There were rumors he had two or three at a time while the Secret Service agents were posted outside his door. Secret Service indeed. But late at night he must have awakened with his Catholic guilt and his aching back and gone alone, penitent, to the window to think it over. Perhaps to justify it as Ross was trying to justify it—this is just a journey, and I am just a soul in the world, a soul falling through space. The journey sweeps me along and I cannot be blamed. And time will mercifully pass. Time will dilute the joy and the guilt. Equally.

When he paused she put her finger on his lips and shook her head. "No more about him," she said. "He was part of the unraveling of our lives, wasn't he? Part of the thick romantic fog, the myth we lost our way in."

"But at the time—" he started to say.

She shook her head again. "How much *time* do we have? How much more time?"

"I don't know."

"I've been wondering," she said.

"About the time?"

"What will you say to her?"

When Casey says this, he thinks she is asking what he will say to his daughter, not to his wife. It is the daughter whose picture he carries in his wallet, whose picture he finds now to show Casey. And what *would* he say to her? Nothing, for she is too young. But later on, when she's grown up, she may understand everything. She may know the motion of the soul. She may know that the spirit longs to be alive, to rediscover what it was that first set it on fire.

"I always had a dream of getting back to you," Ross said.

Dreams drain the spirit if unachieved too long, he tells her. Surely his daughter will understand this, will understand why he came here and made love with this other woman, why he was able to feel connected to the center of life once again. Doesn't blame belong to skin, to flesh and to joints, to lips and to bones? The abyss of sin that opens up before us will not catch our rising, hurtling souls.

"But your wife, what will you tell her?"

"I may tell her everything," he said.

"You know each other *that* well?"

"We trust each other."

"Well, that would be the end of that. Tell me though, do you undress her when you make love to her?"

"What a question!"

"Tell me the truth."

"You keep asking me for the truth. You always thought of me as an imposter, putting on acts."

"No, not always," she said, and saying this, she moved closer to him. Her hair fell across his chest, a nipple brushed his arm.

"I want to tell you something," he said. "Something

—295

I saw. It was in Dallas at the airport. It was very early one morning, I was there waiting for the first flight out to St. Louis."

She had half a smile on her lips and he paused, then smiled back. "You knew me before I became a windbag," he said. "I'm sorry for going on and on."

"No, I'm listening," she said.

"There was only one other person in the waiting area with me that morning. He was the quintessential business type, wing-tip shoes, cigars in his coat pocket, the *Wall Street Journal* on his lap. So it was just the two of us there and then all of a sudden this group of people descended on us, noisy, rearing to go. Forty or fifty people with kids and everything. They were all terribly excited about something and they pressed up against the glass windows watching the runways. I thought they were waiting for a plane to take them somewhere but none of them had tickets. Every time a plane landed they asked each other, 'Is this it? Is this the one?' And the kids couldn't be contained. A couple of them pestered the businessman. He blew his cigar smoke at them.

"Well, a lot of flights were delayed that morning. There was bad weather over most of the West. They kept waiting, and the kids got more and more excited. Finally another jet landed and taxied over to our gate and they all rushed to the door and stood there looking at every person who got off the plane. Then they shook their heads and drifted back to the big glass windows. I was curious as hell, and by now the fat-cat businessman was beginning to wonder too. What the hell were these people waiting for? I mean why were they so excited? It was just another day in the executive's life, and in mine.

"Another plane landed then. The kids went through the whole routine again, yelling, 'This is the one!' Everyone pressed up to the glass windows as the plane taxied in. Then they rushed to the doors. One by one the passengers filed in, and then all at once a great cheer went up. I mean everyone was cheering and clapping. I went on over. There they were, six men, six priests in their white collars coming up the ramp, one after the other. And each of them was carrying a baby. A little, oblong bundle in a blanket. They were Asian babies, orphans, and out of this great group of people waiting for them, six sets of parents appeared, tears running down their faces. It was something to see, and we were all crying before it was over. Everyone in the waiting area was cheering and crying. People had drifted in from other gates and from along the corridors. Airport employees, pilots. Even old Scrooge in his suit was clapping. I thought how wonderful it was that out of all the bad in that part of the world, this much good could happen. They were here, these infants, despite the long odds against them. They were going to have a life. And I know now how they must have felt. I told Jack that having a baby is the one thing in my life I know is right. It's the one good thing I've done."

They slept and woke and slept again. In the morning out on the porch he touched the gray lines in her hair and said, "I've got some gray myself."

"Mine are silver," she told him. And he looked again and nodded and told her that she was right.

She sat down on the steps while he stood there. She made a church out of her hands and pressed its steeple to her chin exactly as she had seen her mother do many times.

"You know what would be great?" he said. "Maybe this is crazy, but I was thinking we should promise each other that when we get old, I mean very old and near the end, that we'll get together once again. No matter how silly I look by then and no matter how our lives have turned out, if we could just get together once more and make love like we did here. What would you think of that?"

"I don't know," she said. "It sounds like another romantic notion. I'd have to think about it. And anyway, I was thinking about something else. I was hoping you and I could spend some time together now."

He looked surprised. He walked down the brick pathway, off into the grass. Then he came back to her and waited. "These children," she said, "these little babies you talk about as if they can redeem a whole life, they don't come out of thin air." She looked at him and waited.

"I should go," he said, but without any conviction.

"This is no time to go," she told him.

Chapter Twenty-Two

The summer ended with a clement fall. The days stayed warm and they seemed unaccountably long, and out over the water each afternoon toward dusk there was still that last burst of sea light Casey had always associated only with summer. She had buried her father and was living alone in his house.

One evening that fall Jack watched Billy Graham on TV. He was speaking from some domed stadium in Calgary, Alberta—a vast, barren structure that made everyone look very small and insignificant. Reverend Graham was much older than Jack remembered him. He had always pictured him a youngish man who had somehow escaped the ravages of middle age. The crowd was thinner too. Well, the people had others to follow now, that fellow out West in the glass cathedral, and the one who named a university after himself. Billy had some real competition. They all talked about faith. They said you should *have* it, as if it was that easy. And they asked, "Are you saved?" Saved from what—boredom, disappointment, death?

Jack wanted to save them all. Casey, Ross, King. He

—299

wanted to save himself. It was so complicated. Why did it seem to him that the world must have been simpler once before? Was he wrong that people once found it easier to be content, that there were fewer questions asked, that answers seemed to be within reach? There must have been, for a while, a great feeling of gratitude. Wasn't everyone grateful that the depression was behind them, that the war was behind them, that polio was finally behind them. There was so much to be thankful for then. A man could hold his modest hopes, he could dream of finding a wife. A woman could dream of finding a husband. They could hold on to each other and dream almost of going on forever. They could get a house of their own and they could fill it with children. And if they never actually reached their own dreams, or if they just became too tired to try any longer, then they could sit back and use their faith and energy nourishing the dreams of their children. And as for God, God was everywhere then. Wasn't it easy to feel close to Him? There was a question then that must have been easy to ask and to answer—"Are you happy?" Oh, it wasn't all roses. There was the trouble over in Korea, and the big scare with Senator McCarthy. But things soon leveled off then.

Was the tranquility he assigned to those years illusory? Jack wondered. A deception? Things were brooding under the surface while people had their backs turned. This is what Casey had once told him. Even then, in those halcyon days, there were men out in the desert bombarding atoms with neutrons, setting up a chain reaction of splitting nuclei that could release energy great enough to destroy the planet. Maybe God saw them out there in the desert mixing up their numbers under a breathtakingly blue sky.

The disillusion soon came. John Kennedy was shot. Bobby was shot. Martin Luther King was shot. The senseless shooting broke out in Vietnam. Then came the descent into confusion and fear and distrust. People asked angrily where God was. But not for long. Ten years passed, uneventful years for Jack, years spent looking back.

Still the turning went on. Days turning into years, children turning into adults, old men turning back into children, plans turning into disappointment, loss turning into meaning, the meaning turning away. . . .

With the end of summer and the change of season other changes had come. Casey stayed with her father until the end, then buried him in August. When Jack had spoken with her she seemed remarkably well to him. She had left King, but he was going ahead with his life. He was running for governor and the election, Jack read, was really too close to call.

It was late October when Jack learned about a passenger train in northern Maine that was to make its last run after one hundred years of passing through the state on the way from Montreal to Halifax, Nova Scotia. He wanted to be on it with Casey. "This is history in the making," he told her when he called. "And the foliage is still great up north."

"So," she said, "there's this man riding on this train after all."

They laughed over this and she agreed to meet him in Montreal.

They rode the train in high spirits and had thirty-four hours together in a doll-house room with a tiny brass lamp under an emerald-green shade, and a wall that opened

—301

into a bed and a wide window looking out at the moon skating for miles across Moosehead Lake.

In the small towns slouching along the tracks this old train had meant a great deal. In towns like Jackman and Mattawamkeag and Vanceboro and Brownville Junction, there were people lining the rails to see the train pass for the last time, people who had learned there was some sort of magic about a passenger train, that a father standing out on the porch of his weathered, stick house will go inside and get his child and hoist his child up onto his shoulders just to watch the train go by. It was something to hear, the roar and the rattle. It was something to see and to think about, to imagine the lives of the people silhouetted in the windowed cars, to think of the places the train could take you if you were to get on board.

They talked a long time about their reunion at Hancock Point. Jack said he was guilty for expecting too much.

"Well, we tried though," Casey said. "It reminds me of a story I read about Stravinsky, the great composer. I'm not even sure it's a true story, but he composed a piece of music and after several days his first violinist came to him and told him he couldn't play the solo part. It was brilliantly written but it was just too difficult, he was terribly sorry. Stravinsky said to him, 'That's all right. I just want to hear the sound of you *trying* to play it.'"

"I guess that's what I wanted," Jack said. "I just wanted you to have the chance to see what was there."

She looked at him and thanked him for that. "There's nothing to be sad about," she said.

She kept looking at him, thinking, "Life is a sticky business. We go crashing along, those of us with wounds. We're never able to breeze along through life, so we go crashing along with our wounds, spreading them around, knocking over innocent people, disillusioning them the way we were disillusioned."

Finally she said, "I told Ross it would have been better if I'd been quarantined after my father. Alone with my wounds. But he tried to soothe me. He said it was people with wounds, the people who couldn't breeze along, who made a difference in the world. People who are wounded, he said, have the humility and the sympathy to help the world somehow. But of course he assumed an awful lot. He assumed you'd survive the wounds first."

They walked to the dining car where they sat for a long time watching a group of young people, college students, playing cards at one of the tables.

"I can't get over the short hair," Casey said. "And the way they dress up. They look so serious."

Jack told her they had to be serious. "They want to make a lot of money, they don't have time to horse around. But I'll tell you, there's going to be hell to pay for us when we get old and this generation is running the show. They're not going to support us, they'll put us all to sleep."

Casey laughed. "Oh, I've heard all about how ruthless this bunch is, but I don't believe it."

"Well," Jack said, "this is the age of personal gain and greed, it only figures."

"But they're not to blame. *We* made them selfish. They're the followers of our generation, and we didn't give them much to admire. We were going to make everything better, we were going to end the wars." She paused and smiled knowingly.

Jack defended their generation. "People cared enough about changing things to put something on the line, to make a sacrifice."

Casey was looking at one of the college girls, thinking

—303

to herself that this girl was probably as lost as *she* had been at that age, and that if she were to fall in love she would throw away all her plans to make money. Watching this girl, Casey thought back to something Ross had said, something she had known at once was true: We all need a place to come to, where things are always the same and where we no longer equivocate or misinterpret, where the train whistle consoles but does not call, and the voice in the wind is uncontentious. What face will watch our face turn old? When our mind strays and comes up empty, who will draw it back for us? Will there be grandsons to bring us souvenirs, or will we be alone, restless, walking about? God help us if this is so, for there is nothing worse to contemplate.

She turned to Jack. "But what you said about making sacrifices—we didn't make any sacrifices really. We were running around in the streets, the cops chasing us, chasing us back to our apartments, back to our nice safe dormitory rooms. It was the people in Birmingham, Alabama, and Vietnam—*they* made the sacrifices."

She gestured to the students and said, "Maybe our time was better though. We were young when the world was saying how fine it was to be young and angry and defiant. We didn't have to be serious about things. It was perfect. I mean, there's no romance in *following* the American dream—the job, the house with the backyard. The romance is in tearing it all down, trying to make a new way."

She thought for a long time. There was only the sound of the train clattering over its tracks. Finally she reached across the space between them and took Jack's hand. She began to smile. She told him it was all clear to her now. The way they were then, the whole generation out in the streets angry and defiant. Defiance was a way out of the past. "It's like there was a whole generation trying to make up for the lousy, corrupted past by being angry enough. And there *we* were, trying to find a way out of our own past. I wanted to find the defiance. And you, you found your faith, Jack. And what is faith if it isn't the ultimate defiance. You believe what you believe without any proof at all."

She said that Ross made her see this too. "Instead of letting the poison in your past kill you, you say, '*Damn it*, my life goes on. I give life to a child and I stop the poison right here. The poison stops with me, it doesn't go any further, I don't pass it on.' You see? That's a triumph, Jack."

For a minute she looked past him as the lights of a town flickered in the windows. She told Jack that she wanted her father to see how she had changed. "He was lying there dying and I was changing right under his roof, changing more than I ever had. I finally felt the defiance. I stood at the end of his bed and pulled up my dress so he would have to see how my body was changing. He never opened his eyes, but you can't be sure what dying people see and hear. It might have sunk in."

Jack started to ask her to explain, but a sudden look of excitement in her eyes stopped him.

"I told Ross that if we pulled this off then we would see each other again someday, after everyone was old enough to understand and there wouldn't be any more broken hearts."

She sat up straight and turned to him, smiling with satisfaction. "I haven't even *told* you yet. Put your hand here and hold still, Jack. This baby only kicks when everything's quiet, when it gets bored and wants some action."

—305

She kept smiling at him. For a long time while they waited to feel the future stir they were as still as could be. And though she knew they possessed together the precious, the irrecoverable past, it seemed to be behind them now.